The Fiction of forever
a stand by me novel

Brinda Berry

Published by Sweet Biscuit Publishing LLC
Edited by Nancy Cassidy of
www.redpencoach.com

Acknowledgments

Back in my naive days, I thought writing a book would be easy. Simply dream up the stories and put them on the page.

So very wrong. Tragically wrong.

Here's the page where I do an inept job at thanking the people who help me make this happen. It's almost like that saying about the best friends you can call at midnight. All I have to do is write a note and these ladies come to my aid.

I couldn't do this without the support of the following writers, readers, artists, and got-your-back people.

Critique partners and beta readers—the people who sweetly point out the good and the you've-got-to-be-kidding me: Abbie Roads, Mandy Dismang, Jen Crane, Audrey Estes, and Holly Goslin.

My personal cheering squad at READerlicious.com: Christina Delay, Kathleen Groger, Jennifer Savalli, Kelly Crawley, N. K. Whitaker, Jenn Windrow, Carol Storey Costley,

Sandy Wright, S. B. McCauley, and Abbie Roads (yes, I know she's listed twice in this piece!).

Thank goodness for the talent of the people who make me look presentable: Nancy Cassidy, editor; Najla Qamber, graphic design; and Scott Hoover, photographer.

You all make the book world a better place.

Thanks to all the readers who give me words of encouragement and especially those who asked for Gunner. He deserves a happily-ever-after.

"That's what fiction is for. It's for getting at the truth when the truth isn't sufficient for the truth."

~ Tim O'Brien

Forever and a Day

High School, Sophomore Year

Gunner

I GET SWEATY HANDS when I look at Kiley Vanderbilt. Another part of me notices as well, but I fight to ignore that awkward fact as much as possible when in public.

In private, I worship the photos on my phone. Worship might sound a little creepy. Actually, it sounds a lot creepy. I prefer to think of my photo collection as our pre-dating album.

Kiley is every guy's dream girl.

In my favorite photo, she wears a tiny pink bikini. I snapped it at her sixteenth birthday party last summer. She'd been standing by the edge of her outdoor pool talking to my friend Aiden, an all-right guy, when he isn't hitting on the girl who should be with me.

I conveniently cropped him out of the photo.

The photo isn't my favorite because she's almost naked. I appreciate all her curves, but mostly I like the shot because she looks happy. Her eyes dance with the pleasure of having all her friends around, or maybe of turning sixteen so she can drive the SUV her daddy bought her. Whatever it is, I want to know what gives her this feeling so I can make her look at me like that all the time.

Tonight is the night I'm going to make my move. I've just played the best game of the football season and everybody's been congratulating me on winning the game.

Kiley sneaks looks from beneath her dark lashes whenever I'm in her line of sight. She smiles that smile where she holds back a little.

Shy. It's not like her and the chatterbox that she is, which tells me a lot. She likes me. Maybe she has a photo of me on her phone.

A hand touches my back.

"Hey, Gunner. Nice pass in the fourth quarter," Jenna says.

"Thanks." I sip from my red plastic cup and hope she'll leave. I like Jenna but Kiley's moving closer to the bonfire. It's my chance to get her alone.

Jenna takes a couple of steps to stand in front of me, blocking my view of Kiley. "I was wondering something."

"What's that?" I crane my head to the left to make sure Kiley's still alone. Dang. Now some douchebag from another school is moving in on her and handing over his football jacket.

"Well, I don't have a date for the dance next Friday."

"Hm." I take another sip.

"Gunner?"

"Yeah?"

"I thought maybe we could go together."

"That's really nice of you. But...um...I was going to ask someone else tonight."

Jenna follows my gaze to the bonfire and Kiley. Kiley who takes the jacket from the guy I don't know.

"I hope you don't mind if I give you some advice." Jenna's voice is low, as if she's giving me top-secret info.

"What's that?"

"Kiley's nice. And she's my friend. But..."

"But what?" I narrow my eyes. It's hard to switch between focusing on what Jenna has to say and making sure Kiley doesn't get away before I can talk to her.

She shrugs. "She doesn't date anyone for long. I don't want you to get hurt."

Jenna places her hand on my arm, as if she's offering me consolation.

"Well, thanks Jenna, but I've known Kiley all my life. I'm not too worried about it." I lift my plastic cup to take a gulp. She drops her too-friendly hold on my arm.

"I'll see you later. All out of drink," I say, holding up my cup to give some kind of reason to get away from her.

"Sure," she says and looks over at the bonfire where Kiley stands.

I guess I'm not very subtle, but I'm limited on time. It's the first time in a while since I've gone out after a game. Mom's cancer diagnosis moved everything else in my life to the unimportant list.

In minutes, I'm across the field and standing before the most beautiful girl in Tennessee. It's been documented. Pageant judges put a crown on this girl every time she steps on a stage.

"Hi." Kiley says. "You were fantastic tonight. You were generous to pass so much. I know you could've run that ball down the field every time."

I shrug and an embarrassing heat floods my face. I'm not good with compliments. Other guys may need them, but I don't. I'm a team player, not a glory hound.

My gut churns with anxiety all of a sudden. Why does she make me so nervous? I've planned everything I want to say and if the douchebag to her left will get out of the way, I can.

Kiley removes said douchebag's jacket and

hands it to him. "I'm warm now. Here you go."

He takes it from her reluctantly. "Are you sure?"

"Yeah. Gunner, can you walk me to my car? I need to get something."

"I guess I can do that." Slap my stupid mouth. Of course I'll walk with her. I'd walk to the moon and back if she asked. Hopefully, I'll only have to master talking to her without saying something stupid.

She leads the way to the area of the field where she's parked. Kiley's dad always lets us set up the field parties on his land. He's the coolest dad I ever heard of.

I walk beside her and look straight ahead, rehearsing my speech about how we should go to the dance together. We're a couple hundred yards from the bonfire when I know it's the right time.

"Kiley—" I say.

"Hey, I—" she says at the same time.

We both laugh. Hopefully, mine didn't sound as nerdish as I feel like it did.

"You first," I say. Look at her. I turn my head and damn if the girl doesn't take my breath away. It's sappy and true and terrifying.

Only the moon and stars illuminate her face, but it still shines with a beauty like nothing else.

She twists her hands in front of her and

then turns to look at me, hopping a little as she walks. It's cute because she seems excited.

I glance at her again. She messes with straightening the bottom of her mini-dress. She's so hot with that mid-thigh dress and cowboy boots. My brain sends an emergency alert message to my dick every time I look at her.

God, I hope she doesn't bend over in that. I have enough problems without adding an aneurism or blue balls to the list.

"Want to sit in my vehicle and talk?" she asks. "It's chilly tonight."

"Yeah," I say in a near croak. Calm down, calm down, calm down. You'd think she asked me to party naked with her.

Is that really what she's asking?

My gut churns. Shit. One aneurism, order up.

We get to her SUV and she clicks the key fob to unlock the doors. Her vehicle's parked behind a thicket of tall brush. Once I'm sitting in the passenger seat and looking at the front windshield, I exhale rather noisily. We're practically hidden from seeing what's going yards away at the bonfire. Even the music sounds dim and faraway.

"So," she says and shivers. "Are you excited about the state fair?"

"Not really." I turn to her. Oh, shit. That was

a stupid thing to say. Does she want me to take her? Now I'll be the dumbass who says he doesn't like fairs and then asks her.

I try to think of something to say. Anything that will help me get past the usual talking-to-Kiley panic.

"I haven't seen you around much. Now that we don't have classes together this year..."

"I've been busy." I could tell her my mom's been so sick that I don't have time to think about much else. If I wanted to put a downer into this conversation, the topic of Mom's cancer would certainly do it.

"Classes are killing me this year," I say.

"Oh."

"I wish we did have classes together. You still doing the pageant thing?" I search my brain for something—anything else to talk about. I don't want to talk about how my home life sucks.

"Yes. I was in one last weekend." She pauses. "I was wondering... Are you dating anybody?" she asks.

"No." Her question surprises me and heat creeps into my face. I inhale and try to stay cool. I don't want to say that I'm not interested in anyone but her. Even I'm smart enough to know that's coming on too strong. Or is it?

"Oh. That surprises me." She gives me that smile I've been waiting for. The one from the photo where all her happy vibes point at me, as if I'm the one who made it happen.

Be honest. That's what I need to do. Make this moment count. "I want it to be the right girl, not just any girl." Great. Now I'm the emo douchebag.

Her grin continues and loosens the worry in my gut. She likes that thought.

"Me, too," she says. "Not the right girl, but the right guy...you know what I mean."

"Yeah. I know."

We sit in silence and look at the front glass. A layer of condensation films across it, hiding the rest of the party.

"Want to kiss me?" she asks.

My heart rams into my throat. "I...um...who wouldn't?"

She straightens the edge of her skirt. "Funny," she says.

But I'm not joking. Doesn't she know how I've wanted to ask her out all year?

"Maybe you don't." She runs fingers through her dark hair, lifting it off her face. "You're in a secluded car with me and you haven't tried anything. So, I'm not sure."

I will certainly die at any moment.

Happy.

Maybe not totally happy, because I'd like more than a kiss.

She's waiting for a response from me and

I'm not sure if I should yell, "Hell yes," or go for it.

"But I understand if you only want to be friends," she says, but doesn't move. "It might be weird since we've known each other forever."

I lean over the top of the console and I'm not sure what to do with my hands. Feeling her up will probably be more than she's bargained for tonight.

Her breathing is shallow, her gaze locked to mine. She smells like the most delicious thing I've ever smelled—something flowery and heady.

Pretty and perfect.

She stares at my mouth as I come closer. The car's console digs against my waist. I can't control my hands.

Without my permission, they move to slide against her neck and pull her closer, linking in her silky hair and capturing the back of her head in my hold.

She licks those full, pink lips.

I slant my mouth to touch hers in a light kiss, then pull back and look at her with our noses barely touching. "You feel like the right girl."

Kiley's eyes dance at my words. She grabs the sides of my jacket and kisses me, her tongue sweeping across the inside of my lips. I move one hand from her neck to snake down her back, her sweater soft as a rabbit's fur.

I press her close to my chest. She skates her hands into my open jacket and around my back. The tension shooting through me rivals running down the football field with somebody on my ass. Our mouths move hungrily against each other's. I graze my teeth along her full bottom lip and there's nothing I'd like more than to eat her up.

Her fingers tighten their grasp on my shirt, her fingernails barely skimming my back. She feels better than I imagined. The console prevents me from pulling more of her body against mine.

We break apart panting, our air mingling.

"We'd have more room in the backseat." I regret my words when her brow furrows. Shit! Now she thinks I'm expecting to get laid. "Only kissing. Promise."

She gulps so loud I hear it. "OK."

I open my door and run around to the driver's side to open hers. She steps out and gives me a shy smile.

Both of us are shaking from the cold by the time we're in the backseat. I take off my jacket and wrap it around her.

She leans against me, her teeth clicking together from the chill. "This is nice."

"Yeah."

"I've always had a crush on you, Gunner

Parrish."

I smile with my head above hers and out of sight. "I've always had a thing for you, too."

"Good," she says. She turns into me, her hands running over my chest and her lips meeting mine.

Our kiss escalates with my tongue darting into her sweet mouth and my hands skating up and down her back, over her sides so near the swell of her breasts.

Her hands find the bottom of my untucked shirt and skim higher on my bare skin.

My heart's beating so hard it's sure to explode at any moment. A kiss was all I wanted, but I think she loves this as much as I do.

More might happen. My life sucks lately, but this night might redeem all the suckage and make it bearable.

Kiley moves a hand to the front of my chest to rest over my pounding heart. She pulls her lips back. "I don't want you to think that I do this—"

"Shush," I say and stroke her hair back from her face. "I don't make out with just any girl. Unless it's the right girl. And this is the beginning, not a one-time thing."

I don't tell her that I'm a virgin. That I'm scared shitless that we'll go too far or not far enough. That I'm scared this thing between us will slip through my fingers and I'll wake from a dream.

"God, you're so beautiful." I whisper the words as I lean forward and kiss the edge of her jaw, the crook of her neck, the base of her throat.

She unbuttons the top buttons of my shirt and stares at the open V of my shirt collar. "Your skin is so warm."

I tentatively touch the top button of her sweater. My gaze flicks from the button, up to her eyes. She nods without me having to ask. I unbutton three buttons of her cardigan painfully slow. If I don't stay slow and steady, she'll see how much I want to race down her buttons and shove the sweater down off her shoulders. Her white lace bra peeks from the top of the opening and my dick gets even harder, if that's possible.

Our eyes lock on one another. Daring each other because our heartbeats match rhythm in time. Ba boom. Ba boom. Ba boom. Then my mouth crashes onto hers and I'm wrestling with her buttons and she threads her fingers through my hair.

Kiley falls back against the seat and I slide on top of her, pressing my erection against her thigh and not caring that she'll know.

We're beyond being coy.

Meeep. Meeeep. Meeep.

It takes more than a second to realize it's my

ringtone—the one that sounds like a weather alert warning. Reserved for only one person in my contacts, the sound causes my heart rate to jump for a different reason.

"Just a sec," I gasp.

We break apart and I struggle to pull the phone from my pocket.

"Hello," I answer. She never calls unless it's important.

"Um...Gunner? Sorry to bother you while you're out."

"Mom. What is it?"

"I'm sick and think I should probably go to the emergency room. That last round of chemo really did a number on me. I can't quit vomiting."

A wave of pure panic washes over me. "I'm coming."

"Don't speed," she says. Her weak voice scares the hell out of me.

Kiley's wide eyes are sympathetic, but I don't have time to explain. "Is everything OK? Do you need me—"

"No. Gotta go." I leave Kiley in the backseat without explanation and run faster than I ever have on the football field. I run because I shouldn't have left Mom alone in the house.

She'd begged me to go and let her have some time to rest. Read a book. Watch a movie without me hovering. But I was wrong to leave.

I don't have time for high school or Kiley Vanderbilt.

I run because Mom wouldn't call me unless it was bad.

Animosity

Current Day

Kiley

THE FITTING ROOM OF VISIONS BRIDAL smells like designer perfume, new fabric, and old money. I fidget in front of the three-way mirror and my wedding gown of silk and lace whispers against my skin. I've dreamed about this moment most my life.

Except, a woozy feeling swirls in my gut. Things are very wrong with this picture of happily-ever-after.

Perhaps my wooziness is only because I'm sweating more than a hardcore dieter in an ice cream shop. Lately, I've drowned my nerves in tubs of mocha chocolate chip, as evidenced by the snug fit of my wedding dress that I naively bought a size too small.

I wave my hand in front of my face to circulate air and ironically crave more ice cream.

The overly cheerful woman working at Visions kneels behind me, fluffing the elaborate train. The gilded mirror of the empty shop reveals my every angle. My fiancé, Mason, ignores me in favor of checking email or texting while he sits in a small velvet chair. Why did he insist on coming if he isn't going to pay attention?

The Visions' store clerk, an attractive middle-aged woman, finally stands, walks around in front of me, then stares at my chest. "Kiley, I think it's gorgeous. Breathtaking. Does it feel all right? I don't think we can take out the bosom anymore. We don't want to ruin the drape of the Leavers lace. We couldn't take the risk."

"Mm hm." I can't say more because I need to conserve my energy for sucking in and shallow breathing.

The pearl encrusted lace bodice itches like a fiberglass bra, and I rub two fingers inside the fabric encasing my cleavage. If I weren't waiting for Mason to look up from his phone, I'd be changing. Pronto.

"Mason? Remind me again why you insisted on coming to this fitting? You're not even looking."

He swipes a finger across his cell phone display. "Oh, of course I am." He lifts his head and eyes me approvingly with small nods of his head.

I attempt to calm down. The last thing I want is to start another fight with him. Unclenching my fists and my jaw, I inhale and exhale and inhale again. I examine the bodice for any signs that one more inhale will bust a seam. Who knew breathing could be dangerous?

Pre-Wedding Disappointment #1: Not sticking to tradition where the groom doesn't see the bride until she walks down the aisle, one of those old-fashioned ideas I had about weddings.

We're the new-age, non-sentimental couple. No secrets between us, he'd said. I'm a little sad that he won't be surprised to see my gorgeous gown.

Disappointment #2, that led to fights one through three of the week: Him telling me how to wear my hair for the wedding, which jewelry is acceptable—a pearl choker he gave me for a wedding gift that's uglier than a hairless cat, and last, his arrangement for us to spend our wedding night at his parents' home in Dallas before we leave on our honeymoon. He's crazy if he thinks I want to spend a night of passion with his parents twenty feet down the hallway.

Disappointment #3: He's taken to buying me gifts instead of apologizing when he is clearly in the wrong. A second wedding gift of lingerie, white sheer panties that will give me a wedgie before I make it to the altar and won't make me forget our huge argument about a prenup.

He clears his throat. "My mother said she's going to have to add fifty people to the wedding list. They're friends of my father's," he says. "It's so late now, they'll know they were forgotten from the original list. You won't mind if she tells them you forgot to send their invitations..."

He keeps talking, but I shift my attention to my reflection. His mother. He's already agreed to what she wants without asking what I thought.

He gives the store clerk a dazzling smile reserved for pretty female witnesses in the courtroom. "Miss, I'd bet you've heard every word I've said." He adds a wink. "But my future bride seems distracted. Do you mind stepping out for one minute so I can talk with her in private?"

The woman flushes and returns an approving smile. "Of course."

He stares at me in the mirror. "You see my point?"

"Oh. Sorry. What were you saying?"

He offers me an impatient smile, so tight his lips disappear. "We have to talk about your dad's show."

"Now? We've been over this." I tug at the confining bodice. He's not going to like it when I strip down naked in the middle of the store.

He smiles again. "I think we need to clear the air before I leave for New York. My flight leaves in a couple of hours."

"You're leaving early?"

"I must've forgotten to tell you." He finally puts the flipping phone in his pocket. "I know you're slated to star in Forever this season, but it's ludicrous. You don't need a career. Being my wife will be a full-time job."

Mason crosses one leg across the other to rest an ankle on his knee. He's not wearing socks with his cream summer suit, and I focus on his tan skin—courtesy of a "work" trip he took alone to the Bahamas last month.

"I can't believe we're going to talk about this again. I'm tired of arguing with you."

"I don't want my wife working instead of concentrating on our family. I've ordered credit cards for you. You'll have an allowance."

"An allowance?" I frown into the three-way mirror. "I'm not a teenager."

"You're acting like one."

I pull the bodice from my skin to give me some relief. Deep breath. "I have wanted to be on the show ever since the first season. This is very important to me."

"For Christ's sake, it's a reality show."

Mason rolls his eyes. "You know I won't be stingy with you when it comes to money. You're accustomed to your father's bank account. I understand."

"I don't care about the money. It's something I want to do with my degree. I know Forever isn't broadcast journalism, but I have a knack for this. I've been matching up my friends with the right guys since high school. I'm good at matchmaking and this will get me noticed. It could open the door to all kinds of opportunities." His expression says he doesn't understand.

Money makes sense to him. I should stick to mentioning what I'll get paid.

He sighs and narrows his gaze. It's a hard look, one I'm not used to seeing from him. "You're not single anymore. You think it sounds exciting to be on television. I get that. But can you think about me for once? What about my needs?"

He gets to his feet and strolls toward the mirror without breaking eye contact. Placing his hands on my shoulders, he leans in and kisses the back of my neck in a brief, perfunctory way.

When he lifts his head, his face is corporate serious. "I'm going to be honest. I should've stated this earlier. There is no fucking way my wife can be on a reality show. It's a bad idea. I'll be the laughing stock of the firm. If you ever

28

want me to make it past junior partner—"

"I can't believe you're asking me to sit at home and wait for you to come home every day." My voice cracks. I stand straighter so I can get some air into my lungs. I can't look at him, with his concerned look, as if I'm the one ruining some perfect plan he has for our life.

He moves both hands to my upper arms and squeezes lightly, the pressure making me look at him again in the mirror.

"I didn't realize you put this reality show over our marriage. I've never kept my career goals a secret. But when I put that ring on your finger, you agreed to a partnership," he says.

"Giving up everything I want sure sounds like a dictatorship."

He caresses my shoulders. The three-way-reflection doesn't lie, portraying how nice we look together—he in the tailored suit, me in the pearl and gossamer, albeit itchy, gown.

Walking around me so we're face-to-face, he grabs my chin and tugs my face upward. "My sweet girl. I love your ambition. I do. But what happens when we have children? Will your wants and needs come before them? Maybe you'll send them off to summer camps and miss their recitals because you were busy."

I'm suddenly a little girl again, hundreds of miles away at a summer camp with strangers. Looking into the dark audience at the ballet recital hall, pretending my dad is out there watching, only to discover my nanny at the end of the performance.

Too many years of being homesick and heartsick. For too long the need to talk louder, be prettier, and basically perform a freaking tap dance overcame me whenever Dad entered a room.

I struggle to control the quiver in my voice. "That's not fair and you know it."

"You're right. It wasn't." He folds me into his arms. "I know you aren't your father."

Mason doesn't even mention my mother— he knows better than to go that far. I nod, unable to speak past the need to rant, but knowing I won't. He's a trial lawyer. Strategy is his game, not mine.

He kisses me gently and steps back. "I want you to know I have a plan for a financially successful family life. I don't want my wife trying to juggle a career and the people she loves. I don't want you to have to choose."

"Women today don't have to choose."

"And who told you that? Your feminist friends?" He shakes his head. "We can talk about it later. I can't miss this flight. I'll see you back in Nashville."

I look at myself in the mirror and pretend to adjust the bodice of my dress. If I don't keep my hands busy, I may succumb to punching him in the throat for the feminist remark.

How have I missed this small yet important attitude about women?

"Don't pout," he says. "Where's my future bride I love so much?"

"Not pouting." I allow one corner of my mouth to lift in a half-hearted smile. I'm overreacting. He's parroting his father and the handful of partners I've met at the firm. All male.

He'll learn I'm my own person and plan to have a career.

"Oh," he says and looks at his cell. "I almost forgot. We have to host a dinner party on Friday night. It's very important that we make a good impression. We can use your father's house since he's on that cruise. My apartment isn't right for this."

"This Friday? As in a few days from today?"

"Plenty of time. Three couples from the firm. And you'll do a fantastic job because you are my incredible Kiley." He tweaks my nose, something I hate but I'm not fast enough to step back and avoid. He walks toward the door of the shop.

I pick up the yards of gossamer fabric circling my legs and twirl to watch him go. "But that's not enough notice. No one can arrange a dinner party of that size this quickly."

He smiles at me with the confidence of a

newly promoted junior partner of Ellison, Montgomery, and Caldwell, LLP. "Of course you can. But if you don't feel up to it, call my mother. She'd love to help."

I bet. She'd love to prove I can't do it alone.

He checks his phone. "I'll talk to you tomorrow. I hope you won't be upset with me. I know you. I know where your heart is and what will make you happy. And see? You thought you could handle the stress of a television show and you're getting stressed out over a meal."

I hear the chime of the door as he leaves the bridal shop. I close my eyes and exhale in a long shuddering breath. Pre-wedding jitters dance around my brain, taunting me. I've known what kind of man Mason is. I wanted a man who wants to be involved in every part of his partner's life.

A family man.

Not a man who wants everything to revolve around him.

I rub the hollow between my breasts, wishing I could tear this gown off. Everything about it chokes me. "Ma'am?" I call out in a choked voice. What was her name?

She doesn't appear.

I grab the silk fabric of the train and tiptoe into the dressing room to close the door. I reach around with one hand to locate the tiny hooks above the hidden zipper. Must break out of the dress before I hyperventilate. If I can cool off, I can think. I skate my fingers along the back of the dress, searching futilely. No need to panic.

I continue my pat-down of the dress back until my arms hurt from contorting. I'm welded into this dress forever. A woman who had too much mocha chocolate ice cream last week and is paying the price now.

But that's silly. It's not only the tight dress. It's the vice-like grip of Mason's words. Does he realize I don't want to bend to everything he wants? Let me pick out my own freaking underwear, even if it's basic cotton panties.

I sit on the padded chair in the corner of the private dressing room. The fabric pinches my waistline in protest. "I need out of this dress!"

OK, my voice sounded way too loud and toddler-like, but I cannot help it. Tears threaten behind my eyelids. I will not allow myself to get worked up and ruin this damned beautiful day of being fitted for my wedding dress. I'm wearing Vera Wang and this dress demands some composure.

Silence.

"Help?" My pitiful voice is barely a whisper.

"Are you talking to me?" a female voice says.

Who else? I think crankily. "Yes." I struggle to get up from the chair.

"Can I come in?" she says.

"Yes. Please."

The door swings open and it's not the clerk from earlier. A very pretty woman my age stands in the open doorway, a pearl encrusted wedding headpiece pinned in her hair.

She holds out a hand to help me up. "Wow, just wow," she says. "Your dress is to die for."

I take her hand and stand. "Thank you. But you don't have to help me get undressed. I thought you were the lady helping me earlier. Where did she go?"

"She probably took a break when she saw me come in. The clerk here hates me. Turn and I'll get the back."

I obey and feel instant relief as she unfastens the hooks. She slides the zipper down.

"Why would she hate you? You're a client," I say and glance over my shoulder.

I examine the girl closer. Her hair is fire engine red, and she has a tattoo of a moon and some stars across her upper forearm and onto her shoulders. The combination of her pale skin, vibrant hair, and blue tattoos makes her pop like an exciting Fourth of July display.

She chuckles, the laugh deep and so contagious that I know I'm smiling back.

"I can't buy a wedding dress in this place," she says. "I can't even afford the headpiece. I only love trying this one on until the day I get married."

"Oh." I'm not sure what to say to that. "So you already have your dress?" She pulls the dress over my head. I'm careful to keep my face away from the fabric. The last thing I need is a makeup spot.

"Yes, I made my own wedding dress. I do alterations for a living and have an obsession with this veil. It's crazy expensive and such a waste of money."

She hangs my gown on the padded hanger inside the protective dress bag, fluffs out the fabric, and grins. "You've got killer taste."

"Thanks. So do you."

"Adam and I decided to marry in a park near here. We're renting a pavilion and our friends will be there. It'll be the best."

"A park sounds wonderful." Soon, I'll be standing at the altar with Mason in the Diamonds Event Hall, a venue that will hold our five hundred guests.

"I told Adam that we should elope, but he said he wants to let the world know that I'll be his one and only forever. He's kind of passionate like that." She giggles, a husky sound that hints at all kinds of unsaid things. "I'd do anything for him. And I love my dress, but this veil. Ethereal, don't you think? But maybe I'll put some flowers in my hair." She touches the veil, as if to assure herself it's still perched on her head. "I won't waste our savings. We need it for a down payment on a house."

"So, you're a seamstress. I wish I had a talent like that. By the way, I'm Kiley." I step into my beige slacks as she backs out of my dressing room.

"Yeah. I'm so rude! I'm Zoey. If you need anything altered, I'm your girl." She reaches into the bag on her shoulder and pulls out a couple of plain white business cards. "If anything comes up last minute at your wedding, call me and I'll alter it."

"Zoey," I repeat. "Nice to meet you." I take the cards. "I'll give you a call if I need something for the wedding. Thanks."

"Good luck. With that dress, you must feel like the luckiest woman alive. I bet your guy won't know what hit him when he sees you walk down the aisle in it for the first time."

"Hm..." I don't bother to say he's already seen it. Mason didn't even say if he liked the dress. Dammit. He was too busy making sure I knew what he expected from me. The prick of tears behind my eyelids increases as they threaten to spill, so I study her card. There's a business address with a little needle and thread running through Zoey's name.

"Nice to meet you. I've got to run." Zoey steps back and glances at the dress hanging on the dressing room wall. "Happy wedding."

"You too."

She lifts the headpiece from her hair, untangling a strand of her red hair. Then she's gone.

I shouldn't be jealous of her, of the way she said her finance's name and the way her eyes twinkled when she talked about her wedding. I have a fiancé willing to give me the world. That is, a world without my own career or my own voice.

I leave the dressing room and browse through a shelf of wedding jewelry. I toss a glance over my shoulder as the clerk comes to stand beside me.

The clerk sniffs. "I hate the riff raff. Girls like that one come in with no intention of buying—"

"The veil she was trying on? Can you box that up for me?"

The woman stares at me. "But you already have a custom piece."

"I know. Please box that up and send it to this address overnight." I hand her one of Zoey's business cards. "I'd like it there by tomorrow."

"But do you know her?" Shock ripples in a wave over her face.

"I do now. Put it on my account."

"Hmph. She's definitely lucky that you were here today." She appears perplexed. "I'll put a gift card from you in the box."

"No," I say. "Please insert a card that says courtesy of the bridal shop. I don't want her to know it came from me. Put something sweet and romantic on the card."

"Like what?"

For someone who works in weddings, she has no imagination. I think about it for a minute. "How about, 'May your marriage be filled with romance and passion, held together by the threads of your love.'"

She looks at me like I'm a loon. "All of that? The gift cards are small."

"Yes," I answer, getting slightly irritated. "All of it."

My cell phone tings and I pull it out of my bag to read the text message. The clerk takes the opportunity to escape.

Mason: Guests arrive at six. I'll send over something for you to wear. I know you won't let me down.

I place my phone back in my purse; a dull thumping in my head warns that I'll have a migraine soon. Romance and passion. It's out there. Zoey is proof.

Ever since I was eight years old and my mother walked out on my dad and me, I vowed to find true love.

I've had this image of what true love is supposed to be—the kind of love that you feel in your bones as you drift off to sleep. The kind that follows you safe and sound into your dreams. The kind where people care more about each other than themselves. Sacrifice.

A season of my dad's reality show Forever only takes four weeks to film. Six weeks tops. Surely Mason can sacrifice his ideas for less than two months, when we'll be married a lifetime.

The woozy feeling in my belly settles down when I think about Dad's reality show. The magic of finding soulmates proves that true love and passion aren't dead.

I'm more determined than before. I can't cancel my spot as Matchmaker on the show. This season is mine to match a bachelor with his forever love.

Mad For Her

Current Day

Gunner

I WONDER IF KILEY VANDERBILT WEARS a princess tiara to bed. It wouldn't surprise me.

Pretentious is her middle name.

She sits in her black Cadillac SUV honking her horn while she waits for me to move my backhoe off her driveway. The bleating sound grates over every ounce of patience I possess. I wipe my sweaty forehead against the sleeve of my T-shirt, and my baseball cap tumbles to the ground.

Dang-it. Now I'll have to get down and retrieve my hat.

"Hold up," I mutter to myself and flash a stiff smile in her direction. I hold up my pointer finger—not the finger I'd like to give her. I drive the backhoe out of her way and wait for her to pull forward.

She accelerates a couple of yards and rolls

down her window and says something at me. Her chestnut hair is pulled back with a scarf thing in a stick-up-her-ass hairstyle. Between the hair and the sunglasses two sizes too big for her head, she looks like some movie star straight off the cover of one of those trashy tabloids.

A rich, snooty star. Rumor has it she's landed a spot on her daddy's TV show this season.

"What?" I yell and then shake my head in resignation. The engine's too loud for either of us to have a conversation, yet she keeps talking. Those ruby lips could hypnotize a weaker man. I shut the engine off.

She tilts her head halfway out her open window. "What are you doing?" Her voice screeches as if she doesn't realize she doesn't have to scream.

The girl always had a motor mouth on her. In school, I'd have sold my soul to have her talk to me. We were from different worlds then and nothing has changed.

Nothing at all. She's still a living doll, but annoying with her demands.

I step down and saunter to the vehicle. Sometimes a guy needs a closer look at a snake. Her head pops back into the SUV. Maybe she's coiling back so she can strike. I grin at the notion.

"I have guests coming tomorrow night. This is a mess." Her eyebrow lifts above the dark frame of her sunglasses.

"I told your dad that the driveway will be out of commission for a couple of days. He said no one would be home this week."

"My dad said what?" She flips her sunglasses up to sit on top of her head as if it will help her hearing. The flash of diamonds on one hand catches my eye for an instant before I notice her red-rimmed eyes.

She must've pulled an all-nighter. Everything about her is polished except for her eyes. Puffy, pink eyelids. For a second I wonder if she's been crying. Girl sits in a fine ride, living with her rich daddy. She can't have a care in the world.

Nah. Not crying. Girl needs to stop her partying and get some rest.

"Ed said he wanted this done. Talk to your dad," I say.

Her mouth purses as if she's sucking on a lemon. "I don't have time for this."

Me either, woman. I stare into her hypnotic gaze for an eternity. I shake my head to break her spell. "I should get back to work."

I turn and walk to the backhoe, feeling her gaze on my back. There's a barking sound behind me and in the next instant, a tiny tug at my jeans. I glance down to find a furry, rat-sized dog attacking my leg.

"Westley!" Kiley steps out of the SUV. "Westley! Come. Here."

Kiley has sure grown up. Her bright green dress ends at her upper thighs. The snake has legs. Shapely legs I remember from our school days. I reach down to grab the dog who has mounted my boot, humping with passion. The moment I lift my foot, the dog falls off, slightly disoriented that I've cut short his hook-up session.

Darting around my feet, he tries to woo my boot once more. He escapes my attempts to grab him and yips in a frenzy until he suddenly stops, his attention on my fallen baseball cap. Her dog runs twice around it, then lifts a leg and with perfect aim, saturates my cap. My favorite St. Louis Cardinals hat.

"Dog, I'm going to—"

"Don't you dare!" Kiley steps over a section of busted driveway, wobbling precariously in her high heels. "I'm coming."

I make another grab at the dog and pick him up. The last thing I need is for the dog to fall into the hole I've dug for the tree being delivered tomorrow.

"I've got him." The words are out of my mouth when a gush of hot liquid trickles down my chest. "Holy hell," I mutter and close my eyes, my nostrils flaring as I attempt to stay calm. I open my eyes and Kiley stands inches in front of me.

"You scared him." She takes the wiggling dog out of my hold. The sunglasses are gone and her eyes flash fury.

I widen my eyes in disbelief. "Your dog pissed on me."

"Yes, because he was afraid." She clutches the evil thing to her chest like she's caught me in an unforgivable act. "You're big, and he's little. Shame on you."

"You should teach your dog some manners. He was getting it on with my boot, if you didn't notice."

I pull my T-shirt away from my skin. It's one hundred degrees in the Nashville August heat, and I smell like a porta potty. I step back and tug my shirt over my head with one hand.

Kiley's jaw drops, her red lips parting. "Put your shirt back on." Her gaze travels down my chest and back up.

I blow out a weary breath. "I'm not wearing dog piss. Don't look if you don't like it."

Her little monster has settled down, his pink tongue licking at her neck. She snuggles him closer and the open V neckline of her dress scoops lower underneath the strain of his feet. I wish I could trade places with the varmint.

"I wasn't," she says, taking one awkward step back in her high heels. She averts her gaze and then returns to meet my eyes.

I can't help but chuckle. Her dog had amorous thoughts earlier. Maybe she has similar ones.

"Don't I know you?" Kiley stands straighter and asks in a citizen's arrest tone of voice.

I could be persuaded to hook-up with her. If she didn't have to talk, that is. Listening to her would be a mood killer. I shrug and wad the T-shirt into a ball. My cap lays wet on the ground and I retrieve it before walking away. Now destined for the trashcan—courtesy of the incontinent terror.

So, she doesn't remember me. I'm not surprised, but I am stupidly disappointed. We were in the same classes. Her locker was twenty yards down on the same hallway. I played football on the same field where she twirled her baton.

It all started in first grade, when she wore those cute red cowboy boots every day and ended after one memorable backseat tango. Apparently, that's all she wanted from me. One hot and heavy make out session was enough for her.

I didn't even get to second base, which to this day sort of irritates me. Hell, I barely got to step off home plate.

"Hey. You!" she yells to my back.

Her use of the pronoun instead of my name

forces me to grind my teeth. I pause and look over my shoulder. She stands in the same spot with a bewildered look on her face.

"You have to get that thing," she says, pointing at the backhoe, "out of here. I need all these holes filled and everything back the way it was."

Since she's not paying the bill, I'm not sure if I should laugh or tell her to get lost. I turn completely and glare at her. "I take my orders from Ed."

Ed Vanderbilt ordered landscaping and lights down his entire driveway. He said no one would be at home all week—five more days. Kiley was somewhere like New York or Dallas. Some city far away where she should be carrying that dog around while someone carries her shopping bags.

"Dad's not here, so you'll have to take orders from me," she says.

I place my hands on my hips and a corner of my mouth quirks. "Is that right?"

She nods, looking a little less sure of herself. "Well, yes. Absolutely."

Her voice is softer. She strokes the top of her dog's head and the diamond on her left hand flashes in the sunlight. Sweat trickles down the back of my neck. We can't stand here all day, arguing. "Please?" she adds in an oddly vulnerable voice.

"Call Ed," I say on a sigh. Damn. This is the way girls like her get what they want. "If he says I need to do anything different, I will."

"Dad isn't available. He's on a cruise ship with a...friend," she says, again with the softer tone and pleading gaze.

For the briefest moment, I rack my brain for a way around this problem. There's not one. This job needs to be finished before Ed returns home. I scold myself for wanting to give in to her. "I can't help you then. I'm really sorry."

"What am I supposed to do? I have guests coming." The panic in her voice certainly doesn't equal the problem. Drama queen. Yes, a tiara is in order.

"So, let them come." I turn and walk to my equipment.

"You move that one inch, and I'm calling the police and saying you're trespassing. And you are, since I've asked you to get off the driveway."

Now she has my attention. Although I have a work order, a call to the police will cause me problems while I try to sort out the accusation, especially since Ed is gone. There's nothing like having to prove you're innocent.

"Give me a break. I'm only trying to do my job. I can leave, and then you'll have these huge holes, unfinished landscaping, and Ed will be pissed off."

She clutches the dog into the crook of her

arm as if she's holding a baby and walks to meet me. "Can't you do some other job? And fill up these holes first?"

I tilt my head back and look skyward. It's better if I don't look into her warm eyes. Eyes like rich soil with glints of amber tree sap. "I could, um...do the back koi pond."

"It's a deal."

I look down to see she's holding out one hand to shake on it. "My hands are filthy."

She drops her hand and shifts awkwardly, studying me again—my hands, my bare chest, and then my face.

If I had a dollar for all the dirty thoughts I can read on her face, I could pay off my expensive new backhoe. "I'll fill this one since the tree hasn't been delivered yet. The others have to go in. The koi pond is on the other side of the pool in back. And this thing of yours is tomorrow night? Then I can get back to this?"

She nods. "Yes. You can do whatever you like after tomorrow night."

"Good." I slap my hands together. "Better get to work then."

"I'll be on my way." She returns to her vehicle and drives toward the house, a sprawling two-story Tudor in the distance. I make fast work of scooping the pile of dirt back into the hole. This delay will cost me a couple of hours, and I'll be working later tonight than I expected.

No matter. It's not as though I have anything waiting for me at home.

DUSK CREEPS IN, the hour when the sun finally drops without notice and hidden night creatures stir. I inhale deeply and take in the beauty of the land that stretches forever past the Vanderbilts' fences, past the creek that runs on the other side, past the mountain in the distance.

The Vanderbilts don't know how lucky they are to possess a back lawn like this—not a neighbor's house in sight.

I finish digging the koi pond and placing the liners inside. I'll have to change the delivery of the stones and medium-sized shrubs, but that's easy enough to do, since I'm the boss. I study the size of the prepared holes I've dug for the camellia shrubs.

"Westley." Kiley's voice travels across the back lawn.

A sudden yipping at my heels startles me. Kiley's dog is in full guard mode while he darts to and fro within inches of my ankles. I know I'm bigger than he is, but he looks like he's a biter with razor sharp teeth. It's a good thing I wore boots.

I place the end of a shovel on the ground. "Hey. Calm your tiny ass."

"Excuse me?" Kiley says to my back.

"I wasn't talking to you." I glance around to look at her. She's no longer wearing the green dress from earlier. She's changed clothes. I only thought she was tempting all dressed up earlier. Now, she's in shorts and a snug-collared shirt. The top button hits deep into her cleavage, and I make an effort to pull my gaze up. All the blood I possess rushes south. I imagine threading my fingers through the dark hair tumbling down her back.

"You're sunburned. You should've said something. I could've given you one of Dad's T-shirts." She's staring at my bare chest again.

"I'm fine. Unless my lack of clothing bothers you." I can't help myself. I smile at her pink cheeks.

Westley the tiny terror gives a low growl, so she picks him up. The dog has her figured out. "Sorry. He's protective of me."

"That's clear. Maybe you should train him better. He thinks I'm a threat to his alpha dog status."

"They teach canine behavior in gardening school?"

"I'm a landscape technician. Not a

gardener." I don't know why I'm so defensive. Usually, I'd joke about being called a gardener.

She narrows her eyes. "You and Westley might have more in common than you think."

"How do you figure that?"

"You both have a chip on your shoulder."

"Honey, you're wrong. No chip here." Now she thinks she knows me. She doesn't remember my name, but now she's going to psychoanalyze me. I glance at my shoulder and return to my task of shoveling gravel around the edges of the pond liner. "Why does Terror the Terrier have a chip?"

The nickname fits the tiny maniac perfectly.

"Quit calling him that. His name is Westley."

"What kind of dog name is that?"

"He's named after the guy in The Princess Bride. Westley came from a breeder. I discovered things about the place after I bought him."

"Puppy mill?"

She nods. I give her a look, then squat down and straighten a piece of landscape material. I've seen enough in the news to imagine the puppy living in tight quarters with a mama only used for making babies. Poor dog.

"What? It's not my fault. I love Yorkies."

"You could've rescued a shelter dog. Instead, you helped support the puppy mill by paying for a dog. Besides, a pedigree doesn't

51

matter when it comes to love." I stand and lean on the shovel. Westley pants, his tiny pink tongue waving at me, and never takes his eyes from my hands.

Of course, it does matter to her. If it didn't, she'd probably remember me from school.

I shake myself out of the trance, hoping only a second has passed instead of the eternity it feels like. "I think I'll head home for dinner. At least I got this done." I nod at the nearly finished koi pond.

"Do you want a sandwich?" she asks. Her velvet voice is seductive and at odds with the practical question.

"What?" I'm positive I didn't hear her correctly.

"A sandwich."

"Nah. I'm good." I remove the gloves I put on this afternoon to use the shovel.

"You have something against me making you a sandwich? I know you stayed late to do this." She waves at the koi pond.

I smirk. The truth might be that I hoped to get a glimpse of her again. "No. It's best that I leave."

"I guess you need to get home to your wife. She probably cooked for you."

There's a weird tension in the air. "No."

"No, she doesn't cook?"

"No, I'm not married."

"Oh. Why not?"

I shrug. This conversation is getting weirder by the second. "I...um...don't know. I'm not the marrying type."

"Hmm..." She absently strokes the top of Westley's head. "Everyone's the marrying type. You simply have to find the right one to marry."

Her tone suggests this is a little known fact from Wikipedia and she's educating me. I laugh and shove my leather gloves into my back pocket.

"I'm serious." She tilts her head to one side as if trying to make sense of me. "I insist you have a sandwich. Come."

I should tell her I need to wash my Jeep. Or organize my laundry. Or pick up a hooker. Anything but spend more time getting hypnotized by the poisonous rattler wearing a rock on her finger.

She pivots on the balls of her feet. I notice that she's barefoot as she strolls past the pool and to the back patio.

I wipe my hands down the front of my work jeans and walk toward the French doors. My footsteps slow as I near. I haven't been inside the house before. Now, I stand at the threshold of the open door, uneasy as a vampire waiting to be asked inside.

"Hello?" I yell. She's nowhere in sight. I knew this was a mistake.

"In here," she yells back.

I follow the direction of her voice, walking through the back sunroom and reaching a hallway. "I don't know where you are."

"Kitchen."

That tells me absolutely nothing. I make a guess and take a left since there's more light coming from that end of the hall. When I get to the end, Kiley stands with her head stuck fully inside the refrigerator.

"You don't need to make me anything. Really."

"Are you saying I don't know how to make a sandwich? What do you think I am? An idiot?"

I press my lips together and glance around the kitchen area. I take a seat at the long wood table. It's one of those distressed things that's supposed to look old. I wonder if anyone ever eats at it.

Her head pops above the refrigerator door. "Prosciutto?"

"Mmm...I don't know what that is. Do you have turkey?

"No," she says. "We have prosciutto. I've never made a sandwich with it, but I'm sure it will work." She pulls the package from the fridge. "Mason—that's my fiancé—he expects me to host a dinner party here with no notice. Tomorrow night for three couples. He says it will be my job to whip up catering or whatever at a moment's notice, because that's what his future wife should do. Can you believe that?"

I don't answer. So that's why she's throwing a fit over the landscaping in front. It's clear to me now why I'm sitting in the kitchen. She needed to vent and I'll do for a sounding board. Rich people problems. She'd better get used to her fiancé treating her this way if he's doing it before they're even married.

I hold back from stating my last thought. Surely, there's a more neutral topic that won't lead to a fight. I glance around the kitchen. "Where's Westley?"

"I put him in the laundry room while you're inside. I don't want him to bite you." She pulls a plate from the cupboard.

"Don't want him sneaking up on me." I peer to the left and right, then back up to watch her making the sandwich and cutting it diagonally. "You don't need to do anything special with it. Bread and meat is fine."

She ignores me, pulling some fancy pickles and shit from the fridge. "You can tidy up in the mudroom."

Tidy up. Why is she pretending we're good friends and she's casually making me a bite to eat? Clients don't make sandwiches for me. "Listen, Kiley. I really should go."

She freezes, her back straightening and shoulders tensing. Then, she turns and leans back against the counter. "Are you sure we don't know each other from somewhere? What did you say your name is?"

"Gunner. Gunner Parrish."

"Gunner," she repeats. "I knew that was you!"

Sure, she did.

"Why were you pretending we didn't know each other? I couldn't place you. You should've told me earlier."

She has got to be joking. As if I want to acknowledge that she ignored me after the night of the bonfire. I'd have cut my heart out and offered it on a platter to her. But all that was before my life went south.

Literally. I went southwest to Arkansas in a move that changed my life.

I inhale. "I don't think you really want to reminiscence about old times, do you? I think you've got some little party to worry about now and you want to make sure I stay on board to make it happen without a hitch."

Her expression says I've hit a raw chord. "You're kidding, right?"

"It's OK. I still get paid, but let's not pretend that we run in the same circles."

She abandons the sandwich prep and stalks across the kitchen, still holding the knife. "You haven't changed one bit. You were a broody, sulky teenage boy who stopped speaking to me all of a sudden. I'm seeing that same sulky boy all grown up."

But after that night at the bonfire, I called you and texted you over and over, I want to say. You never answered when you could've made my world better than the hell it was.

Silence.

The slam, slam, slam of my heart as it speeds up.

The sounds of both our breathing in the otherwise silent kitchen.

"So what's your excuse for being a sorry SOB when I kept trying to talk to you?" She crosses the room to stand too close.

I'm not going to tell her how much I wanted her to make my world better that year. It was a long time ago.

I get to my feet. "Yeah. I was rude. Sorry about that. Mom had cancer that year, and your hurt feelings didn't rate very high compared to that."

Surprise, embarrassment, and regret take turns flickering across her face in succession.

"I'll finish the koi pond early tomorrow so I won't be around when your guests get here."

I can't leave her house fast enough. For a split second, I'd returned to my youth, wondering if my life would ever get better. Kiley, the girl I had a crush on for years, took my heart and tossed it aside when I needed someone the most.

Now, she needs to know how unimportant she is to me.

Current Day

Kiley

A MAN LIKE GUNNER PARRISH has to know the effect he has on women. His broad shoulders and massive chest taper down to a trim waist. The white T-shirt hugs him like a second skin, perspiration from hard work shows in the center of his back when he turns around. His back muscles flex against the damp fabric.

My maid-of-honor, Josie, and I stand at the window of my bedroom on the second floor of the house. I started out showing her my wedding trousseau. Since noticing Gunner outside, we've reverted to our teen years and can't tear ourselves from the view.

A faded red ball cap hides Gunner's face. I hope he hasn't noticed us, because we're gawking. There's no other word for it. I tear my gaze from the manly form working hard to finish the koi pond in the back lawn. "We should really get busy," I say to her.

"Five more minutes..." she murmurs. "My brother said Gunner was back in town. I don't think I would've recognized him. He was tall and lanky back then. That man filled out."

Perfect. She's as captivated by him as much as I am. "We're going to get caught watching."

Josie doesn't even turn her head away from the window. "We need a break from this wedding talk. Gunner Parrish. Huh. I don't think I've drooled over a man like this since my freshman year of college."

"Who was it?"

"Brad Delamark. Football player. Tight end. Real tight end." She mutters this with perfect timing as Gunner bends over to pick up something.

I furrow my brow, attempting to remember this Brad guy. "Is he the one you followed around campus for weeks?"

"Yes. Good memory. Hey. I think I need a koi pond. It's a beautiful sight. How much do these things cost?"

Although I know she's ogling Gunner purely for fun, the thought of her ogling him without me sends a nasty jolt through my veins.

"Mmm..." I give in and look down at the lawn. "I made out with Gunner one night in tenth grade. He moved soon after that."

"I'd have to ask him for a trip down memory

lane." She grins. "I need details. Is 'made out' code for sex?"

"No. It's not," I answer with a hint of regret.

"At least tell me there was heavy petting involved."

"What exactly qualifies as 'heavy'?" I smirk at her. "No, you don't have to be jealous. I barely remember it," I lie. "Besides, he was a jerk then and sort of a jerk now."

"I remember liking him in school."

I lift one shoulder as if it's no big deal. "Yeah, I did, too."

"Where does the jerk part come in?"

"I don't know. I thought he'd ask me out and he never did. That doesn't really make him a jerk, huh?"

"No, not really. Unless you had sex and you're withholding information. Then he's certainly a jerk." Her head thumps against the window. "His muscles have muscles. I do not remember him looking like that. I'll have to ask Leo for an update on what Gunner's been doing." She grins at me. "OK. Backing away from the window and the beautiful man now. Slowly, so I won't have withdrawals."

I glance at her. "About the bachelorette party. I don't care where we have it. You choose."

"New Orleans is my first pick. Or Vegas." She strolls across the room and sits on my purple velvet chaise.

"Why can't we have it here?"

"You are kidding, right? Nashville is boring. Let's go somewhere wild and crazy."

I sigh. The pressure of the past few days makes me want to fly away somewhere. Maybe I can find a remote island where I can hide from the world. If I fly to Vegas, I may never come back.

I force myself to leave the window and walk to the chaise. "I think you're more excited about this bachelorette party than I am."

"Heck yeah! All I ever do is work at the bookstore." Josie scoots over and pats the space beside her. "Sit. Talk to me. What's wrong?"

"Nothing," I lie, and take a seat. As my best friend and first cousin, she knows too much about me to be satisfied with my previous answer and I know it.

She points at me. "Liar."

"Everything." I drop my head down and place both hands over my face.

"You're scared. It happens. I always hear people talk about pre-wedding jitters. They're normal."

"I hate him. Is that normal?"

"What?" Her eyebrows draw together.

"I hate the way he talks to me—like I'm supposed to take notes so I do everything he says. He's so anal about certain things. He takes better care of his cuticles than I do, for God's sake. Ugh."

"Oh, sweetie. It's nerves, that's all."

"He thinks my career plans are a joke. He wants me to break my contract to be on Forever this season. He said I'll be too busy after the wedding. That if I love him, I'll understand that he needs me."

My throat threatens to close shut. I attempt to swallow past the lump in the middle of my esophagus. I don't want to cry, but it's too late. My tear ducts have gone renegade. A small tear escapes to roll down my face. "I'm afraid it's not nerves. What if it's the beginning of a hate that grows until the day I'm standing in the back lawn with a shovel in my hand trying to figure out a way to bury him next to the koi pond?"

"You'll call me and I'll help you figure it out. The koi pond is a bad location. We'll take the body out to the lake and sink him. If the body's too heavy, Leo can come help. A twin brother should be good for something. He's my accomplice for life."

"Can we do it now and get it over with so I don't have to live with him?" I begin to laugh, a hysterical sound even to my own ears. I gasp for air in-between giggles. "Because I swear, if he tells me one more time what he wants me to wear at this dinner tonight, I'm gonna kill him."

"You're kidding." Her eyes widen and she

grins. "What does he want you to wear?"

I get to my feet and stride quickly to the closet. Tossing a look over my shoulder as I enter the walk-in, I say, "A dress that will make me look sexy, but not whorish—his words. He gave me a dress to wear so I wouldn't choose one of my own. Shoes that make my legs look long but won't make me taller than he is. My hair should be in an updo, but nothing too fancy."

"I'm surprised he didn't tell you what jewelry to wear." She follows me into the closet.

"But he did. No costume jewelry. Let me quote. 'I forbid you to wear any of that fake stuff you made.'"

"He can't be talking about the beaded jewelry you make." She picks up one Louboutin platform shoe from my rack and tries it on her bare foot.

I nod. "He is. He gave me a necklace and insists I wear it, since it matches the non-whorish dress." I stand on tiptoe and retrieve a jewelry case. Opening the lid, I stare at the large sapphire pendant on a choker. The necklace box feels leaden as I hand it across to her.

She puts the shoe back in its spot and takes the box. "I had no idea he was so…domineering. But I haven't really been around him." She places a hand on my arm. "I said it was jitters. I was wrong. Forgive me for what I'm going to say."

"Forgiven. I'm sure I've thought it already.

"If you're not sure, call the wedding off or tell him you need more time. But don't marry him because some invitations have been ordered or some other whack reason. I couldn't marry a guy trying to make me into a perfect robot wife. I'd tell him where he could shove this necklace along with the diamond." She signals with one finger to my left hand.

I stare at the engagement solitaire on my shaking hand. I was so sure the day I said yes to his proposal. We'd gone on a midnight riverboat cruise and everyone on the boat had witnessed Mason going down on one knee. I felt loved that day.

Things are changing and I see how my life might be with Mason. He's planning our life the way he prepares a legal brief—detailed and unemotional.

I give myself a mental shake. He says he loves me. He says I'm the most important thing for his happiness.

People don't call off weddings four weeks out. I have a dress and wedding presents. Caterers and a string quartet. Dad's approval that I'm marrying a solid guy.

"Mason isn't horrible. He has some good qualities. I swear he does. Every person has annoying personality traits and I'm letting his get to me."

"Tell me about it. I haven't dated a guy I can stand after the third date. That's about when I notice all the things that drive me crazy."

I attempt a smile. "Yeah, I know. Right? Mason makes these sucking sounds when he eats. Every guy is going to have something like that. How petty am I for pointing it out?"

She puts the necklace box down on a shoe rack and grabs me by the shoulders. "That's why I'm not getting married. Mason sucks his food, huh? You are talking about a lot of meals in a lifetime. Do you really want to be the one to fly across the table someday and fork him?"

My heart pounds faster as I imagine the sucking between bites of breakfast, lunch, and dinner. My stomach churns.

She continues. "I hate to say it, but that's not the worst thing you've listed about him. That alone is grounds for divorce in my book. But the controlling thing. I know you. You'll be miserable. Oh my God. I've realized something."

I lift a questioning eyebrow.

"I was trying to figure out why you are marrying this douchebag. I know." She leaves the closet with me tagging along behind her to hear the rest.

"I've made him sound worse than he is. It's pre-wedding jitters. You were right when you said it. Everyone gets them."

"He's sort of like your dad."

We're both silent for a full minute.

"Shut up," I finally say. I laugh, the sound of it forced. "You don't know what you're talking about."

"I'm sorry. I shouldn't have said that about Uncle Ed." She gives me a sad smile, her look filled with pity.

In a flash, I'm taken back to a single moment when I was five. Sitting on the top step of the staircase, I hid so I could listen to Mom and Dad arguing about whether she could open her art gallery.

Usually, Mom did what he said, quietly and without any argument. Not that day.

I glance at the clock. "Look at the time. Wow. I should get ready for the caterers to bring the food. They'll be here any minute. And then I have to shower and change. Can I call you next week?" I walk toward my bedroom door, hoping that Josie will follow me.

"Sure." She pauses and whirls around to hug me. "I'm so glad to see you again."

"I've missed you," I say into her mass of red hair. "This bachelorette thing will be fun."

Josie pulls back and looks into my face at arm's length. "We can do a party no matter what happens. Don't be mad about what I said. I want you to do what's best for you."

The sound of the doorbell saves me from

responding. "I wonder who that can be." We smile at each other, some of our earlier camaraderie missing. I walk downstairs faster than necessary.

I open the front door, only to find Gunner. "Oh, it's you." You. Tall, tanned, and toned. The one I dreamed about last night instead of my fiancé.

"Hi." Josie beams at him. "I was just leaving. I'm Josie. You were friends with my brother Leo when we were in school. And I used to follow you guys around everywhere."

Gunner looks her over as if he's not sure.

"Yeah. Sure, I remember. I've known Leo for a long time. Nice guy. But you look different." A corner of his mouth lifts.

"No braces or glasses. Figured out the bad hair issue." She winks. "I didn't even get boobs until my senior year."

Gunner stays silent as if he's not sure how to respond.

Josie stops ogling him. "You guys have details to work out. Come on in," she says and steps aside. "I'll let myself out."

He shifts his gaze to me with a relieved expression. "I wanted to find out what time the shindig starts. I'll stop work at least an hour before people arrive."

Last night, Gunner left as if he had a fire to put out. He hates me. He thinks I'm insensitive and cruel. I wish I'd known about his mother back in high school and last night.

But when I get as nervous as I was last night, my mouth gets me into trouble. Words fall out of their own accord.

Now I step back and watch Josie leave. She hops into her white Mercedes and waves at me. Then she gives me a thumbs-up sign. Unfortunately, her thumbs-up occurs at the same moment Gunner turns to look at Josie.

He turns back to me with a confused look on his face.

There's no explanation for Josie's signal to me. Not that I need to make one. "What can I do for you?" I tap my fingers against my bare legs. As if he can hear my fingertips hitting skin, his gaze travels down the length of my body.

"I asked you when the party starts."

Whenever you want, my body says. "Um...it's at..." My mind is like a squeaky-clean marker board—white and blank as the day it came off an assembly line.

He nods slowly. "You did tell me it's tonight. But maybe I got that wrong. You don't look dressed for a party." His gaze travels once more over me, trailing down my legs in a slow burn.

"Oh for heaven's sake. You too? I've had it up to here with men trying to dress me."

Gunner gives me a bewildered look as I glare at him. Then the most unexpected thing happens. He gives me a sly grin. And it's like a freight train knocks into my body.

"I'd be more likely to undress a woman than dress her," he says. His soft voice travels across the space between us and my knees knock together.

If only.

My mouth morphs into a dry piece of sandstone and my heart vibrates with hummingbird wings against my breastbone. I'm going to begin talking. I have no doubt my mouth will open and there's no way to stop it. It's either babble or jump him. One or the other, because there's no in-between.

I swallow past the sand in my mouth. He's freaking me out with the flirting. "That would be something. You and me. Really?"

I know my comment came out wrong. All wrong. When I get nervous, I pretend I'm overly confident.

That sly grin disappears and the hard, flinty look in his eyes returns. "No. You're right. I like my women a little less frigid."

And I like my men a little less...hot. Apparently true, if I compare Mason to the man before me.

But I stop myself from blurting that lame reply. "I like my men a little less dirty."

He chuckles, as if I've said something totally funny. "That doesn't surprise me at all." One corner of his mouth continues to quirk skyward.

I'm glad for his cutting comment. It clears my head of all the things I was two seconds away from saying. Crazy things. This is real life and not some music video where Gunner smiles at me, I smile at him, and we run away together.

"Are you going to tell me what time or do I have to guess?" he asks.

Westley, who'd been napping in the kitchen, comes wheeling around the corner at warp speed. His high, vapid barking fills the room. Gunner eyes him cautiously.

My cell phone rings. "Give me a second. The caterer might be lost."

Gunner exhales. "What time?"

I race to find my phone in the other room. Finding it on an ottoman, I breathlessly answer. "Hello."

"Miss Vanderbilt? This is Five Star Cuisine. We need to confirm the arrangements."

"Great," I say, and peek around the corner to see why Westley is so quiet. My dog sits five feet from Gunner, eyes trained on him for any sudden movements. Gunner leans back against the front door, arms across his chest and an unhappy look on his face. It's an official showdown. Giant versus small beast.

"The delivery will be at 6:00 pm," the voice says.

"No. It's supposed to be at five." I glance at the ornamental clock hanging across the room. "Five is better."

"It won't be ready then. You'll have to wait until six for the delivery."

I inhale and attempt to stay calm. "My guests are arriving at six."

"Then we'll be there on time."

"No," I say, my voice rising. "It can't be at the same time. I need everything here before then."

"It's not possible. Are you canceling it?"

"No!" I wave a hand in front of my watering eyes. "No, no, no. Not canceling. Bring it."

"Good. We'll be there on time at six." The caterer ends the call. I hold the phone and listen to the dead silence. With my free hand, I place my palm against my forehead and squeeze my eyes shut.

"Kiley? Did you forget I'm waiting?" Gunner sneaks up on me and I twirl around.

"Sorry," I mumble. "Um, the time. Yes. The guests will be here at six." My voice strains, thin and reedy.

Westley follows Gunner into the room, then trots over to stand guard beside my feet.

"Do you feel all right?" Gunner's gentle voice unlaces the tight hold I have on my composure.

"No. Not all right. I cannot do this." I sit in the nearest chair. "I should go throw myself off the second floor balcony. Now."

"What is it you can't do?" He raises a brow, but he's not mocking. He's actually concerned. I must look as though I'm serious about planning a swan dive to end my misery.

"The caterer is getting here at the same time as my guests."

Gunner shakes his head. "I'm not understanding the problem."

"This is a big deal. It's my fiancé's clients. I can't instruct the caterer about the food while people are here. And I didn't hire people to serve it."

"You're losing me. You can let your people visit with each other. They're grownups, right? So, what exactly is the problem?" Gunner fidgets with the brim of his ball cap, certainly out of his element talking about a dinner party.

"I should've called Mason's mother for advice on a caterer like he asked me to. But, no. I was going to do it my way. I didn't want to do what he asked. I was going to set out a buffet in the dining room. I wanted it to look like I did everything. Well, not everything, but most of it. And it would be rude to ignore the guests. See, my fiancé needs..." I squeeze my eyes shut and swallow the lump in my throat. "I'm screwed. I can't do this. I can't."

He holds up a hand. "Calm down. What if you had help?"

"Mason thinks I'm this perfect woman who knows how to do this stuff. He assumed...he expected..." My eyes tear up. Great. Why can't I be normal? Why do I have to keep talking?

"Want my help?"

"You'll help with the dinner?" I attempt to imagine Gunner setting up a dinner service. No matter how hard I try, it doesn't work.

His mouth quirks at the corner. "Not exactly. I have a friend who owns a bar. He can probably come up with some help for you. You might have to pay them overtime wages. Maybe double their pay."

"Done."

"Would two or three people be enough?"

I nod frantically. "Yes. Make sure to tell them to wear black slacks and white shirts. I don't want them showing up in bar clothes. This isn't a barbecue I'm having and—"

He lifts his hand a second time to cut me short on my talking. "And you'll owe me a huge favor."

"Like what?" I gulp. I'd like to do a lot of things for him, but most would be indecent—especially since I'm supposed to marry another man in four weeks.

He shrugs, drawing my attention to the broadness of his shoulders. "I'll think of something," he says in a slow drawl.

His words are innocent, but the look in his

eyes makes my pulse sprint. I suck in air and smile as if I'm not turned on by the thoughts I have. "You name the deed, and it's yours."

ONCE GUNNER MADE THE CALL to his friend and sent people to help, everything else fell into place. I owe him. I had time to take Westley to the dog-sitting service and plenty of time to get ready.

Mason didn't plan to do anything for the dinner, as was evident by his arrival a half hour before guests are to arrive. I check my lipstick in the stainless steel server on the buffet table.

"Mason?" I walk through the kitchen and into the entry. He's disappeared, so I wander around the main floor to find him.

There's a sound from Dad's study, so I reverse directions and head that way. He should be helping me instead of sneaking off to make business calls.

I stare at the wooden door of a room that is normally open. Frowning, I place my hand on the knob and slowly turn it.

Mason sits in Dad's chair while he faces the window. He rocks slowly in the chair, his foot tapping on the wood flooring. "Kiley and I talked it over. She doesn't want to do the show." Pause. "We realize it will leave you in a bind, but surely you can find someone else." Pause. "She asked me to call you because she knew you'd be disappointed."

"Mason? What are you doing?" It's a stupid question. I know exactly what he's doing.

Lying. Manipulating. Dictating.

Devoted

Current Day

Gunner

PRETTY GIRLS ALWAYS MEAN TROUBLE. They bat their eyelashes, drum up a tear or two, and you find yourself rearranging your schedule.

I've spent an hour worrying about her dog falling into the holes I dug near the koi pond. One false scramble after a leaf or frog, and the dog will be trapped in the bottom of a deep hole—the kind I usually cover until a tree is planted, but didn't, since I was so distracted.

After I finish dressing, I hop into my Jeep and drive the short distance to the Vanderbilts'. If I hadn't inherited my own property from my grandfather, I'd never be able to live in such a beautiful place—green pastures and blue sky everywhere. Two horses graze along the white wood fences that parallel the road.

There are only a few vehicles parked out

front, including a white van with a catering logo on the side. She must've convinced them to come early after all. I park on the side of the garage so I won't be trapped in case someone pulls in behind me. I figure I don't need to go to the front door. Only guests will be entering the front of the house. The kitchen is closest to the rear of the house, so I get out of my vehicle and walk around back. The sound of the waterfall I created as a water feature in the koi pond gurgles pleasantly.

From somewhere near the patio arbor, voices carry in the still evening. The conversation punches with anger—each word staccato and strained. I freeze before I make the turn, wondering if I've arrived too late to check on things or if some guests are already here.

"You had no right to say those things to Dad." Kiley must be holding her temper in check, because her words have icicles hanging from them.

"I only did what I thought was best for you."

"You don't get to make that decision."

"I do, as your husband."

"You aren't my husband, yet. It's not too late to back out," Kiley says. "If you can't respect me and my decision to work on the show, then I think we need to reevaluate."

"Sweetheart. Baby. What are you saying? You're stressed over tonight. That's all it is."

He's using pet names, but they sound false to my ears. The manipulation of a guy who tosses around endearments he's used with every girl he's dated—even the one-night stands.

If she buys that load of crap, they deserve each other. I don't hesitate any longer. Walking around the corner, I glance up and act surprised to see them. "Oh, hi."

She appears embarrassed for a split second when she realizes I must've heard them. Her shame is raw and real. My chest tightens to see her so vulnerable.

In the next second, Kiley puts her emotions away. She's a damned actress.

"Gunner. I didn't know you were coming by." She gives me a genuine smile—a grateful smile—and something loosens within my chest. I take in her dark hair that falls in gentle waves around her bare arms, the navy silk material of her dress that clings to every curve, her bare long legs and high-heeled sandals that bring her closer to my height.

She's more gorgeous than a sunset over water and as blinding. I kick myself for staring. "Wanted to make sure Dane sent some help for you." I nod at the guy beside her.

"Hi, I'm Mason. The kitchen is through that door." He turns and looks at the door as if pointing me in that direction. "And there are still some things to be unloaded from the caterer."

"He's not here to work," Kiley says to her fiancé. She takes an almost imperceptible step closer to me, but I see it and Moneyclip does too.

He sizes me up, trying to put a label on me. "I don't understand. Then why are you here?"

"Only to check on things. I also left an uncovered hole in the back lawn that the dog might fall into."

"No, Westley's not here." Kiley takes another step toward me. "That was thoughtful of you. That's so sweet. Thank you."

"As long as you're here, you could make a few bucks if…" Moneyclip trails off as he looks at my face.

I rub my hand along the back of my neck instead of punching the asshole. If a guy isn't wearing a designer suit, he must be the hired help. "Mason, right? I—"

She puts a hand out and touches her man on the arm. "Could you go inside and put the wine into the wine case? We want it to stay chilled." Kiley stares at him with raised eyebrows. "Oh, and I think I heard the doorbell. You'll want to get that."

He hesitates for an instant, giving me a last, assessing look. Then he turns and enters the house.

She shakes her head and closes her eyes briefly. "Sorry about him. He's not happy with me right now. We were having a disagreement." Kiley immediately blushes and I can see she regrets revealing this fact to me. She looks out at the back lawn as if searching for something to say. "It's so pretty back here. I almost wish we were having this thing outside."

I exhale a long breath at her change of subject and give in to her need to pretend everything is normal. "It's too warm tonight. Maybe in a month or two, it will be nice...if you have another dinner party."

She cuts a look in my direction. "I hope you're kidding. I wouldn't wish this on my worst enemy."

"And yet your fiancé..."

"Mmmm. Good point. I can't thank you enough for what you've done to help me. But I need to check the food and make sure we have everything on the buffet table. So, I'll see you when you come back Monday to do the landscaping in the front."

"I won't be back."

"Why not?"

"Because I was only filling in for someone," I say. It's not a good idea to return next week. I already want to beat her fiancé for being such a shit.

"What if I tell your boss we need you? Will

he let you come back?"

"Listen. You can tell the boss, but it won't make a bit of difference. Travis is showing up on Monday."

"But I want you." She fidgets and looks behind her at the back door. The sounds of opening and closing doors tell me that her guests are arriving.

Lord help me. This woman is used to getting her way. Was she this spoiled in school? Probably. But I was so blinded by my crush I couldn't see it. Although I'm my own boss and can decide who works a job, I suddenly don't want to explain why I won't be back. I already can't seem to stay away from her—a very engaged woman—and the more I see her, the worse it gets.

I shake my head. "I'm real sorry about that. See you around, Kiley." My legs feel shaky as I walk away from her toward the front of the house.

A definite regret settles inside me that things can't be different. But I'm no thief and she belongs to another man.

Besides, I like women with more substance and heart than Kiley Vanderbilt. A person who gives more than they take. I've only known two women like that in my life: my mom and my stepsister. One no longer graces this earth and the other lives in Missouri.

I get into the Jeep and pull out from the side of the garage. A woman stands next to the catering van, attempting to balance a large cardboard box and some sort of rolling cart. I stop and cut the engine.

"Ma'am? You need help?"

"Si. Por favor."

I jog over to her and take the box.

"Drinks," she says.

"Ah." I wait for her to lead the way. She walks to the side entrance, a door I'd missed in my time working outside the house.

We walk down a corridor and into the kitchen. I glance around for empty counter space and place the box on the nearest empty spot next to stacks of white china, white napkins, and silver platters. I back away carefully so I won't knock into anything breakable. Jesus. You'd think this is the makings of a wedding reception.

"Gracias," she says.

I smile at the woman and turn to leave the house, going the same way we came in. I'm walking down the short hallway when I hear Kiley's voice from somewhere. She's irate, if the barely controlled timbre of her voice is any indication.

"You called my dad and lied," she says. "I never agreed to quit the show. You made the choice to—"

Moneyclip interrupts her. "I think you need to start acting like the wife of an attorney. That's all."

They both come into sight from a doorway in front of me. Kiley walks in front, her head down and studying the floor.

"Maybe I shouldn't get married to an asshole attorney," she mumbles.

"What did you say?" Moneyclip grabs her arm from behind.

My heart pounds in my ears, my temper riled by what I've seen and heard. I cannot tear my gaze from his hand on her arm. If there's one thing I won't stand for, it's Moneyclip laying his hands on her.

Kiley's gaze flicks up and she sees me. Her face flushes and she gives a confused smile. "Oh. Gunner. What are you still doing here? Are you looking for me?"

"No. I helped your caterer carry a box to the kitchen."

Moneyclip steps to her side. "Thank you," he says with a fake pleasant look on his face. "You know the way out?"

What a dick. If he thinks he can dismiss me so easily, he's wrong. "Everything OK here?" I look at Kiley as if we are the only two people in the hallway.

She furrows her brow. "Sure. Only having a little disagreement."

Her fiancé's mouth twists. "I believe this is private. We don't require your help for anything else." He drops his hand from her arm.

"Kiley?" I still ignore him.

"I'm fine," she says. Her tremulous smile, only a tipping at the corner of her mouth, does crazy things to my instincts. She's not fine.

I nod. "If you say so."

My footsteps slow in the distance to the side door. It's not as though I belong here, lurking in her house, but I don't want to leave.

I strain to hear their conversation, but I can only tell her voice from his. Turning around, I pause and stare toward the kitchen area where the voices are. Their volume increases or maybe I've stepped closer without realizing it.

"Say that to me one more time. I dare you," Kiley says.

"You're used to being a daddy's girl, and you're throwing a tantrum at the wrong time," he says. "You're spoiled and don't know what's best for you."

"Don't you ever speak to me that way again." There's no mistaking Kiley's words, but now her voice lowers. "I want to talk about us. I think we've made a mistake. We want different things in life."

"You're being dramatic," Moneyclip says. "Honey, you're not that bright. You're on your daddy's show only because of who you are.

85

What happens after Forever ends? Next season, you're out. It's not like you have a future in television. I'm not going to put up with this crazy talk. You pick now when we have a house full of the people who matter—"

"Do you think I care about those people? We're talking about the rest of our lives here," she says. "Get your hand—"

I don't need to hear more. I stride away from the back door and toward the kitchen. When I turn the corner and see them, his hand grips her upper arm. Again.

Holy shit. "Take your hand off her," I say only inches from both of them.

"How did you get back in?" He releases her. "I suggest you turn around and leave before I make sure you're off this property."

"He's not leaving." Kiley rubs her arm where he grabbed her.

"What? Something is going on here. Kiley, have you been messing around with the lawn boy?"

She doesn't respond, her face surprised and ashen at the accusation.

Moneyclip misinterprets her expression of shock. "I know you're stupid, but I didn't peg you for a cheater. You cunt. I should've known, since you put out anytime, anywhere."

The surprise is gone from her face. She shoves him in the chest. "You stuck-up, smallpenised bastard," she screams, loud enough to be heard two counties over.

If I weren't so pissed, I'd laugh my ass off. The guests in the house heard that one. There's a moment when I consider the consequences of my next words. Oh, what the hell. "She hasn't done anything with me. Yet." My lips part in cocky smile that says I certainly know how to please a woman. "After tonight, I'm thinking I might be able to persuade her."

He lunges toward me, his right hand balling into a fist. Before his elbow lifts, I step forward with an uppercut and his teeth click together with a sickening pop. He falls back three steps and his body hits the kitchen counter.

"No!" Kiley inserts herself between us. She grabs my hand and yanks. "Come on. Please." She pulls at me. Her hand is small in mine.

I search her face, trying to figure out what I should do about the mess I've made.

"You'd better leave before I call the police." Mason pushes away from the counter.

"Take me away from here." She tugs once more and we're running through the back of the house and out the door. Her shoes make clipping sounds as they hit tile and then brick.

I turn and the guy still isn't following us. What kind of idiot would take a punch and then let a guy leave with his woman, the one he had planned to marry? "What about your guests?"

"I didn't invite them. He can deal with dinner." She tugs at my hand again. We're at the edge of the grass and she takes off her heels. "Where's your vehicle?"

I point. "Beside your garage." I'm not sure what to think about the way she's holding my hand as if she's afraid to let go.

"Hurry. Before I chicken out." She does let go now and runs faster than I'd thought she'd be able to in a dress.

Her long hair streams out behind her in the moment before I move. Then I'm chasing after her to the Jeep.

She stands beside the vehicle in her dress, those high-heeled shoes dangling in one hand and her other hand on the sidebar. I grin and grab her by the waist so I can lift her into the passenger side.

She settles into her seat and the dress rides high on her thighs. I'm glued to the expanse of tan skin. She lifts one perfect eyebrow brow. "You coming?"

"You bet." I run around to my side and hop into the driver's seat. My grin makes the corners of my mouth hurt. How long have I been smiling?

I glance sidelong at the woman beside me—a rich girl with no idea of the mess she's making for me. Her dad has a good head on his shoulders, but he'll likely fire me for running off with his daughter during a swanky dinner party. I work hard for a solid reputation in my landscaping business. I would hate to lose Ed's respect more than the fact that I could lose his business.

But if Ed Vanderbilt thinks I could persuade his daughter to do anything she doesn't want to do, then he doesn't know Kiley.

"You sure about this?" I ask.

She widens her eyes and laughs. "You have no idea. I'm one hundred and fifty percent sure."

I start the engine and drive straight over the lawn and around the cars parked in the driveway. It's a long, paved drive to the highway, and we pass the hole I dug the other day and had to refill at her orders. I stop at the end. "Where are we going?"

She looks panicked for a second. Then she regains her composure. "Drive to your favorite place. Where is that?"

Is there such a place? My initial instinct is to respond that I don't have a favorite. I love being under the open sky, and I'm a total blank on where to take her.

Then it hits me. I take a quick left turn, almost as if I should hurry before she thinks better of leaving with me. The tires protest at the acceleration from zero.

When I look across at her, she's smiling as

widely as I am. My heart stutters for an instant, forgetting to beat. I look back to the road and pray I won't regret this.

Because Kiley choosing to be with me instead of placating her fiancé—even if he's an asshole and it's only for this night—is too good to be true. And all really good things don't last.

Yearning

Current Day

Kiley

I'VE SPENT THE LAST FIVE MINUTES in a happy daze, as if Gunner broke me out of a maximum-security prison. The deserted highway has never looked better as we put miles between us and my dad's house. Gunner slows the Jeep and turns on his signal.

I grab the strands of my hair that whip into my mouth. Pulling them aside, I yell, "Where are we going?"

He flashes me a mischievous grin. "Changing your mind?"

"No."

"You'll see." He turns the Jeep left onto a narrow paved road. "Almost there."

The trees are thick and the road curvy. After

only minutes, we pull up to a small cabin. There's a porch light on, even though it's still light outside. He cuts the engine.

"I didn't realize someone lived so close to our property." I unbuckle my seat belt and hop out. I glance around curiously. A patch of sunflowers stands to the left, humongous sentinels of good cheer. A wind chime hangs from the porch and tinkles in the slight breeze.

"Let's go around back." He strides ahead and doesn't wait to see if I follow.

"Wait a minute," I say. "How do you know anyone's home?"

Gunner turns the corner and I run after him, past the sunflowers and a silver washtub made into a fountain. He walks up a set of stairs leading to a deck on the back of the house. "Have a seat. I'll be right back."

He opens a set of sliding glass doors and lets himself in.

The land beyond the deck drops, so all I'm looking at is the valley for miles. I sit in one of the Adirondack chairs, wondering whose deck we're crashing. He must know them well, if he can come and go as he pleases.

I turn at the sound of the doors sliding open again. Gunner steps forward holding two bottles of beer. He hands one to me and drops into the other chair. "I don't have fancy drinks."

"This is fine." I tip the bottle and drink.

When I lower it, I give him a sharp look. "Who said I need fancy?"

He shrugs. "So you like beer?"

"Sure. Doesn't everyone?" I smirk. "You didn't answer me. Whose house is this?"

"Mine." He takes a long pull of beer and doesn't look at me.

"No. Seriously."

"I'm your neighbor."

"No. Really." I sit forward and look at the house. "Really?"

"Uh huh." He chuckles under his breath. "Don't like the lawn boy so close?"

He's ribbing me without any nastiness in his tone. I purse my lips together to fight an embarrassed smile. "No. I remember the Wilsons owned this land when I was younger. I didn't even know there was a house on it. I guess I missed you moving here when I was away at college."

"Hmm..." He nods and stares straight ahead. "I inherited it from my mom's family."

"Oh." I relax into my chair and listen to the evening sounds. After a good ten minutes of silence, I can't keep quiet any longer. What is he thinking? That I'm wild? I ran off and left my fiancé—soon to be my ex-fiancé—with a houseful of guests. That I'm a pushover? He heard the way Mason talked to me. How do I explain that I didn't see all the parts of Mason

93

before we got engaged? "I don't want to talk about Mason and what happened."

"I didn't ask." He doesn't look at me, but a slight smile tugs at one corner of his mouth.

"Why aren't you asking? I mean, you barreled in and helped me escape. You told Mason we might have something going on, which is not true and...then you hit him."

He sighs. "Are you mad that I did it?"

I picture Mason, rubbing his chin and glaring at Gunner. "No. But I don't get it. I thought you sort of hated me."

Gunner lets his head loll to the side and studies me. "Would you have come if you honestly thought I felt that way? We're just very different kinds of people. Always have been."

I suddenly notice he's not wearing a hat. It's the first time I've seen him without one. His dark blond hair is short, nearly a military cut. His face is all sharp angles and serious. He's more handsome than he was in high school. Even though I had the hots for him then, it was more about his aloofness that got to me. That and the way he seemed more mature than the other boys.

I fight an urge to run my hand over the back of his neck, to caress the five o'clock stubble, to be close enough to gaze into his eyes, and this all overwhelms me in a heartbeat.

"I always wondered what happened to you

after you moved. You sort of disappeared." I don't tell him I pined after him for months.

He stiffens for an instant, then leans back. "I wondered about you, too."

"My mom grounded me for a month after that night." My lips smash into a bitter smile that I can't hold back.

"That night?"

"Oh, the bonfire night. You probably don't remember." I snicker. "My parents had dual custody and I was staying with my mom and her current husband at the time. I went home with my sweater buttoned in all the wrong buttonholes. You can imagine how that went over."

He grins. "Maybe I do remember."

"Oh, did that trigger your memory? I'm not sure it was worth getting my phone taken away for a month."

We're silent for several minutes and I wonder if he's thinking about that night. It's something I've never forgotten.

He examines the beer bottle in his hand and nods. "That would explain why you never returned my calls."

"You called?" My heart thrums at the serious note in his voice. He did call. And he does remember.

"Yep. I did."

"Why didn't you just talk to me at school?"

I wiggle uncomfortably at the thrill that he called me so many years ago.

Stupid, stupid, stupid. A lot of time has passed, and we were kids then.

"You weren't taking my calls. Do you really think I wanted to humiliate myself with you blowing me off at school?"

I put the beer down beside the chair, irritated with him. "I would never do that. Get a clue. I spent my Friday nights twirling that baton on the football field, hoping you'd notice me." I twist my hands together in my lap. "So, yeah. I thought you weren't interested after that night."

He takes another drink but doesn't respond. Instead of babbling, I listen to the sound of a bullfrog croaking in the distance. The scent of Gunner's cologne and the dark woods meld together in a decadent way, making me lean my head back and relax.

Can someone bottle this smell? Because I may have to roll around in it every day to start the morning right.

"I knew you weren't a beer drinker," he says and motions at the nearly untouched drink I hold.

"I'm OK."

"Want something different? I can get you a soda." He sits forward as if to get out the chair.

"I'm not thirsty." I pause, wondering when

it's socially correct for me to ask him the one thousand questions about him I have to know. I glance around and return my gaze to him. "OK. You caught me. I really don't drink a lot of beer. I mean, I did in college—I went to Loyola—but that was because everyone drinks a lot of beer. And other things. But anyway, I'm going to just hold on to this to keep you company."

He peers sideways at me. A corner of his mouth teases up. "Are you nervous about sitting here with me?"

"No. I mean. A little." I think about Mason and what I've done in the past hour. "It's over between me and Mason. I can't believe I finally did it. And do I seem nervous?"

"You're talking a lot. I thought that topic was off-limits."

"Right."

"But since you brought it up... How did you meet that dickhead?"

My mouth quirks at the hostility in Gunner's voice. "My dad introduced us. Dad was in the same fraternity with Mason's dad. Mason and I dated for two years while I went to college in Chicago. He was at Cornell Law in Boston. We didn't actually see each other much."

"Long-distance, huh. Bad idea."

I tilt my head, staring into the woods. "Yeah."

"So, how's Ed going to feel about tonight?"

I squirm in my seat. "He'll deal with it."

"Ed's a nice guy. He'll want you to be happy. Don't worry about it."

"I'm not worried."

Gunner chuckles, a husky sound that elicits pleasant goosebumps along my body. "Let's do something to take your mind off it."

"What?" I realize I sound breathy and suspicious and hopeful. Oh God. What do I think he means?

"I didn't have anything particular in mind when I said that." He grins and I'm positive he has read my thoughts.

"Oh." My face heats. I don't think I've blushed this much in my life.

"What do you like to do? I brought you here, to my favorite place. What's your favorite thing for fun? Something we can do here. Poker? Television? Twister?"

He's teasing me, and I love it.

"Dance. I love dancing."

Gunner lets his head fall back with a thud. "You've got to be kidding. Anything but that."

"What? You don't like to dance?"

"Does any man?"

"Yes. They do."

"It's not my thing."

"You have to let go and feel the music. That's all there is to it."

"I didn't say I couldn't dance. I said I don't."

I get to my feet. "Give me your phone. We'll put some music on and dance here."

"Forget it."

"No. I want to dance."

"Sweetheart, you need to work on your hearing. I said I'm not."

I grab both his hands, hoping to pull him to his feet. "Come on. Please."

He stares at me so long I'm positive he's regretting that I'm here. "All right," he says. "But I choose the music. None of that hip hop stuff."

"Deal."

Gunner stands, his knees bumping mine at first because I wasn't expecting his agreement. He towers above me, the top of my head barely reaching his chin. I take a step back.

He pulls his cell phone from the pocket of his slacks. Wearing his dark slacks and white dress shirt, he looks like a different guy from the one who spent time working on the koi pond. Both looks are sexy and confident.

My belly tingles while I look at him. "What kind of music do you have? I like all kinds—R & B, pop, alternate—"

"Kiley," he says without looking up from his phone. "Relax. I've got this."

Gunner moves his finger along his screen. How much music does this guy have?

"I—"

"Shhh," he says, a grin tipping the corners of his mouth as he continues to scroll.

I'm going to combust from anticipation. Those science stories about people who automatically incinerate? I'm going to join them. Gunner will tell the police, "One minute we were going to dance, and then she went up in flames in the next. I have no idea why."

He presses the screen and places the phone on the arm of the chair. A slow country song begins. "This will do."

"Oh. It's slow."

"Yep." He steps forward and pulls my hands up so they rest on the back of his neck. "You do know how to slow dance, right? Or do I need to teach you?"

I swallow. "Of course, I do."

"Good. I didn't want to have to talk." His hands rest on my hips and there's only an inch between our bodies.

It's all very innocent on the surface, except I can't quit wishing the inch of space would disappear. The heat of his big hands sears through the silk of my dress. His touch is light, but each flex of his fingers sends a bolt of desire right to my core.

"Is this OK?" he says, his gaze searching mine.

"Sure. It's..." Do not admit anything. If I

start talking, there's a chance I'll say something stupid and truthful. "This is good."

"Can we dance closer?"

"Oh. Um...sure." I swallow, his touch leaving trails of heat along my skin.

He pulls me to him so our bodies are flush; his hands glide around to rest on the small of my back. "Much better."

My nipples perk at the contact of my chest against his. Settle down, I command. Only dancing here. No one is getting naked.

We move to the slow beat. I recognize the singer and song. Sam Hunt croons about how much he wants to take a girl's time. "What are you thinking about?" I ask.

"Fourth grade."

"What?" I laugh and smile against his shoulder. I breathe in his scent and hope he doesn't wonder what I'm doing.

"Do you remember you sat behind me and bugged me all year?"

I nod. "Sure. Sorry your last name ends in P. But in my defense, I was bored in the backseat. I mean, come on, teachers. It's a curse to have a last name like Vanderbilt. Who does that to a kid? Always assigned to the seat in the far corner."

"I assume your dad had some evil plan to keep you hidden in the back. Damn him for that last name. But I'm not complaining. Only, I was too young to realize you were flirting."

"Was not." I feel his smile against my hair. "OK. Maybe I was."

"That's what I thought." His hands slide up for a moment in a caress, then drop lower to rest above my waistline. I've never been so aware of every movement, every breath from another human being.

The song changes on Gunner's phone. It's a faster beat and a song I don't recognize. He pulls back and places his right hand on my shoulder blade. "Two-step?" He holds out his left hand.

I put my hand in his. "I thought you didn't like to dance."

"Depends on the partner." He steps forward with his left, twice. Then once with his right foot. And he's flawless. We're moving around a small area of the deck, taking care not bump into the chairs or the railing. Moonlight reveals his grin and he's enjoying himself. Or maybe he's mirroring my face.

Gunner twirls me once, spinning me quickly. He smirks at my surprised expression. "Keep up."

My face hurts from smiling. "I could do this all night." Then my smile fades when I remember what awaits me at home—Mason.

"You don't have to go home. We could hang out here on the deck until the sun rises. Or go inside and watch television." He lifts one eyebrow as if saying he dares me to take a chance on him.

"I think you'd best take me home."

His mouth tightens and the lightness of the moment fades. When the song ends, Gunner releases my hand. "What are you going to do about that ring on your finger?"

It's not that I don't want to answer him. But I don't feel right telling a guy I haven't seen in years what I should tell my soon to be ex-fiancé.

"What I should've done weeks ago."

"Maybe you should wait until tomorrow, so he can cool off. If he's still at your house, I'm not dropping you off."

"I'll be fine."

Gunner nods. "If he's gone, I'll leave. If he's not, we'll see."

We walk to the Jeep and although I don't need help, he places gentle hands on my waist and lifts me up.

During the drive, my thoughts are too crowded to talk about old times in school or anything else. When we pull up, the house is dark and all the cars are gone—even Mason's.

"I'll wait a minute. Flash the porch light that everything's OK," he says.

"It's fine. He's not here."

"I'll wait," he says in a streak of stubbornness I remember from our school days.

"Thanks," I say. "Really. You have no idea what you've done for me tonight."

Then, I hop from his Jeep and run into the house. Run away from the confusing temptations I've felt for this man tonight.

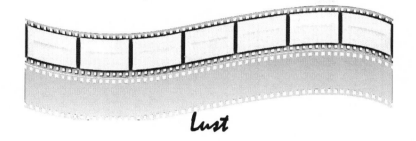

Lust

Current Day

Gunner

THE MORNING SUN GLINTS THROUGH AN OPENING in the canopy of trees. A mocking bird swoops low, angry that I'm encroaching on his territory in the Vanderbilts' back lawn.

Kiley's SUV was already missing when I pulled into their driveway. I tell myself that I didn't come here for her.

I tell myself that I'm here because of the empty holes in the ground I need to fill with trees. Ten sugar maples fill my long trailer I brought from the nursery.

It's dangerous for her tiny dog to run around the holes. I don't want to be responsible for an accident.

But then I remember how good she felt in my arms last night and I'm that teenage boy from so many years ago with his eye on the girl of his dreams.

All I need is a little hard work to get her out of my system. I complete the work this morning, I'll send one of my guys from here on, and my life will return to normal.

No problem.

Except that my heart begins to rival one in cardiac arrest at the slam of a car door.

Kiley. Or maybe it's Ed and I'm acting like a lunatic, looking at my T-shirt to see if I've gotten soil all over it from working this morning.

She bounds around the side of the house with the dog in her arms. "Gunner! You're back. I thought you said you wouldn't be."

She's all smiles and glory with her dark hair loose on her shoulders and a fresh-scrubbed face. I like her without so much makeup.

"I like to finish things I start." I remove my gloves and tuck them into my back pocket. "You all right after last night?"

Kiley looks everywhere but at me. "Yeah."

"You sure?"

"I..." She puts two fingers on the bridge of her nose. "I broke off the engagement this morning. I've never been called so many names in one hour."

Her hand shakes and the dog whines. She puts him down and he immediately goes for the leg of my jeans, tugging with his tiny teeth.

"Hey," I say, shifting awkwardly and ignore

the dog. "You're upset. That's normal when a girl breaks up with a dickhead."

One corner of her mouth lifts, but her eyes fill with water. She turns away, as if to shield me from her emotions.

Jesus, don't cry. "You have some coffee in there?" I nod toward her house.

She sniffs and turns back to me. "Oh yeah. Come on in. Westley. Let go of him."

When she bends over to pick the dog up, her low-cut pink V-neck top reveals the tops of her full breasts and the edges of her white lace bra.

She pops back up with the dog and I frown at the frisky animal so I can do something—anything—besides think about her breasts. She's luscious. Not a word I tend to use, but I've discovered a reason to now.

Of course, now I seem to be frowning at her luscious chest. She tugs the V-neck higher while the dog's paws seem determined to pull the fabric lower.

I follow her as she walks past the gated pool and through the back patio. She places the dog on the tile when we're inside and it happily trots off, no longer interested in molesting my leg.

"I have flavored coffees, but I'd bet you like the plain stuff," she says in a sunny voice that I know dang well is fake.

"I have a sweet tooth. Probably why I like you." I wait for her response, but I'm disappointed. It was meant to be flirty, not crass. Maybe she's distracted.

Once we're in the kitchen, she sniffs again. Her back is to me and I wish she'd turn around so I can see if she's OK.

"Did Moneyclip go ahead with his dinner?" I look around for signs of the dinner party last night.

"Of course. He told the guests I was ill. Apparently, he's an expert liar."

"Hmph." I sit in the nearest chair and fold my arms over my chest. "Sorry."

She sniffles twice and doesn't turn around. "He's really upset. He's positive I cheated on him with you."

"You want me to tell him I was goading him? Would that help?"

She threads fingers through her hair and winds it up off her neck, massages the muscles as if she's noticed how tense she is. "Let him think what he wants. It doesn't matter if I try to deny it. He's going to think whatever makes him feel better." She keeps her back to me and places both hands on her hips as the single-cup coffee maker drips into a mug.

"When's Ed coming back?" I worry about her in this state, alone in the house. Women are known to be emotional creatures and Kiley seems one sniffle away from a breakdown.

She waves away my question about her dad.

"I'm glad you're here. I..." Her voice breaks and she turns around to look at me.

Tears course down her cheeks, careening with her trembling lips. She covers her face. "Sorry. This is embarrassing."

Turning back to the counter, she pretends to do something to the coffee. But her hands and shoulder shake.

I get to my feet and walk softly to her, putting my hands on her shoulders. "It's going to be OK."

I'm surprised when she pivots and folds herself into my arms. She places her forehead against my chest. "Why do guys have to be such jerks?"

"I know," I say with a smile into the top of her hair. "Shitty men."

"Yeah, shitty men," she says. "Well...except for you. You're sort of nice."

"Most days," I agree.

"Especially today." She begins sobbing into the front of my shirt.

I stroke her hair. "You're sweet and funny and a knockout. Any man would be lucky to have you. So don't settle for a shitty one. You have to be more careful next time."

"Tell me how."

"How what?" I hope we stop hugging before her nipples give me an obvious hard-on. Then I'll be in that shitty category without intending to be there.

"How to be careful." She's silent, waiting for my answer. When I don't give one, she laughs—not a happy sound, but the kind that tears at my heart because there's a sob mixed in. "He said, he said..." Then the tears start anew.

"He, your ex?"

"Mason says I'm messed up. That he knew I'd bail on him because I don't think of anyone but myself." She throws an ineffectual fist onto my chest, allowing it to slide down as she cries. "He said so many awful things to me. He said I'm a self-centered bitch. But I know I'm doing what's right. I don't love him and he certainly doesn't love me."

She lowers her head and mumbles something intelligible.

"Hmm?"

Kiley looks up at me. "I was going to marry Mason and probably end up divorced. He said it'll be no big deal to replace me."

I tilt my head, getting earnestly pissed off. "There's something wrong with him. Women like you don't come along every day. He didn't know the real you if he thinks that."

"Stop trying to make me feel be...be...better."

She won't stop crying. Her breasts and body melt into mine, her arms wrap around my waist and her hands rest close to my belt. Dammit.

I'm getting aroused, and it's not the right time for that shit. Not funny, I tell my body. Not funny at all.

I try to distract myself from the way she presses even closer. "You're special. Smart and funny. Feisty. That's what I like about you. You go after what you want."

"You've always been such a good guy."

"I'm not saying it to be nice. It's the truth."

"I wish I'd talked to you after that night in high school. I thought you blew me off. What's wrong with me? I'm no better than my mother—the way she can't tell the good guys from the bad."

She's sobbing harder now and I don't know why her last statements cause this, but they do.

"I think maybe we should go sit." I'd like to save myself the embarrassment of full wood knocking against her belly.

She lifts her head and I think she's going to pull away, give us both some space, but then she tiptoes and places her hands on the back of my neck. "What if I asked you to kiss me?"

I stare down at her, too surprised to move back or think of what's smart.

Then my heart restarts, firing on all cylinders and in overdrive.

"You don't want to?" she asks in whisper. "Sorry. That's so inappropriate. I just…"

Instead of answering, I lower my mouth to

hers. Her lips part and I gently kiss her bottom lip. A whisper of a kiss. Tentative and tender.

True.

She pulls me closer, not satisfied with my attempt at being a gentleman.

I feel the desire of a sixteen-year-old and the wisdom of an adult. A kiss isn't going to be nearly enough.

Our mouths crash together, teeth bump, tongues tangle. Her skin is hot to my touch as I pull her toward me so she can feel how desirable she is.

She gasps into my mouth and I push her backward to the kitchen counter. Her hips hit the edge and she grabs the belt loops of my jeans, forcing me to press against her. With one hand, I caress her breast.

"Oh," she moans around our kisses. "That's good."

Her nipples pebble through the fabric of her bra and her shirt, but I want bare skin. "You're beautiful."

I skate my hand inside the bottom of her shirt and up to one breast. One tug on the bra cup and I run my fingertips along the swell of her breast.

I've got to have more. I want to smell her skin. Taste her. I lift her shirt and pull the bra down to expose her, sucking the pink tip of her nipple into my mouth and grazing my teeth over the sensitive bud.

Shivering, she runs her fingers over my short hair and grasps for purchase. "Don't stop."

My dick strains against my zipper. It's pretty happy about that request.

"We should stop," I grind out, trying to find control over the situation. Ed Vanderbilt's kitchen, I tell myself.

"Ed," I sputter as she runs her hand along the front of my jeans, over the full length of my dick.

"Two days," she says, not needing to say more.

I nod and reach around with one hand to unfasten her bra. Heat fires through me at the wanton look on her face. My gaze sweeps down to her exposed breasts and my dick aches. Blood surges to my balls. "Good Lord woman."

"We shouldn't do this." She shakes her head. Her eyes and nose are red from crying. "But I don't want to stop."

I reason that I'm not a self-serving jackass. Even though I'm not the one who caused her tears, I'm glad to be one who can help them disappear.

She's the girl who got away, the one I dreamed about through my teen years. And now she wants me—not some rich prick.

Her dilated pupils and swollen lips scream

desire and need. "Maybe we should slow down," she says.

"I want to touch you. Do you want that?" When she doesn't answer, I tip her chin up so her eyes meet my gaze. "Sweetheart? It's you and me in this room. No judging or over thinking. I won't do anything you don't want me to."

Her cheeks turn pink. "I'm a little nervous."

I glance down to her open shorts, white panties peeking out. Licking my lips, I inhale. She's unsure. I'm certain that I could blow by simply looking at her half-dressed state. "Tell me to stop. Talk to me. I'll do whatever you want."

She watches wild-eyed and quiet. "No. Don't stop."

I lift her to sit on the kitchen counter so I have better access.

"Good." I slide her ass back farther onto the countertop. Tracing one finger along the wet fabric between her legs, I shake my head. "Let me taste you."

Will one taste lead to addiction?

"I've never..." she hesitates, her legs trembling underneath my touch. "I mean, I haven't...Mason never..."

A darker bloom of pink steals across her cheeks.

Damn. Not only is the guy a dick, he's out

of his mind. I've never wanted to pleasure a woman more in my life.

I spread her knees apart and slide my rough palms up her smooth thighs. She moans and her legs open up for me. "Lift up, baby."

She obeys and I tug her shorts down, then her panties follow. She places her forehead on mine. "Ummm..."

I skate one finger across the nub of her center and her entire body jumps in response. "Is this good?"

"Yes," she murmurs. Her head falls back, long hair swinging across my hands that now bracket her sweet ass.

I lower my head, kissing and sucking along her belly, dipping my tongue into her navel, until I reach her core. She smells of scented soap and musk. I trail my fingers along the skin of her inner thigh, and she squeezes her legs against me.

I give a tentative lick and she trembles. My tongue darts in and out, while I place wet, wide kisses on her center.

She's wiggling her ass, her fingers digging into my shoulders, alternating between pushing me away and pulling me against her folds. "Gun...Gun."

I love the desperation and affirmation in her voice. The connection between us fills me with pride and longing to make her lose control.

Her body is slick and ready, the workings of my fingers in time with the increasing movements of her body. "I need you inside," she says in a high tone.

I pull away and whisper against the satin skin of her thigh. "Let yourself go."

This moment is about her, not me. She needs to know she's desirable. I've wanted her since I laid eyes on her the other day.

Who am I kidding? My infatuation goes back to fucking middle school.

I return to my ministrations—hell, my worship of her body—until she shudders and makes a sultry sound of pure ecstasy. A thrill courses through me, her orgasm more pleasurable than mine could be.

Her body continues to quake, her short nails biting into the flesh of my shoulders. Finally, she stills and there's only the sound of her quick intakes of air.

I stand and run my knuckles across her flushed cheek. Her wide eyes search mine.

"Gunner," she pants. "That was, that was..."

"Intense?" I grin and lock my hands around her waist so I can bring her flush to my chest.

"What about you...do you want to..."

I like that she can't quite put her thoughts together. Leaning forward, I nuzzle her neck. "Some other time. Let me hold you right now." Words I never thought would come out of my mouth. I should feel like a pussy for saying I'm content with holding her. Should, but I don't.

She's offering herself to me. Why am I turning it down?

I know why. Because it's too soon after the dickhead had his ring on her finger. She needs to be sure about me. I don't want to be the rebound guy.

And I need to be certain I can handle her. Because as far as I know, there's no Kiley rehab.

Uncertainty clouds my thinking. I don't know if I'm brave enough to start up something with her.

Guys like me don't get to keep the Kileys of the world.

Heat

Current Day

Kiley

A WATCHED CELL PHONE NEVER RINGS. Gunner doesn't call.

Fifteen days and I've waited to hear from him every flipping day. I don't have his phone number or a way to reach him. A different guy shows up to work on the landscaping.

I'm worried that Gunner regrets everything with me. Otherwise, wouldn't he have called?

Unless he's not interested now. Or he thinks I'm the type who gets naked with every guy she meets.

What kind of girl breaks up with a fiancé and runs into the arms of another guy? But he's not any guy. He's Gunner Freaking Parrish, the boy I daydreamed about my entire sophomore year of high school.

"Kiley? What do you think?" Dad chuckles because he's well aware that I have no idea what he's asked me.

I scold myself for not having my mind in the right place. Dad's agreed to talk about the show schedule and it's time for me to get my head in the game.

He stands beside the fireplace mantle in his Armani suit, looking strangely identical to the images of him in last year's Vanity Fair photo shoot. I've interrupted an informal meeting between Dad and his director, Tony Tolino.

Dad shakes his head at me. "I think some bad publicity is inevitable. The news reporters will key in on what's happened with you and Mason. I can see the headlines now—— Matchmaker Loses Her Own Man." My dad's matter-of-fact words clip out sportscaster style. "Not to be tactless, dear." He adds the endearment to soften his words.

Right. My dad wouldn't know tact if it hopscotched over and kissed his ass. Doesn't he realize how cold he sounds? I lift my chin and form my lips into the Miss Tennessee smile that's become second nature to me. "I don't want to talk about Mason. I want to talk about when we begin filming and why we haven't chosen the substitute bachelor for Forever. What's taking so long?"

Last week, our bachelor for the season

broke both legs in a skiing accident. He's out and we need a replacement.

"We have five contenders for screen testing tomorrow."

"Oh." I sigh in relief. For a few seconds, I was afraid he might want to discuss postponing the season.

Tony studies me from his seat in the wingback chair to my right. He's always liked me, and I know he generally agrees with my opinions. He's closer in age to me than to my dad, and he's been around for years.

Once, I had a crush on Tony. He was an intern with my dad at Rolling Hills Productions. I was a senior in high school and he a senior in college—an older man.

Those days are long past

He turns away from me to look at my dad. "Forever is in its eighth season," he says. "The ratings still bring in the advertisers, but it's not what it has been. We need something different this season. More challenging."

"What if we change the rules?" I ask. "How about this: let's give the guy a dilemma—choose love or money. Offer him either the perfect girl or cold, hard cash."

Tony narrows his eyes and nods slowly. "I like it. It makes it a challenge for both the Matchmaker and the contestant."

"How much do you have in mind?" Dad

asks.

I shrug. "A million?"

Dad laughs. "You're feeling pretty confident if you think you can tempt a man away from that."

"I can do it."

Tony taps fingers on his knee, looking as if he's doing some mental calculation. "It's not a bad idea. But what's to say the guy won't cut a deal with the match? He could promise her half the money if she waits for him."

"No," I answer quickly. Some people think beauty contestants can't think on their feet. Wrong! As a former pageant queen, I can fix a high heel broken minutes before walking on stage or answer a question about solving world hunger. Each equally high pressure. "The show contract would have to be clear. If he chooses the money, the couple cannot have a relationship of any kind with each other for five years."

"Five, huh. You think that's long enough?"

I smile. "Sure. Would you stay away from the woman of your dreams for five years so you could keep the money?"

Tony and my dad give each other that look that says I'm naive.

"You would think you guys don't even believe in soul mates or true love," I say.

"I believe in ratings," Dad says. "If you keep

our audience engaged, I'll let you have your own show next season." Dad moves to the window. "If you two will excuse me for a minute. One of my contractors has pulled into the drive. Let me take care of him, and we'll continue." He strides across the room and disappears into the foyer.

Tony gets to his feet. "I'm on your side. I think the show needs something different. Viewers aren't satisfied with the same thing every season."

"That's what I'm saying. Thanks, Tony."

"I'm on the same page. You're more than a pretty face." He looks away from me to the doorway.

I hear the voice I've wanted to hear for days. Gunner.

He steps inside and the air whooshes from my lungs as if I've been punched. I didn't expect him to be so gorgeous. So tall. So beefcake. Dad follows a couple of steps behind him, coming into full view. "Let's see what an unbiased person thinks." He motions at me. "My daughter has my director twisted around her little finger. I'd like to know what someone else thinks."

Gunner nods, still staring at me. My belly continues to flip at the sight of him. His dark blond hair gleams with some highlights from the sun. His white, starched, cotton shirt stretches across a wide chest and tucks into dark jeans. He's a Greek god wearing clothes—all muscle and power. If I were a model scout, I'd have a pen and contract in his hand faster than he could blink.

My gaze travels back up to meet his and there's a glint in his eye. My appreciation doesn't go unnoticed.

"Oh, is this necessary?" I murmur. I don't want to talk about Forever right now. I want to grab Gunner by the arm and haul him outside to find out why I haven't seen him for days. I want to know why he hasn't called. I want his phone number because maybe he thinks we had a one-time thing and he doesn't know how I feel.

I want him.

"If a man were given the choice between a woman and a million bucks, do you think he'd ever choose the woman? Would romance win over money?" Dad asks.

Gunner's brow furrows. "Well, Ed. I don't know much about romance." He shifts a little and folds his arms uncomfortably.

"You don't have to. Simply answer from your gut instincts," Dad says. "If my daughter tried to find your soulmate, the one woman you are meant to be with, do you think she could?"

Gunner glances from me to my dad and then to Tony. "Definitely not. I don't believe in that soulmate stuff or love."

My heart shatters inside my chest, piercing my chest wall with tiny barbs. He doesn't believe in love. I swear it's blasphemy. Of all the things in my life that I hold tight, it's the belief that I'll find someone who'll love me with his entire being.

"I could find someone for any man. But him," I say with a motion toward Gunner, "he's not the ideal guy to ask. I, um..."

Dad grins. "So, Kiley, you're saying you couldn't."

"Not for him. We have to find someone in the market for love. Someone who..." Gunner's dark gaze doesn't break from mine for a second. If looks could kill, I'd be ten feet under. "Can we use anyone else as an example?"

"Let's stick with Gunner," Dad says. "The unbeliever. Could you find a woman he could walk down the aisle with or not?"

Fixing Gunner up with another woman is about as appetizing as week-old leftovers after Thanksgiving.

I shake my head. "Nope. Not him."

"Are you saying something is wrong with me?" He folds his muscular arms across his chest and tilts his head. His beautiful eyes narrow into disgruntled slits.

I swallow and choose to nip this in the bud. I will not, cannot, won't fix Gunner up with a woman. "Yes. That's what I'm saying."

"Are you gay?" Dad asks Gunner.

"Dad! He's not gay. I can assure you."

They all look at me as if waiting for me to say more. I press my lips together.

"Not as far as I know." Gunner says, still staring at me.

"Nothing wrong with being gay or straight or bi," Dad says to him. Then he glances over at Tony as if I don't even exist in the room. "We could do something exciting on the show with that."

"No, Dad. He's not the right material for a reality show. He's...he's..." I search for the word. I wave my hand in the air. "He's a confirmed bachelor. He's not really the type you normally have on the show."

Gunner shoves his hands into his worn jeans pockets. "Type?"

Dad studies me. "I think I see what she means. Last season, we had a brain surgeon who put me to sleep every time I tuned in. You'd be intriguing to the audience. A man who isn't afraid of hard work."

"So, you mean I'm too blue collar," Gunner says, his unhappy gaze flicking to me. "Is that what you mean?" He directs the question at me.

"Well, no. That's not exactly what I meant." I fidget, something I never do.

"This show sounds more interesting all the time. Does it involve women throwing themselves at me?" Gunner asks.

"Ugh. Listen to him. Confirmed bachelor with a chauvinistic attitude." Is that what he thought I did the other night? I scan my memory for how desperate I may have seemed.

"Then you must not be up to a challenge like me. I'm not the kind to settle for anybody. I'd need a woman who challenges me. I like to chase a little. I'd like a woman who doesn't expect everything handed to her on a silver platter."

My chest squeezes. If I were alone, I'd succumb to tears. But I'm not alone. The audience before me is watching this like it's Wimbledon. My serve. "I've changed my mind. I could find your true love. No problem. Give me four weeks and you'll be down on one knee proposing to your true love."

Gunner takes a step back. "That's never going to happen. Dream on."

Dad's face splits into a wide grin. I haven't seen him this happy since the show won an Emmy. "You are exactly the type of guy we need this season."

My dad tilts back his head in a laugh. "I love the sheer animosity between these two. Sparks are what we need. Gunner, how about being the next bachelor on Forever?"

Challenge

Current Day

Gunner

IT'S ALWAYS BEST TO MAKE SURE your mouth is big enough before you insert your foot in it. I hadn't intended my comment about the reality show to be taken as a challenge. But pride is a funny thing. A guy can either have too little or too much.

I'm obviously packing heavy in the pride department. Shit.

We stand in the Vanderbilts' living room. This place makes me nervous, with its off-white furniture waiting for a dirt stain and breakable stuff on every table. I only dropped in to talk with Ed and maybe secretly get a glimpse of Kiley. Now, I'm somehow trapped in this conversation with Kiley, her dad, and this stranger in their living room, who look at me with all this expectation.

"I could do the show if I didn't have to work." I smile, hoping my backpedaling isn't too obvious. "Reality shows are for those guys who don't have jobs. I don't think my clients would appreciate me taking off." I can't think of anything more excruciating than being on a television show. I have better things to do.

Owning a small business at my age takes a lot of hard work and capital. Long hours and pure determination.

"Oh, come on," Ed Vanderbilt says. "You're the boss. Surely you can make arrangements for any time we'd be filming."

"Wait a minute. You're the boss?" Kiley couldn't sound more surprised if you'd said I was king of a small nation.

I nod and I'm positive I'm wearing the same face I do in poker when I put down the straight and rake in the winnings.

"It's his company. He can set his own schedule." Ed gives me a smile that says we're equals in the world of business. This is why I respect the guy. Even though Ed's net worth is a couple of billion times mine, he still treats me the same as he does the suit standing next to him. "Also, you'd get paid a sum that would be well-worth time away from clients," he says, his speech getting faster. "Or the show can help you find someone to sub-contract the jobs taking place in your absence. Not to mention the prize money if Kiley fails to find your match. A million dollars."

The guy I haven't met, the slick-looking suit, strides across and holds out his hand. "I'm Tony Tolino, the co-producer of Forever. Maybe you could drop in the studio and we could discuss the show. Take a few test shots."

"Gunner Parrish," I say, taking his hand and shaking it. "I haven't agreed to anything."

Tony has this smug air about him. No bullshit with a lot of eye contact, strong grip, but smooth hands. He's confident and well dressed. I'm not sure I like him, but I can't isolate which part of him bothers me.

"Sure, sure," he says. "But there's nothing wrong with considering it."

"He doesn't want to do it." Kiley says to Tony.

She's fighting this awfully hard. You'd think she believes I'm a lost cause. This hurts for some reason.

"I can talk for myself," I say.

She looks like a colt ready to jump the fence. "We can't use you. You're not the right sort for this kind of thing. I mean, I want someone I can find a match for and win."

"I get it." My voice grates in irritation. I'm not good enough for the show and certainly not good enough to be someone's husband.

"Gunner." Ed steps between us. Somehow, Kiley and I are only feet apart, as if we're magnets pulling toward each other. "Kiley," he says.

"What?" We answer in unison.

He faces Kiley. "If Gunner will agree to do the show, I'll leave you on as Matchmaker this season. That's my offer. There's a chemistry between you two that would work for this competition idea that Tony has. If he doesn't agree, we're probably going to postpone filming and I'll put another show in the slot. I'm afraid our ratings will fall if we rush in and put just anybody in as our substitute bachelor."

"Thanks for your vote of confidence," Kiley mutters.

Ed gives her a patronizing smile with a consoling nod. "All I'm saying is this: If I can't find the right bachelor to co-star with you, then we may have to rethink this entire season. I know what's best for your career."

Damn. I'm not crazy about the way Ed treats his daughter as if she's some kid. Also, I'm going to decline and now Ed's made it my fault that Kiley won't get to do the show. Thanks a lot, Ed.

"Ed," I say, avoiding Kiley's gaze. "I have to meet a client."

Kiley's mouth purses into a little bull's-eye of tension. Her picture could be in the dictionary beside "pissed-off woman." Her hands ball into tight fists at her side. She's probably not even aware she's doing it, but I notice everything about her.

"OK," she says. "I'll do it." The sound of ambition is palpable.

"I won't." I take a step back.

"Scared you might find the woman of your dreams and end up walking down the aisle?" she asks, sarcasm dripping in her tone. "Buying a house in the suburbs and having a couple of kids?"

One minute she's arguing that I can't do the show, the next minute she's arguing that I must. Typical woman.

Also, if I wanted to argue with Kiley—which I do not—I could mock her in light of her own recent dilemma with Moneyclip. I involuntarily glance at her folded arms and her ring finger. Still bare.

"Well?" Kiley widens her eyes and then lifts one eyebrow as she waits for my response.

Oh yeah. She mentioned weddings. "I don't believe in marriage."

Kiley flinches. You'd think I had made some jab at her personally.

"But if you found someone you loved, you'd reconsider. Wouldn't you?" she asks with this hopeful expression.

"Nope. A man asks for trouble when he gives

his life over to a woman."

"I'll give you overnight to think about it," Ed says. "We'll need your answer by tomorrow. Tony can send you the compensation packet by email. That will surely add some incentive."

"I appreciate the offer, but..." I look away from everyone in the room and then back at Kiley. "I'll think about it tonight," I lie.

Lord help me, but there's only one thing I'll be thinking of tonight.

I'll think about how she makes my blood run hot every time I look at her. I'll imagine showing her my new hot tub on the other side of the deck. We could have fun if she would forget about getting me on the show.

I half-turn toward the entry so they'll know I'm done with this talk about a show that has nothing to do with me. "I have to get back to work now. Ed, I wanted to let you know we're finished with everything. Let me know if there's anything else you'd like done. Otherwise, I'll send you a final bill."

I walk from the room, ready to have some time alone to plan how get her back over to my place. These people talk too much.

All she's worried about is whether or not she can make the damned show. I stayed away from Kiley for days to give her plenty of time to be sure about me. Time to make sure she doesn't regret what happened between us in her kitchen. I refuse to be her rebound guy—even for a hook-up.

But I knocked on that door today knowing she'd be inside and I couldn't wait.

I'm infatuated with her, the same as in high school. Now she's ready to sacrifice me to another woman to further her career. Won't I ever learn?

This is why a man should only look out for himself.

A SOFT RAPPING SOUND startles me. I glance up at the clock. It's almost midnight and I never have visitors, unless you count the raccoon that raids my trashcan and periodically attempts to break through the back deck.

The first thing that pops into my head is Veronica, my stepsister. Maybe something bad has happened. A wreck. A shooting. Something with that new fiancé of hers.

My life has been too much on the upswing lately and I'm due for a swift kick of reality. In two seconds, I'm at the door. My heart pounds, despite the fact that I know I'm overreacting. I jerk the door open with sweaty palms.

"Hi." Kiley says, appearing disheveled as if

she's recently crawled out of bed. She tucks a strand of hair behind her ear and folds her arms over her body like she doesn't know what to do with her hands.

Fear squeezes around my chest, making it hard to breathe. "What's wrong? Are you all right?"

And even though Kiley didn't cheat on her ex, that fucker Moneyclip couldn't stand the thought of me getting his girl and he's done something to her. He'll be sorry he ever laid eyes on me.

"Sure." She smiles, a real smile, not that wide fake one. "Couldn't sleep. Are you busy?"

I gulp to grab a bit of air. She's fine. Dragging one hand over the top of my head, I step aside so she can enter. I'm disconcerted by how scared I was that something was wrong with her.

I need to get a grip. She's OK, but here for some other reason. The only one that springs to mind is the conversation at her house today with her dad and that director fella.

My heart and voice harden in defense. "If you're here to try and convince me to do the show, you can go home."

"You think that's the only reason I'd talk to you?"

"Maybe." I've spent today thinking about how she threw me under the bus in favor of keeping her spot on the TV show.

She takes timid steps into the cabin. "Thanks for the vote of confidence. You have a low opinion of me."

I shrug. "So, talk."

"It's usually polite to offer someone a seat when they visit."

I motion toward the sofa. "By all means. Can I make you some hot tea? Cookies?"

"That would be nice." She sits in the middle of my sofa. Due to the limited space, I only have a sofa in this room. It's nice to fall asleep on while I watch television.

"Now, I'm joking. You think a confirmed bachelor like me stocks up on tea and cookies?" I sit next to her on the sofa, which seems too intimate in the dimly lit room.

"Beer?" she asks.

"Always." I stand and go into the kitchen, glad to have something to do. Is the girl here for some other reason than the reality show?

When I return, she's going through a stack of hunting magazines on my coffee table. "How long have you lived here?"

"Why?" I frown at the way she's examining the mailing labels and the magazine dates. Our fingers brush as I hand her the beer bottle. A pleasant rush of adrenaline shoots through me.

"These magazines are all new. Did you move in recently? Also, you don't have anything hanging on the walls." She motions around the room. "Usually people hang a picture or two."

"Moved in earlier this year." I sit beside her and lean back. "Are we doing small talk?"

She shrugs. "I guess. Am I being too nosy?"

"I don't mind. You can ask me anything."

"Oh." She sounds pleased. "Do you have other family here?"

"No." I study her lips, so dark pink and full. Erotic.

"Your dad?"

I take a long pull of beer without answering. She continues to stare, so I give in. "No. My dad's in prison. I don't know his family. They live in Nebraska. Got more questions?"

"What did he do?" She takes a drink of her beer and raises one eyebrow.

"What didn't he do is more like it."

"Murder? Robbery? Treason?"

"Maybe. I wouldn't know. He did get charged with drug manufacturing, intent to sell, assaulting a police officer, possession of a deadly weapon." I expect a shocked look from her, but it's strangely missing. Instead, she seems interested.

"How long will he be in?"

"I don't know and I don't care. Can we talk about something else?"

"Sure."

"Have you talked to Moneyclip lately?"

Kiley has taken a drink of beer and begins choking. I pat her gently on the back. A stupid gesture. I'm not sure if that actually helps a choking victim.

She begins laughing and wipes moisture from the corners of her eyes. "Oh, I forgot you called him Moneyclip earlier. No. I am so done with Mason. I swear, that is my new favorite thing—you calling him that."

I grin, her response spreading a warm feeling into my chest. "How are you doing?"

"About like you'd expect. I thought I had a future planned and now it's all up in the air. No wedding. Possibly no show. I'm living with my father. I have no idea what I'm doing with my life."

"It'll work out."

I slide a little lower on the sofa and prop my feet on the coffee table. Kiley does the same, except she kicks off her flip-flops and wiggles her pink polished toes. "Why don't you want to get married?" She lifts the bottle to her lips.

"Are you proposing to me?"

She struggles to swallow the beer in her mouth, her lips holding a smile in. Finally, she gulps it down and exhales while shaking her head. "No."

I place my beer next to hers and give an unmanly sigh for effect. "Maybe you and I are all chemistry, and you came over here to take advantage of me."

"Yeah. We have chemistry. We always have."

I grin at her blatant admission. "Chemistry ever since you poked me with pencils in the back of the neck back in second grade."

"You said it." She jabs me in the arm with her finger.

I glance down at the spot where she poked me. "Don't start flirting with me now."

"That's not flirting. I've grown up a lot since grade school."

"I've noticed." I lay my arm along the back of the sofa. A faint scent of tangerine drifts my way and I'm tempted to bury my face in her hair, along her neck, wherever that fantastic smell lives on her.

Although we both stare straight ahead, as if afraid to look at each other and see too much, my hand rests on the back of her head. I give in to my instincts and stroke the back of her silky hair.

"You're not regretting your break-up with Moneyclip, are you?"

She doesn't move away. "I could've married Mason. It's what my dad expected. What everyone expected. But I knew deep in my heart that I'd regret it. He wasn't the one."

"The one." I take a piece of her hair and allow myself to play with it. The texture alone is enough to make me imagine all the things I've wanted to do to her. With her. If I had her naked underneath me, I'd wind her hair around my hand and tether her to me.

"Yeah," she responds. "I think there's a soulmate out there in the world for everyone."

"That's nuts. Is the soulmate the person who makes you happy or sets your world on fire?"

She sits straighter and I miss the feel of her hair as it slides out of my grasp. "Both. You think that's impossible?"

"If you believe two people could be struck by one bolt of lightning."

"What's happened to you to make you so cynical?"

"Life. You of all people should know that it's damned near impossible for a person to find that one who is perfect for them. I'm sorry to be blunt, but you almost married a guy you admit couldn't make you happy. You aren't exactly the one to be handing out fictional promises of one man for one woman."

She hangs her head, looking at her bare ring finger and I'm immediately sorry for what I've said. It's not her problem that I'm so jaded. Not her fault that I've loved people who left me.

"I shouldn't have said that." I reach out and tilt her chin up with a finger so she can see I'm earnest.

"It's OK. But it's the reason I broke up with

139

Mason. You see, I know he isn't the right one for me. Even before I discovered I couldn't trust him. I think when you find the right girl, you'll know. Your world won't be right until she's part of it."

I pull my hand back. "I can tell you really believe what you're saying. It's...I don't know. It's tough to give over your happiness. Because that's what happens. You put yourself out there, put your sanity and well-being in the hands of someone else."

"You know, you're right. That's what so flipping wonderful about it. You said it right earlier. Like being struck by lightning—it's magical."

Dammit. Her eyes practically sparkle as she says the words.

My breath catches at the way she radiates, making me want to move near her. She's a warm fire on a chilly night, drawing me closer.

I reach out a hand and grasp the back of her head in a light hold, drawing her to meet my lips. The light scent of her perfume, a fresh citrus smell reminding me of sunshine, assaults my senses. I breathe her in during that brief second between knowing I'm going to kiss her and then my lips touching hers.

There's not a bit of hesitation from her. I drag my hand through her hair, a sensation I've dreamed of all week.

A groan.

I'm not sure if it's me or it's her, but the sound sends desire slamming into me. Common sense escapes and my heart pumps blood in anticipation of more.

Her hand lands on my chest, gripping the fabric of my T-shirt like she'll never let go.

I feel her opposite hand suddenly high on my thigh, inches away from my dick that pulses to attention.

The taste of her mouth and the oh-so-right feel of her body pressing against mine is that elusive magic she's mentioned. My tongue strokes the softness of her mouth. I suck her bottom lip into my mouth, amazed at the powerful rightness of a kiss.

It's as if I've waited all my life to experience this kiss and I've kissed hundreds of girls. Girls who didn't send my system into shock and scare the shit out of me.

I'm so tempted to carry her to the bedroom.

But neither one of us is ready for that tonight. First, she needs to understand that I can give her everything in the bedroom, but I can't give her my heart. I'm not a forever-after kind of guy. Some guys are like a wolf mating for life. Not me.

I touch my lips gently to the corner of her mouth and sit back a little. We're both breathing hard. Her hand releases the tight grip on my shirt and I drag both my hands from her hair.

My body aches for her and the physical connection that's damned near electric.

She pulls back. "I think I'd better head home."

Crazy warring thoughts fill my head. I have to think of a way to get her to stay.

She checks the time on her cell phone. "It's late. Thanks for the talk. I don't want to be accused of trying to seduce you onto the show. It's actually for the best that you aren't interested."

Is she trying to pull some reverse psychology on me?

I stand, straightening up and aware that the wood I'm sporting certainly tells her how much I want to keep her with me. "I'm sorry I don't want to be on TV. But there are millions of guys out there who'll jump at the chance. How soon do you have to find someone?"

Her crestfallen expression is enough to make me want to change my mind, if only to please her. Crazy talk. But I know one thing. Her body was made for mine. That kind of lightning strike I understand.

She gets to her feet and doesn't meet my gaze. "The show isn't your problem. Hope I didn't keep you up too late."

"Kiley—"

"No, don't say anything. It's OK. I should really go. I have a big day tomorrow. I'll see you around," she says as she strides to the door without looking back at me. "Take care, Gunner. You're a special kind of guy and any girl would be lucky to have you."

With those words, she leaves my cabin. Five minutes later, I'm still looking at the door.

"A guy would be lucky to have you, too," I mutter to the empty room. I need more time with her. The time I was cheated back in high school. I picture her dancing in my arms, laughing at my lame jokes, responding to my every touch.

I slide back onto the sofa and kick my feet up on the coffee table. The cabin practically echoes with the ticking of a clock on my kitchen wall.

She's only been gone a few minutes and I already want her back.

I open the drawer underneath my coffee table and remove the DVD of The Princess Bride. The cellophane still covers the new disc and I carefully tear it off. I flip the package over and read the description on the back.

So, Kiley named her dog after the character in this movie.

Maybe she wants to live in a fairy tale, thinking that some guy will rescue her. I could be that guy...if real life were different. If people didn't disappear as soon as you cared too much.

I'm an idiot. Worse than an idiot. A dreamer. She's not asking me to ride in like a white knight and rescue her. She only wants to keep her role on the TV show. That's it.

And what will it hurt? Doing the show would be easy—a little like the school play from junior high. If I don't do the show, I might not see her again.

Worse, some other guy will be on the show spending time with her. I rise from the sofa and stride across the room and insert the DVD in the player.

The movie begins and I return to the sofa. My cell phone buzzes with an incoming call. I check the number.

It's like a strange emotional telepathy that I thought about my stepsister earlier and now she calls me.

"Hey Nicky-girl," I say.

"Hi. Am I calling too late?" She sounds relaxed, her voice a low hum.

"Everything OK?"

"Everything is great. Quit sounding so worried all the time."

"Good." I grimace at her scolding. I do expect bad things to happen. Some habits are harder to break than others.

"Thanks for sending the money. I told you

144

the wedding is small, and I don't need it." She pauses. "But thanks anyway."

She's always turning down help, so independent. "I didn't know how much weddings cost. You have to tell me if I should send more."

"Stop. Gun. You've done enough. Too much. Collin—"

"This is my present to you."

"Show up with a suit on and give me away. That's all I want."

I groan. Loudly.

She giggles, as I knew she would.

"I already said I'd be there."

"Gun?"

"Yes, Veronica?" I say teacher-like, as if responding to a question about the lecture. I rarely use her full name. It's always been Nicky-girl to me.

"You remember when you came to the hospital and saw me?"

My stomach bottoms out.

An ex-boyfriend had almost killed her. I flashback to how small and defenseless she looked.

It was a cruel lesson. Life can be over in a flash. Everything taken away the moment you aren't looking.

"Gun? You still there?" she asks.

"Uh yeah. Just got distracted."

"Are you happy? Please, please tell me you are. You promised me in that hospital room that you'd be happy. Remember?"

"Yeah," I say, rubbing one hand over my eyes. "Sure."

"That's why I called. To make sure you keep good on the promise."

There's a smile in her voice. A distinct note of relief.

"Thanks for calling. I'll see you at the wedding."

"Bye for now."

"Bye." I toss my phone to the cushion and lean my head back.

And that's when I decide I'll do the show, tempt Kiley Vanderbilt into my bed, and take the cash.

I'm living for today.

Solidarity

Six Years Ago, Shelby City, Arkansas

Gunner

THE SMALL APARTMENT that I'm supposed to call home reeks of cigarette smoke and wet dog. Dirty ashtrays litter the end tables and empty pizza boxes fill the space behind the kitchen trashcan.

There's no dog, and I can't figure out the source of the smell.

How could Dad fall in love with a person like Jodie after having a life with Mom? Mom was a clean freak and our house smelled of clean linens and evergreen.

I've gone from a house filled with hope and life to one a step removed from hell.

I think about this disparity often, a mystery I'm determined to solve, but never do.

I'm prepared to hate both Jodie—my dad's new wife—and her daughter, Veronica. Within a month, I waver in my plan.

It's easy to dislike Jodie. Although she doesn't do anything to me to directly, she treats the girl with a disregard that pisses me off. It's as if Veronica is an afterthought. I can take care of myself, but Veronica? I'd guess that she's been self-sufficient all her life.

I sleep on the sofa because the apartment only has two bedrooms. When Dad and I moved in, he said we'd find a bigger place for all of us. Soon. The sleeping arrangement would be temporary.

Soon doesn't happen.

I never go into the bedrooms. Sometimes, Dad and Jodie sleep all day and night. Or maybe they're doing other things in there.

I really don't want to know. I've mentally checked out, sitting on my sofa bed and playing video games in marathon sessions. No more football practice or games. Nashville seems like a distant dream.

Veronica hovers in the background, watching me all the time but never saying much. I don't talk to her, either.

It's Christmas break, but we don't have a tree. Not one twinkling light or piece of decoration. Dad and Jodie left days ago and haven't returned. I'm playing Silent Hill and

Veronica rises from an ugly orange recliner and goes to stand in front of the refrigerator.

She's so damned skinny, her T-shirt swallows her. The light of the fridge reflects off the sharp angles of all her bones. I know she's thirteen and still growing. But shouldn't she have hips and boobs? Maybe not. I try to remember if the girls back home did.

Veronica closes the door and turns to me. "What will we do if they don't come home?"

I glance from the TV to her and back so I won't get killed in my game. "They'll come back."

"What if they don't?" She walks to a stop in front of the TV.

"Move," I say, waving at her.

She doesn't listen. "No. We need groceries. I'm going to get a job or something."

I roll my eyes. "Who's going to hire a thirteen-year-old kid?"

"Don't call me a kid. I can babysit in the building. We need something to eat. I don't mind. I'll buy enough for you, too."

I shake the video game controller and lean my head so I can see around her. "Look. You killed me."

She gets a hurt expression on her face, her eyebrows knitting together in the middle. "Don't you care if we starve?"

"No," I lie.

"Why do you hate me?"

I'm shocked. "I don't. Why do you think that?"

"You never look at me or talk to me."

I exhale and my shoulders drop in defeat. "I don't hate you. It's...you're a kid. I don't have anything to say to you."

"You never ask me to play with you." She signals at the television. "I'm not a kid. I'm almost the same age as you."

"There's a huge difference between sixteen and thirteen."

She sits beside me on the sofa, something she hasn't done since I made it my bed. "I'm sorry about your mom."

"Hm," I say. My throat closes up instantly. Why'd she have to say it? I forgot the bulk of my misery until she had to say it aloud.

"You can talk to me," she says. "Or not."

I ignore her and begin a new game, pressing the controller buttons harder than necessary. "If you want me to like you, don't block my game again."

"OK," she says, but doesn't leave her seat beside me.

"And forget about getting a job. You're not going anywhere. I'll call my grandpa. He'll get us some groceries."

She tucks her feet underneath her body and nods. I try not to notice that she's crying.

Fucking shit. Why is she crying?

"What?" I put the game controller down. "What now?"

Her tears need to stop because I can't deal with it. My chest contracts and I can't breathe seeing them drip down her cheeks.

"Nothing," she whispers. "I don't hate you either."

I don't answer. Instead, I get up and hunt for my other controller.

When I hand it to her, she takes it and places it in her lap. "I'll watch for now," she says softly.

"Sounds good." I continue to play until she falls asleep in her seated position. Her head droops to the side and I push her gently onto my pillow. It's not so bad having company while I play video games.

Later, I call Grandpa Tom. I don't really know him, but Dad gave me his number in case of emergency. I decide this is it. Who knows if Dad and Jodie will return. I sure don't.

Grandpa doesn't ask tons of questions when I call. I ask if he'll bring me some groceries, and he says he'll be right over. Instead, he shows up empty-handed.

"You and Veronica can come home with me. Get your things. Write your dad a note," he says with a curl to his lip. "Tell him that you and the girl are with me."

Grandpa Tom has a small three-bedroom house. There's an anorexic, artificial tree in one corner with silver tinsel strewn over the branches. My dad's mom died before I was born, but I'd bet he's had the tree since Grandma died.

Veronica doesn't speak during the drive to Grandpa's. It's as if she's afraid to mess up a good thing. I give her an encouraging smile so she'll stop looking so worried. We follow him inside the house.

"Where does Veronica sleep?" I ask Grandpa.

"You take the good bedroom," he says to her. He points to the hallway. "First door. There's a bed and a dresser. Check the closet for blankets."

"Go on," I say in a gentle tone, when she doesn't move. I feel like the adult coaxing a child forward.

She rubs her fingers over her mouth, scrubbing hard enough to hurt. I've noticed her doing it when she's anxious. I'm confused. Isn't she glad to be here? I sure am. This beats the hell out of the smelly apartment.

I put one hand on her shoulder. "Are you afraid your mom will be mad?"

She shakes her head.

"Come on," I say. It's evident that she's not going anywhere without me, as if she's afraid of

Grandpa.

We walk down the narrow hallway together, side-by-side. She hugs her overnight bag to her chest. "I can sleep on the sofa," she whispers to me.

"He doesn't want you to sleep there. You have a room."

She's like a shadow behind me as I walk into the bedroom. It's plain, a patchwork quilt on the bed and a white shade over the window. I pick up a photo from the top of a cherry dresser sitting against the far wall.

I recognize my dad as a kid. He's on one knee beside a shaggy dog.

"That's Jerry," Grandpa says from the doorway.

"Yeah." I slide the photo back in place. "How long can we stay?"

"Son, I'm not taking you back to that place. You're staying here now."

Veronica wipes her hand over her mouth, her blue eyes huge in her pale face.

I look away from her to Grandpa. "She stays if I do. Please, sir."

He's quiet for several minutes. I'm sweating at the thought he'll think I'm too much trouble or that she is.

He lifts the John Deere tractor hat from his head. "She can if her mother will let her. I'm not her family."

"She stays with us," I repeat. I don't know why, but I need to know that the whole world hasn't gone to shit. She's not really my family either. I barely know her. But she has no one. Jodie is a sad excuse for a mother. At least I have the memory of my mom.

Veronica needs me.

Infatuation

Current Day

Kiley

"PINCH ME." I FROWN AT TONY and hold out my arm. "Go ahead. Do it. Because there is no way I'm awake."

He reaches across and bypasses my arm to give my cheek a friendly tweak. He lingers a second longer than I expect. "Yes, Gunner says he will be our star bachelor."

I drop into the patio chair and rub my bleary eyes. The coffee doesn't help to perk me up after a night of tossing and turning. "Why would he change his mind?"

Tony takes the seat opposite me. "I forwarded the compensation package yesterday. He emailed me this morning. He's a guy of few words. Didn't even ask the usual questions. I advised that he have an attorney look over the contract before he signed it. He said he'd do that today and get it back to me tomorrow."

"So, it's final. He'll be on the show?" My heart sinks. I'm so screwed. I'll have to watch him with other women until I want to gouge my own eyes out.

"You aren't happy about it?" Tony's forehead wrinkles into fine lines. "Ed made it sound like Gunner Parrish is your only chance to be on the show. You know how Ed is. He thought it would get him what he wants."

I shrug. "It doesn't matter now, does it? It's decided. So, me and Gunner."

"We haven't done the studio tests. If he comes across the wrong way, I can advise that we find someone else for you."

"No. If Gunner wants to be on the show, then so be it." It confirms everything about last night. If he wanted to pursue a relationship with me, he'd have declined the show. My head begins to pound. What the heck do I want? The show. Of course, I want the show.

"Kiley, how about I make some lunch reservations. We could talk about the show and your ideas for this season. I liked what you said before. You've got a great sense for what the viewers want and how to make this fresh. How to reinvent Forever."

I rub a hand over my forehead. "OK. I can meet you."

"That's not necessary. I'll run back out here and pick you up."

Tony's voice barely cuts through my miserable state. "Sure. Whatever you want," I answer, standing with my mug in hand. "I think I'll take something for my headache. Make yourself at home. Dad should be back any minute. He said he had a quick errand to run."

He studies me. "Are you up for lunch? If you don't feel well, we can make it another time."

"Lunch is great. I'll see you then." I smile with every ounce of energy I possess and hope he can't see through my facade.

After I leave Tony to his coffee on the patio, I retreat to my bedroom. I need alone time to pep talk myself into feeling better about Forever. I don't look forward to discussing all the ways I'll find Gunner's future love.

Twenty-four hours later, I conclude that Gunner can be a jackass. We spend only one hour in the Rolling Hills boardroom signing contracts and discussing the schedule, but I'm ready to kick him in the balls—something I've never in my life done. I could pop the violence cherry on him.

And to think I'd been crushing on him for days.

I bite the inside of my mouth to keep from

screaming. OK. I inhale slowly. Then exhale. Every Matchmaker probably faces this sooner or later. I give my pageant queen smile, the authentic one I practiced for hours as a teen. "I think we should film some shots of Gunner in his element. His cabin could use an interior design update, but it would make a great opener. He—"

"You've been to Gunner's house?" Tony looks up from his notes.

"What do you mean an update?" Gunner ignores Tony and glares across the table.

Sweet Fanny Adams. He's like an obstinate five-year-old who doesn't want to get rid of his blankie. "You know. Maybe some woodsy-themed furniture, fabrics with rich golds and greens, some..." I trail off under the glacial look he continues to give me.

"No changes to my place. It's fine. If a woman doesn't like me the way I am, then she can get lost."

I tamp down my frustration. It's only the third thing I've suggested in preparation for filming and Gunner continues to hate every idea I have.

My dad's absent; he never participates in the pre-show arrangements. Tony sits to my left, his mouth tightening after each protest from Gunner.

"Do you trust Kiley?" Tony folds his hands

in front of him and waits for Gunner's answer.

"I don't know," he says.

"Thanks for the vote of confidence." I close my eyes for a second and inhale. This isn't going as I'd planned. If he disagrees with one more item on my list, I'm going to fly across the table and throttle him.

I open my eyes to Gunner's stare. He's grinning at me.

"Maybe Kiley should come over and show me some of the changes she has in mind. She could bring some pictures because I don't know anything about this decorating stuff she's mentioned."

Tony glances between the two of us. "Good idea. You need to get comfortable with each other. The first show is all about Kiley going through the list of candidates for the speed rounds and then planning the follow-up dates for the remaining ten contenders. It helps if there are no awkward surprises in what you like."

"Makes sense to me." Gunner nods and looks to me. "What do you think?"

Now he's agreeable? "Perfect," I say. "Let's do that. When?"

"How about tonight?" he says. "I have some landscaping business to take care of this afternoon and then I could meet you at my place. You have the address?"

"Memorized." I kick him underneath the table. Yes, violence is definitely the answer.

He jumps as I connect with his shinbone. "I look forward to it."

"Seven o'clock?"

"I'll be there."

As I get up from my seat, Gunner stands and says, "I'll walk with you to your car."

Tony places a hand on my shoulder and squeezes. It takes me off guard for a second. "I'll call you later," he says.

"OK." I'm sure he's questioning Gunner's negative responses to every idea I've had. If he's going to be this difficult during the show, we're in trouble.

I grab my bag and Gunner opens the door for me. We walk in silence out to the parking garage of the production studio.

"What are you playing at? Why do I need to come over tonight?" I stop suddenly and face him.

He stumbles into me and his hands go to my shoulders. "To talk about the way you want to change all my stuff."

His fingers tighten for an instant and my nipples—with a mind of their own and little common sense—perk up and ask for more.

I wrench away like he's stung me. "I didn't say I wanted to change everything. But my real question is why you went from disagreeing to everything I said to playing some kind of game now."

"Who's playing games? Isn't that why you came over the other night? To see if my house fit with your show concept?"

I gasp. "I did no such thing. I came over because...I wanted..." I don't really know where I'm going with my explanation. He's grinning because he knows I didn't come over for that reason.

"Wanted what?"

"Never mind. The point is that I dropped in with no ulterior motive."

"OK."

"OK? That's it? I think you owe me an apology."

"Calm down."

"Hey," I say with an edge to my voice. "I'm not asking that you be anything but honest. Do you really think that's what I did? I don't know if this is going to work if you accuse me of underhanded—"

He takes a step forward, so close I can see the anger in his eyes. "I didn't mean what I said. I'm pushing your buttons because I'm frustrated and a little insulted."

His low voice disarms me. "I wasn't trying to hurt your feelings."

I lick my lips and his gaze instantly flicks to my mouth.

"I'm a grown man and I'll be fine. It's... It riled me when you were judging my place. I couldn't give a damn about what anyone else thinks of my place. But you, I..." He shifts from one foot to another and tucks his hands into his jean's pockets.

"Me what?" I soften my voice. "I like your place. I do. It's comfy and it's you. But I want to help you make a good impression on the people who will judge by a first impression. People say it doesn't matter, but it does."

"Maybe tonight you should see the bedroom."

My face heats and my eyes narrow. Oh, he is a wily one. I take a gulp and turn to walk the few remaining steps to my car. "Why is that?"

"To see what you think. Maybe you'll suggest it needs a makeover, too."

Right. The bedroom and Gunner's bed. My belly clenches as a thrill shoots through me. I glance from beneath my lashes to see if I can read him.

"'Will you walk into my parlor?' said the Spider to the Fly."

This fly will keep it professional.

With shaking hands, I unbuckle my bag and remove my key fob. The SUV beeps as I hit the unlock button. "I can guess it's similar to the living area."

"I don't know. I'm not some designer. I really

need your expert opinion."

We both reach out simultaneously to open the car door. I jerk my hand back as if he's branded me.

"I've got it." He opens my door and waits for me to climb up into the driver's seat of my SUV.

My short skirt rides up and I catch him staring at my legs. I tug the hem down, my blush deepening. "I'll see you at seven," I say in my most business-like tone.

"I'll be waiting."

His answer isn't seductive in the least, but the look he gives me makes me hope I can make it through the rest of the day without jumping him and ripping his clothes off.

I am in so much trouble.

At seven, I pull into the driveway of Gunner's cabin.

He's standing on his front porch as if waiting for me, shirtless and wearing jeans that hang far too low on his trim waist. I gulp and point the air conditioning vents toward me for a second.

He saunters over to my door and waits for me to kill the motor.

My hand shakes as I turn off the ignition. I get out of my vehicle. "Am I late? Early?" In God's name, is he trying to torture me with his bare chest?

"Nope. Let's go inside," he says and places his hands on his hips, pulling my gaze to the perfect V of muscles disappearing into his jeans.

Did I imagine a purr in his voice? He's like a tiger, all dangerous and lethal.

"You don't look ready for me. You're not wearing a shirt." Did I have to point it out? Of course, he knows this. People don't accidently forget half their clothes. Do they?

And can I be here next time he does?

"You were on time. I didn't expect that," he answers casually.

"If now is a bad time, I can come back tomorrow."

He ignores my non-stop chatter and walks toward the door. "Hungry?"

"What?"

"I grilled some steaks. I hope you like yours medium well. We can talk about this decorating thing while we eat."

"I don't usually eat dinner."

He stops and I run into the back of him. My hands automatically grab his waist to steady myself. My fingers tighten on the muscles of his waist, a place I've never really considered to have muscles.

My knees weaken at the sheer jolt of energy that surges from my fingertips all the way to my toes. If I fell on him accidentally, I'd probably electrocute myself.

"Why?" he asks. He gives a puzzled look over his shoulder.

I concentrate on whatever he's saying about dinner. "I watch my weight and it's something I've always done. Dad was never home at night and it seemed silly to eat by myself."

"You're perfect, so that's a bunch of nonsense about your weight."

"I won't be this size if I eat meals all the time."

He frowns. "I don't get women. Eat good food. Work off some calories. That's what I do."

I huff at his dismissal of my concerns. "I'm in television, looking ten pounds heavier than real life. People judge. If I gain a couple of pounds, the tabloids say I'm pregnant."

He shakes his head while opening the door for me. "You shouldn't care what people think."

We go inside and there's a bouquet of sunflowers in a vase on the table. "Who did that?"

"Me."

"Are you expecting someone?"

"You."

Me? This is more than a meeting to discuss

plaid pillows for his sofa or a new painting for the wall. This is something more. "Gunner...I don't want you to get the wrong idea. I'm your Matchmaker on the show. We can't..." I wave a hand between us. "You know." One corner of my mouth lifts in a sad smile.

He looks away from my gaze and pulls out a chair at his kitchen table. "It's not a big deal. You made dinner for me once. Remember?"

I grimace and cover my face with my hands. When I let them drop, he's smiling at me—a beautiful show of straight white teeth.

"Oh, come on. That was not a meal. That was a sandwich," I say, mortified that he's teasing me.

"If you think I care what it was, then you're wrong. It's been a long time since any woman fixed something for me. It was nice. I'll be back in a minute."

I stand, because I'm too nervous now to sit quietly as this guy does a number on all my expectations of him. The heavy sunflowers droop over in a glorious riot of yellow and brown. He must've clipped them from the massive group I noticed the first time I visited.

While he's gone, I glance around at the cabin. The last time I visited, only one lamp lit the end of the large room with the sofa. I hadn't paid much attention to the side of the room with a small kitchen. There isn't any decoration, but it's tidy.

A large pink cookie jar, a pig with a curly tail, is the only thing on the counter. It's not French country décor, but more a cartoon pig. For some reason, this makes me smile. Manly guy needs his cookies.

I should make certain the pig jar stays.

His soft footsteps signal his return. "There," he says. "I know it bothered you that I wasn't fully dressed."

"Much better." Not really. He wears a pressed white button-down, but the same jeans as earlier.

He pulls out my chair. "Here you go. Let's eat." I sit and twist around to watch him while he walks from the oven to the counter.

"Can we talk while we eat?" I get a notebook and pen from my bag. "I want to ask you some personal questions. Turn-ons. Turn-offs. Those kind of things."

"Shouldn't the women I date ask me these things?"

"No. We have to find women whose personalities mesh with yours from the beginning. The TV season goes quickly, but filming is even a shorter time span. A friend of mine wrote a computer program for matching people for compatibility. We'll build your profile. Then put it up against the profiles of the women in the dates. I'm also going to score your interactions with them."

"OK, go ahead. What do you want to know?" In seconds, he's placed a steak and baked potato on a plate before me.

"Describe your perfect girl."

"Tall, but not taller than I am."

"Got it." I jot down 'tall' and frown. He must be six-two. That rules out no one as far as possible dates go. It figures he'd start with physical characteristics instead of personality.

Men.

He cuts his steak and points at mine. "I'll answer if you'll eat."

I decide it's a fair trade and begin eating my meal. "Mmm mm mm m...," I mumble, not caring how unladylike I sound. "This is so good. I would never have guessed you could cook."

One corner of his mouth quirks up, but he looks away as if suddenly shy. My stomach flips pleasantly.

"I might surprise you about a lot of things."

I flip the page of my notebook and jot down 'likes to cook.'

"What are you writing?" He leans across and the corners of his mouth dip. "Are you going to make notes of everything I say?"

"No." I put my pen down. "Sorry."

"Can't we talk instead of this feeling like an interrogation?"

I nod and take another bite of steak. "Tell

me about your favorite place for a date."

He studies my face and looks mischievous. Pointing with his fork, he indicates the sofa. "I like to be at home."

My stomach drops as I remember sitting on it with him the other night. "All your dates can't be here. And don't you think that's going to give a girl the wrong impression?"

"What do you mean?"

"You need to wine and dine her. Take her to fun places. Be romantic."

"Like dancing."

I remember the way we danced on his back deck. His hand in mine, a hand lingering on my back. The way he smelled like man and woods and life. The twinkle in his eyes when he twirled me unexpectedly and I returned to his arms, closer than before.

That night was the most romantic thing I've done in my life. I sigh.

"Not dancing?" he asks, clearly confused by what he considered a correct answer.

"Yes, like dancing." I'm not happy to concede. I don't want to imagine someone else dancing with Gunner.

"I also like outdoor activities."

"Examples?"

"Hiking, fishing, camping."

I nod. "I'm sure I can find a woman who likes doing things outside."

"What about you?"

"What about me?"

"Do you like fishing and camping?"

"I've never done either one. So I don't know."

"That's a shame. You should try it once so you'll know."

"Hm..." I grab my pen and write 'outdoor activities.' Then I remember I said I wouldn't take notes during the meal. I put the pen down.

"I could take you so you'd know the kind of things I would do with a date. It could be research for you."

"Oh, I don't think that's necessary." My pulse ratchets and my palms grow damp. Camping? A tent? Alone with Gunner in the woods?

"How will you know what I'm looking for if you don't understand it? Me, you and camping. It's a good plan."

"Not a good plan. Gunner, I'm not going on some backwoods trip with you."

"Why not?" he asks, his tone dripping innocence.

"Oh, come on. Are you flirting with me? This is serious. I'm going to find the woman you'll marry."

"You can try." One corner of his mouth tips. "But you know I'm going home with that cash prize."

I grab the napkin from my lap and place it

on my plate. "There's no doubt about it. I'll find the right woman for you." I get to my feet and he stands with me. I'm all business now. Enough of the shirtless, T-bone steak tango. I'm done here. "We start filming next week. We want to do some speed dating so we can narrow down the field."

"Fast dates. OK. I bet I can cull the herd."

Herd? "It's best if you refrain from referring to women as cattle." I shake my head and grab my portfolio I'd brought. I'm too shaken up to stay here alone with him and go over the transformation of his man cave.

"Sorry if this gig is going to be tougher than you thought. Why else would I sign up? Friends?" He holds out his hand like we're going to shake on it.

I tilt my head and smile. "Oh, it won't be easy. But know this. The bigger the ass, the harder they fall."

Rescue

Six Years Ago

Gunner

GRANDPA DOESN'T TOLERATE what he calls
nonsense. Video games and television qualify,
so he tells me to store my console in the closet.

He wakes early and takes me with him to
feed his horses. It's not a hard job for me, but
he's old. Veronica cooks breakfast before we
both go to school. Even though Grandpa
complains that she's making him fat, he eats
everything on his plate. After we eat, he lets
me drive his old farm truck to school and he
goes to the convenience store he owns called
Gimme Gas, the world's stupidest name for a
business.

On the fourteenth day of living with

Grandpa, Jerry and Jodie show up at the door.

Thirteen days without so much as a phone call.

Both Dad and Jodie stand on the front porch. "I need my girl back," Jodie says as if I don't exist. "She needs to get her things. Gunner can stay with you."

I never expected her to treat me like a son, but I'm still surprised that they only came for Veronica. It shouldn't be a shock.

Veronica doesn't argue. She walks into the bedroom and picks up the bag she brought. She's ready so fast I wonder if she even unpacked it.

A knife twists in my gut to see her go. I've gotten used to her presence in the house. She's been talking to me, even if I rarely answer.

I look at Grandpa's face, wondering if he feels the same way I do.

"Why can't she stay with us?" The words spill from me. I don't know what makes me say it.

"Because I need her. She's my daughter. She has no business here." Jodie walks across the threshold of the house and grabs Veronica's bag.

Veronica holds onto it. But her mom is stronger and certainly more determined, if the rigid unsmiling set of her mouth is anything to go by.

When the car leaves the driveway, I go to my room without a word. Grandpa knocks on the closed door. He opens it without waiting for me to ask him inside. "You're lucky they didn't take you."

There's a knot in my throat that pisses me off. "Yeah. Sure."

"She'll be OK."

I lie on my bed, lift my body on one elbow, and shake my head. "Why do you care?" The knot is too big.

He pulls the door closed with a hard thump.

Five days pass without any words between us. On the sixth day, the phone rings, an alien noise in the house. It's seven o'clock. Grandpa turns down the volume on the television and answers it with his gruff voice. Maybe it's a telemarketer. They'll be sorry they picked Grandpa's number.

I strain to hear his side of the conversation, because I'm so curious. He never talks on the phone.

"Yes," he says. Pause. "Stay put. Veronica? Lock yourself in the bathroom." He shuffles around in the kitchen. "Gunner, I'll be back," he yells.

"Wait." I jump from my bed and scramble to stop him before he leaves. "Where are you going?"

He stands with his hands on his hips. "You always eavesdrop?"

"Yeah. Here I do."

"I'm going to your dad's."

"What's happened?" I run back to my bedroom and grab my tennis shoes.

Grandpa gives me a steely look. A look meant to freeze the ballsiest man. "You're not going anywhere."

"Why not?" I tug one shoe on and then the other.

"Because I said so."

"That's a reason to give a kid." I walk outside to the truck and hop in.

He slides into the driver's side. "You're as stubborn as your dad."

"I'm nothing like my dad."

"Small miracles happen."

The drive across town tortures me with a constant replay of the one-sided conversation I heard.

When we pull into the apartment parking lot, he turns to me. "Stay in the truck. I'll be back in a minute." He studies my face. "Don't test me. There's going to be enough trouble in there without you getting into the middle of it."

He slams the door and runs up the outside stairs to the second floor apartment. He's pretty spry for an old man, his shock of white hair bouncing with each step.

The minutes tick like hours as I wait for him to return. I waver on whether to push my luck on his order.

I push open the truck door and close it quietly, so I stand beside it. Better. I can breathe now and maybe hear something from the apartment. The closed blinds hide whatever happens inside.

What's taking so long and why did Veronica call?

I'm moving toward the building without conscious thought of how mad Grandpa will be or what it will be like to look my dad in the face after he's discarded me so easily.

A loud crash sounds from the apartment. I run up the metal steps and fling open the door. A broken lamp lays in the center the floor. Dad pushes Grandpa against the wall with one hand and then presses a hand against his throat.

Fuck.

I don't even notice where Veronica and her mom might be. I can't hear the yelling or interpret the words. All I see is the war happening in front of me.

"Let go!" I bark out the plea, scared and pissed at my dad. Grandpa's an old man. What the hell.

I bolt forward and grasp Dad by the

shoulders. He whips around with bloodshot, wild eyes.

"Gun, this is between me and him. Go to your room," Dad says.

"I don't live here. Remember?" I stand glaring at him, our bodies almost touching we're so close.

His eyes widen. "You always think you're so smart. Of course you don't live here. I can't stand the sight of you."

A hurt slices soul-deep, and I'm surprised. I didn't think I cared anymore. "What is wrong with you? Have you gone crazy?"

He's unshaven and smelly, his hair a whirl of bedhead like I've never seen. Then it hits me. This isn't drunk-Dad. He's hopped up on something else.

Something really bad.

Grandpa moves away from the wall. "Veronica? Come on. We're leaving."

The bedroom door opens and she comes out. She looks like hell with her tear-stained face. She's carrying the same bag she'd packed the other time she came to Grandpa's.

A movement from the kitchen catches my attention. Jodie stands with a fucking butcher knife in her hand. "You're not taking my baby."

"Go," Grandpa says to me. "Take Veronica to the truck." He puts a soothing hand up to Jodie. "We're leaving with the girl. You don't want her to be unhappy. She's scared here. Be a good mother."

Jodie leans against the threshold and slides to the floor wailing. "No, no, no, no..." she blubbers.

I open the apartment door and Veronica stares at her mom, but only for a second. Then she runs for the truck. Her feet pound down the stairs so quickly, I'm afraid she's going to fall.

Dad makes a grab for Grandpa again, but I'm faster and more alert than he is. I twirl him around and punch him in the nose.

He screams like a wild thing and tackles me. His knee rams into my balls and piercing pain shoots through my entire body. Hot blood from his nose drips onto my face.

And then he's lifted from me. Grandpa pulls him up and drags him across the floor by one arm.

"You ever touch Gunner again, and I'll break both your arms." Grandpa reaches down to give me a hand.

I get to my feet and Grandpa looks me over for a second. "You all right?"

"Yeah," I answer through gritted teeth. We walk out together. I shove my hands into my pockets so they'll stop shaking.

Inside the cab of the old truck, Veronica sits in the middle of the bench seat with her face in her hands while she sobs. Each sound thumps against my heart. I've never seen anyone look more broken and alone.

Grandpa peels out of the parking lot as if making a statement. The squealing tires grate on my already frazzled nerves. I glance around for cops.

"Next time I tell you to stay somewhere, you stay," he says.

I sit quietly for several seconds, not knowing what to do about Veronica. Garbled, gulping sounds from deep in her throat make me want to open the windows for fresh air.

I throw an arm over her shoulders and hug her to me. Stop crying. Please stop because I can't listen.

She's stiff and unresponsive at first. She didn't expect me to do that and I sure didn't plan on it. She says something low and muffled by her hands that are still over her face.

"What?" I ask.

"I tried to stay. I tried."

She begins rocking and puts fingers over her lips in a rubbing motion. I grab her hand with my free one and hold it lightly. "Yeah. I know."

I realize I'm rocking with her. Leaning to her side, I catch a glimpse of myself in the mirror. Blood smears across my cheeks. Dad's blood.

Grandpa gives us both a side-glance in the dark truck interior. "You're supposed to be with us," he says in a gravelly voice. "Gunner and I need you."

She lifts her head from her hands and turns to him. "Thank you."

He nods and returns his attention to the road.

"Do you think Mama will be OK?" she says, her voice barely above a whisper.

Grandpa doesn't answer and I don't either.

How can she even be worried about Jodie? Dad and Jodie proved to me way before tonight that they're losers.

She nods as if we've answered her question with our silence. I take my arm back from her shoulder and release the hold on her hand. I don't move completely away and she leans against me.

Veronica falls asleep within minutes. I wonder how long she's been awake.

Her head falls against my shoulder, long blonde hair trailing onto my arm. I'll let it stay until it's time to wake her at the house.

"This will be your last shitty day. I promise." I don't care that Grandpa hears me say it or that I'm not sure what I'm promising.

Grandpa shakes his head. Maybe he's thinking about what happened at the apartment or about what I've said to the girl sleeping by my side.

For the first time since Mom died, I don't feel absolutely alone.

100 Dastardly Dates

Current Day

Gunner

IT'S THE FIRST SPEED DATING NIGHT. I suggested Dastardly Bastard's Bar as a meeting place for all the dates, all one hundred of them.

My friend Dane owns the bar—a college graduation gift from his dear old dad—and he loves the idea of having free publicity thrown at him. The place serves decent food during the day and hosts some bands at night. It's nice to have the moral support of my buddy, who stands behind the bar.

It's early morning before Dastardly's would

normally open. Although it's not the best time for me, since it interferes with my work hours, I've agreed to it for this round of dating.

Each woman gets me for five minutes. All of them look good, according to the computer program that Kiley used to match me with a love interest.

You have to love technology.

Forever's film crew stands around our booth and I force myself not to look at them. The girl across from me is hot. Not Kiley hot, but I have to admit I'd normally look twice.

She wears a tight shirt with a low neckline, giving me a good view of her breasts. A sparkly diamond necklace glitters in her cleavage, an arrow emblem pointing down like a marquee sign advertising the goods.

It's a little desperate for attention, if you ask me.

"What do you do for a living?" Talisa asks. She flips her blonde hair away from her tits. I hope I'm not staring at her cleavage. It's not that I'm leering. Only, I can't quit looking at the arrow necklace.

"Landscaping business."

She nods. "That's wonderful. I love flowers. Especially roses. Red and pink are my favorites."

I have no clue why she thinks it's important to tell me this. "What about you? What do you do?"

"I design jewelry. I have major distribution nationally and hope to gain international clients soon. I also create custom pieces for the boudoir. If a bride to be wants..."

My gaze flicks up to meet Kiley's. She stands off to the side with her arms folded and an unhappy look on her face. Is she as bored as I am with this woman? What is Kiley wearing? Her legs go for miles and those red shoes are fuck me heels if I've ever seen any. Good God.

The woman could teach a class on seduction, beginning with shoe selection. Director Tony watches from her right and I wish he'd put a damned inch or two between them.

Kiley points at the blonde across from me. I return my attention to her.

Talisa appears to be waiting for my response. "That's nice," I say.

She smiles. "Thanks. I'd love to introduce you to them."

Seeing that I have no idea what she's been talking about, I can only nod. "Maybe."

"I have a large family and five cats."

"I hate cats. Allergic," I lie.

"Oh. I love my cats. They sleep with me and I couldn't live without them. They're like my kids."

I picture us in bed with five cats snuggled between us. "It was nice meeting you, Talina."

That's the agreed upon cue to end the round.

"Talisa," she corrects. "Hope to see you again."

Talisa stands and I see how tall she looks from my seated position. I wonder if she played basketball in school.

Kiley walks over and escorts the girl away. When she returns, she leans down to my ear and whispers. "Pay attention to your date."

"Cats," I reply and lift an eyebrow.

She rolls her eyes and leaves me.

I glance down to take in Kiley's long legs in those heels. I'd love to feel her wrap those legs around me, preferably still wearing the shoes. "You look nice today."

Her eyes widen and she blushes. "Stop trying to distract me."

She straightens and walks across Dastardly's to escort the next one over. My gaze follows her sexy walk, then moves over to director Tony. He's watching her also.

Prick.

Behind him, my friend Dane gives me a thumbs-up from the bar. He laughs and says something to a female in front of him. She turns and I recognize Josie, the one who was at Kiley's house. Josie grins, enjoying whatever Dane has said to her.

The next speed date is again a tall blonde. Did I say this is my type? I can't remember.

I stand and hold out my hand. She goes in for the hug instead. Her perfume makes my eyes water.

"I'm Gunner Parrish. Thank you for coming."

"I'm Zander," she says, her tone a lot lower than I'm used to hearing from a woman.

I'm not able to stop the look I give her. "Zander?"

I lean in a little closer, looking for an Adam's apple. None. I sit back and try to relax. Maybe I'm paranoid.

"Yes, it's my daddy's given name." She smiles sweetly. "Daddy owns Piccolo Farms and breeds horses."

That actually piques my interest. "I've heard of it. Do you ride?"

"I love riding. What about you?"

I nod. "What are you looking for in a guy?"

"Someone stable. Honesty. I like country music and movies."

"Who's your favorite country artist?"

"I have too many to list."

I guess that's a fair answer. "Do you have cats?" I ask.

A throat clears from somewhere. I glance over and Kiley glares at me.

"Do you?" I persist.

"No cats. No dogs either. And I don't want children."

"Why not?"

"Why would I?"

I think about Kiley's little dog. Sort of looks like an oversize rat, but it's cute. "No children?" I ask.

"I think I would make a fantastic mother. But I know kids are demanding, and I'm not sure I can give that. My career takes a lot of time. I'm constantly fine-tuning my craft."

"What do you do?"

"I'm a mime."

Hell-to-the-no. This has got to be a joke. My gaze whips to Kiley and my mouth splits into a grin before I remember I'm being filmed. I can't help myself. "Sorry," I say, hoping they can cut that from the video.

She furrows her brow. "You have something against mimes?"

"Not at all. It was nice meeting you." I can't even remember her name.

"Is the date over? You're not calling me back for a date, are you." Her lips flatten against her teeth in a wooden, yet evil smile.

Very mimish.

I look to Kiley for help. Someone get me out of here. I get to my feet since I'm a gentleman, even if the girl across from me looks like she's contemplating mime murder. "I don't think so," I say as politely as possible.

She slowly raises her hands above the table

and extends two middle fingers. Even I can interrupt the meaning of that mime movement.

I raise my eyebrows at her. She gets out of the booth and stomps away, her cowboy boots making a lot of noise in the stunned silence of her departure.

At the bar, Dane and Josie bend over laughing. No noise comes from them, but the entire body shaking tells me how they think it went.

The camera crew look away, but I can still see their smiles.

Kiley approaches from the side and puts a hand on my shoulder. "How about a break?"

"Overdue." I get out of the booth and stalk outside. I swear I hear laughing as I exit.

"Now, Gunner—"

"No 'Now, Gunner.' What in the hell are you thinking?" I'm not actually mad. I'm more baffled that she really thinks a guy like me would be into the women she's picked for me. Not that I care who she picks, because I'm walking away when this is all over. But is that how I come across to her?

I do have some pride.

"I...um..." She rubs her eyebrows with a bent finger. "None of that came out in the extensive interviews we did. The cat thing? I knew she had cats. A lot of women do. But she never mentioned she slept with them. Even if

188

she did, I might not think anything. I sleep with my dog and—"

"What about our mime friend?"

"She was cute. She loves horses and country music. It's a match made in heaven. Mime heaven." Kiley turns away and starts laughing. When she faces me again, there are tears in her eyes and a smile on her face. "Wow. I am so sorry. That was freaking awful."

"You think this is funny?" I'm smiling with her. "I'm going to make it to the finish line of this show with a bucket of cash."

"No." She stops laughing and sniffles. "We have eight more of these to go. The first two weren't the strongest contenders."

"I hope not. Otherwise, Forever's audience is going to think you suck at this."

Kiley looks away and runs fingers through her bangs. "I know." She closes her eyes and takes a deep breath. "We have to go back in now. I promise to do better."

"You're doing fine. At this rate, I'll be joining a monastery. A monk with a bankroll."

AFTER ONE HUNDRED ROUNDS OF SPEED dating over two nights, I am exhausted from all the fake smiling. Being nice. My eyes glazing over while

189

listening to the most boring women in Nashville.

We sit at a table in Dastardly's, the film crew pulling in for close shots of me talking to Kiley about how it went.

She asks me questions about each woman. I choose ten women to talk about more than the others—all petite blondes. Why? Because I really don't care which ten make it to the next round. I barely remember their names.

I enjoy Kiley's expression as I point to the headshots of all the petite blondes—a definitive physical type and very much the opposite of her. Her mouth grows pinched and she even rolls her eyes on the tenth photo I pick up and study closer.

Kiley put me in this position, so a little jealousy serves her right. But now it's time for me to make my move so she'll admit she wants me.

Even though I've thought of half a dozen ways to get Kiley alone, only one works and only because she thinks it's related to the show. I'm OK with my plan. I've earned this weekend. I have it all planned. Camping with Kiley will be great.

The getting-her-alone adrenaline has me high, like hiking to the top of a mountain peak. I'm so buzzed, it takes me hours to fall asleep.

The next morning, I pull up to the front of Ed's house and cut the Jeep engine, ready to gather up Kiley and haul her ass to the woods. I'd like to find an area with wilderness where we won't have a cell signal or chance of seeing anyone but each other.

She stands waiting, dressed in what I assume she thinks are camping clothes—a red and black plaid shirt buttoned too high and jeans. She looks like she could be on a commercial selling pancake syrup. Her dark jeans mold to her curves. She wears hiking boots and a ball cap with her hair in a ponytail pulled through the back.

Even though I'm sure she bought new clothes for this trip, she's enough to make me want to pull out my phone and take a picture. And that's something I don't do. The whole selfie and snapping photos of every minute craze is for the people who need a life.

I drink her in from head to toe and take the snapshot in my mind, filing it away for later. I could get used to her lumberjack-temptress look.

"Ready?" I ask and examine the three bags at her feet. I grab the largest. "What's in here? Rocks?"

"I didn't know what to bring. Is it too heavy? Are we supposed to keep the luggage light?"

"There is no 'luggage' in camping." I set the bag down. "I'm carrying the tent and supplies. You don't need all this stuff. Let me see what

191

you have."

She purses her lips. "See what?"

"The contents."

"I don't want to show you everything."

Kiley shy? Without a doubt, I can't make the drive without knowing what she has in the bags. Lingerie? Not likely. A wardrobe change of stylish hiking boots and more lumberjack themed shirts in case she gets sweaty? Probably.

"Open 'em. I brought you a backpack for necessities." I stroll over to the Jeep and retrieve what will now be her new suitcase—an old Army backpack.

"I...um..." She balances on the balls of her feet while pilfering through the closest unzipped bag. "This."

I take the stack of clothing. She's handed me a couple of T-shirts and a pair of shorts. "We're only going overnight. You can bring one T-shirt if you can't live without it."

She studies the stack and removes one cotton tee. "OK."

A front door of Kiley's house slams and I look up to see Tony and one of the women from the speed dating round earlier in the week. A guy with a small video camera steps out from behind them, pointing it at me.

No way.

I've been ambushed.

I clench my jaw and glare at her.

Kiley finally meets my gaze with a sullen look. "What? You didn't think I would go camping with you alone, did you?" she asks while still going through her bag.

"I didn't sign up for this." I glance over to Addison, one of the ten blondes who made the cut in the speed dating rounds. "No offense, but I only brought enough supplies for two."

"It's fine," Tony says. "We've packed our things." The guy smiles at me calmly as if he pops up uninvited all the time.

I grab Kiley's hand to still it from pulling more things from the suitcase. "You should've told me."

"We're skipping the date research and going straight for the fun," she says. "Plus, this was the only way you'd agree to do it. I have a job to do."

I bet.

Addison walks the few feet to stand next to me. "I'm looking forward to this. When Kiley called last night, I couldn't believe she'd chosen me. I really couldn't sleep after that."

I smile, all stiff and irritated. Addison's eyes widen.

Instead of attempting to pretend I'm not pissed, I tap Kiley on the shoulder. She looks up from her crouching position, a clear bag holding a book and electronics in her hand.

"Can we have a minute to discuss this? In private?" I stride away from the group to stand near the garage. The camera guy eyes my every move, but he's smart enough to stay beside Tony.

"I don't like to be tricked. You agreed to go camping. You never said that this would be part of the show."

She puts her hands on her hips and her chin comes up. "You said you liked outdoor activities. You picked Addison from the speed dates. You guys clicked. She's great. She loves camping. Told me she goes all the time. That's all I needed to know for this decision. You contracted to go on all dates I arrange as long as it doesn't interfere with your landscaping business. I—"

"Kiley, I don't—"

"And you probably would come up with an excuse not to go since you would give me no feedback about the women from the speed round, even though—"

I put my hand over her mouth, a pretty little mouth that tightens into a rose bud underneath my fingers. "Shush. OK. I don't like surprises and not being asked. But I'll deal with it. But next time, don't expect me to trust you."

Fuck.

I drop my hand and glance over at the waiting threesome, all staring at us. "We can't

194

all go in my Jeep. I only have one tent. Did you think about how this will work?"

Her nostrils flare and she points at an SUV parked on the side of their circle drive. "Tony's brought everything."

"I bet," I mumble.

"That's why you saw three bags. One is Addison's."

"Hmph." I eye Addison and she waves at me. I nod my head in response.

"She's funny. You'll like her," Kiley says evenly.

"You're sleeping in my tent." If I weren't about to strangle her, I'd enjoy her blush.

"No, I'm not. Definitely not. Are you nuts?"

"Then you expect me to sleep with Addison. 'Cause it's a two-man tent and I'm not sleeping with your metro-sexual director or the camera guy."

"The director is Tony," she corrects. "You don't have to sleep with anyone." Her throat works for a second and she looks away. "Unless you want to invite Addison into your tent."

"Are we ready?" Tony yells across the lawn.

I ball my hands at my sides. "That guy has to come along? What's his deal? Is he your chaperone?"

"He's the director," she says as if I'm dense. "You're lucky we aren't bringing another camera guy. I put my foot down when they wanted the whole crew."

"He wants to sleep with you."

She narrows her eyes. "You have it all wrong. I've known Tony for years. He's like an older brother. He is not interested in me."

I shake my head at her naivety. "Mm hm. You keep telling yourself that."

"What's that supposed to mean?"

"Trust me. I'm a man. I know these things."

She turns from me to study Tony. I thought women could sense these things. Some kind of attraction intuition.

Her radar's obviously jammed. What if she has no clue that I'm trying to spend time alone with her? My plan for a weekend in the wilderness went right over her head.

Or did it? Is she deflecting? Fighting the pull we have for each other since we're on this show together? Because no one else has to know if we see each other. She could've disappeared with me for a weekend of research about matching me with someone, a perfectly plausible explanation.

Then she seals the deal on my suspicions that she's forcing me into the friend zone because she's scared. She does know how I feel, because she holds out her hand for a fist bump. I've never been fist bumped by a woman in my life.

I'm positive it's as awkward for her as it is

for me.

I grin at her effort, enclose her soft hand in mine, and rub my thumb along the knuckles. "I'm glad you're looking out for me. It gets cold at night where we're going. Think you can convince her to sleep in my tent?"

"This is a first date." She jerks her hand out of mine. "Are you really such a horndog? No wonder you're still single." She turns to walk to the group.

Behind her back, I smile. "That must be why you're still single, too. I was only talking about sleeping. Get your mind out of the gutter."

Savor

Current Day

Kiley

CAMPING GEAR OCCUPIES EVERY SPARE inch of Tony's SUV. Cameraman Roy sits in the backseat of Gunner's Jeep so he can film them talking and flirting and who knows what else. I close my eyes in the passenger seat and feign sleep so I won't keep staring at the Jeep ahead, wondering what Addison and Gunner are doing.

"That guy is hardcore," Tony says with a hint of amusement in his voice.

I open my eyes and glance at him. "Hardcore?"

"I thought he was going to blow a fuse when

I insisted on Loretta Lynn's Ranch."

"Maybe we should've let him take us to the camping spot where he planned. You know he didn't realize what we were doing. I feel like we deserve his bad mood."

Tony shakes his head. "He wanted some backwoods scene where we'd have no electricity and no bathroom for miles. That's not going to cut it. America wants to see both of them looking fresh and attractive, not grubby."

"I don't know. It could've been interesting. Real."

"This is as dirty and real as you'll want to get. Admit it. You haven't ever been camping and I'm rescuing you with this idea." He chuckles under his breath.

I stare out at the Jeep, wishing I were riding with Gunner instead. I close my eyes and drift off to sleep.

I wake when we arrive at the campground check-in. After paying the camping fee, we decide to do a quick hike so we can film it. Gunner suggests a shorter route, and Tony and I follow along in the rear with Roy filming behind the couple.

Addison begins whining about two miles into the hike. I swear by my favorite Gucci purse the girl told me she does weekend hikes all the time.

"It feeds my soul to walk miles in God's

199

country," I repeat her words under my breath. Women like her give us all a bad reputation.

"How much farther?" she asks. "Can we take a break?"

"Not yet," Gunner answers, since we took a break half an hour ago. He glances back at me and widens his eyes in an exasperated expression.

"Addison?" Tony edges around Roy on the narrow trail and touches her back. "Are you feeling OK?"

Ugh. He's babying her. I'm wearing brand new boots, my jeans are too tight, and I wish I'd skipped the makeup. Still, I'm not complaining.

"I think I may be dehydrated," she answers. "Can I have a drink?"

"Of course." Tony signals to the cameraman. "Roy? Let's cut video. We don't want some idiot at the studio sneaking this into a blooper reel."

Tony passes her a flask. "Here you go."

I avoid Gunner's gaze. After promising I'd select a good match from the speed dating rounds, Addison makes me look bad. I'm not doing it on purpose, but at this point, I couldn't blame him for thinking otherwise.

"Is this wine?" Addison tips the flask up again.

"You can't give her wine." Gunner's expression grows murderous. "She really will be dehydrated."

"I can give her wine so we'll all have a good time as we go the last mile or two." Tony winks at me behind Addison's back.

Gunner throws up his hands. "Fine. You're in charge of this circus."

My back hurts and I hate the way Addison puffs out her chest every time Gunner looks her way.

Ugh. I might need that wine before long.

Roy adjusts the camera on his shoulder. "Turn the camera back on?"

Tony makes a rolling motion with his finger. "We're good to go."

"Addison, take this." Gunner hands her a water bottle from his pack. "You should always drink plenty of water while hiking."

She beams at him. "Thanks. You're so sweet."

"Not really. I don't want you to pass out before we get there," he says, control in his polite tone.

I hang back a little to tie the laces of my boot and Gunner stops and lets the others walk ahead. "Don't fall behind," he says.

"If I had an attraction barometer for the looks you give Addison, it would sink to ten below. I'm going to be the laughing stock of television and worst Matchmaker in the history of Forever."

He chuckles. "Sounds like your problem.

Not mine."

Addison lied to me about her love for the outdoors and hiking. Surely, the audience will sympathize with me.

Gunner pivots and walks ahead, moving at a clipped pace. He probably wishes he could lose us all.

I stare at his fine ass. OK. Hiking into the wild blue yonder with Gunner in the lead definitely has its perks.

An hour later, we've arrived back at the trail head. Gunner slows and turns around, walking backward. He lifts his red baseball cap from his head and wipes his brow with his forearm. "We should probably set up camp before it gets dark."

Tony glances around. "You're the boss. Kiley can help with my tent."

I wonder if Tony's camped a lot. He appears comfortable with it all. "OK." I follow Tony to the right of our assigned clearing.

To my surprise, Gunner allows Addison to help him set up his tent. Roy shoots footage for a while, but it's actually boring from what I can see. He puts his camera down and busies himself with gathering fallen limbs and small sticks. Men must come out of the womb knowing this stuff, because Addison and I wait around for direction on every task.

When the camp is prepared, I stand back

and look at our work. Roy has a tent so small I can't imagine that he'll fit inside. The other two tents are similar in size.

"Now what?" I ask, standing over Roy as he makes a neat little pyramid of the sticks. He's a big man and I divert my gaze away from the inch of crack peeking above his non-working belt.

"We have a good time. Or the lovebirds over there have a good time," he answers between blowing on the flame he's started in the tiny branches.

"Oh," I say, my stomach doing an uneasy flip at the thought.

Addison and Gunner stand to the side, talking. They've finished putting his tent up. Now that Addison has stopped whining and everything has settled, Gunner doesn't seem to mind her so much. Roy videos their conversation and Tony sits in his SUV taking a phone call.

I glance around our sparse campsite.

Three tents. Well, two and a half if I'm honest. Roy's tent doesn't look like it could sleep a dog, much less his bulk.

Two small tents. Four adults.

I should've done the math before this point, but I was so caught up in trying to make sure I could pull off this date for Gunner that I didn't think ahead to this situation.

I guess I'd assumed we'd segregate by

gender—a guys' tent and a girls' tent. What am I? Dumb as dirt?

Gunner walks across the camp toward me and Roy follows him. "I brought some food in the Jeep. Want to help?"

"Am I supposed to be on tape?" I ask Roy. He shrugs and continues to film.

Addison watches us with a predatory eye, as if I'm about to steal her man. Seeing he's her date, she has a right to wonder why he's talking to me. "Maybe Addison should help."

"If you want me to keep smiling, you'll pretend to be thrilled to help me." He walks to his Jeep, expecting me to follow. Roy again follows.

Gunner gives him a dirty look and motions to me. I catch up in two strides.

"Is something wrong?" I whisper to his back.

"Yeah."

"Cats?"

He glances at me over his shoulder with a wide-eyed look, then over at her. "No."

"Her whining during the hike?" I ask, forgetting that Roy still points his camera at us. I lean against the Jeep while he sticks his body across the backseat and grabs a soft cooler.

"No," Gunner answers.

"Then what?"

"She drinks."

"So do you."

"It was the middle of the hike. I don't consider that wine o'clock."

I roll my eyes. Oh well. All of America will be entertained with this exchange. "Maybe she was nervous. Or thirsty."

Gunner puts a hand on the top of the open Jeep door and leans down, shielding his face from Roy and the camera. "Quit making excuses for her. I have certain standards and she doesn't meet them."

"Come on. She's bright. She wants kids. She's as thin as a supermodel..." I wave my hand in the air. "Just the way you guys like them."

All these reasons sound lame to me once I voice them. Lame laced with catty.

Both his eyebrows jack up. He smirks, the corner of his mouth twitching. "She's too skinny. I like my women to have hips. I'd like to think she's eaten a couple of burgers this year. Sort of like you." He steps back and his eyes rake down my body to rest on my hips.

My face tingles with warmth. I'm not sure whether to be insulted or complimented. "Stop it. You're not funny."

"Maybe I'm a little pickier than you thought." He closes the Jeep door and strides toward the fire pit. "Time to eat," he announces.

I try to figure out if he's mad or simply bent on proving how difficult my job is going to be.

There's no way to know for sure, but I'd bet on the second.

Gunner unloads his cooler of drinks and cold hot dogs. He spears the wieners onto metal roasting forks and never says a word as he prepares them.

Addison and I again stand to the side looking pretty useless. Night falls and a chilly night breeze sprays embers from the fire pit. We both step back and wait for dinner.

The smell of food cooking at our camp and those around ours makes my mouth water. I didn't know a hot dog could smell so great. We eat like it's our last meal, or at least I do.

Addison picks at her food and spends her time staring at Gunner. I'm tempted to advise she eat if she wants a second date. But I keep quiet. The last thing I need is to look catty on national television.

"I'm going in," Roy says, cradling the camera. He states this like he's an undercover cop, all serious and determined. He'd better think that way. It will be a miracle if he can squeeze himself into the compact tent.

We watch in amazement as he does manage to caterpillar inside.

Gunner turns to me and Addison. "I'll be back in a minute. I'm going to the showers."

We both mutely nod at him and watch him head in the direction of the communal campground buildings.

Addison raises both hands above her head and yawns. "I think I'm ready to call it a night. Hope we don't keep anyone awake."

She heads toward Gunner's tent. My mouth drops open and my heart begins to pound. Gunner's going to return and find Addison in his tent. I'll have to sit on the other side of thin nylon walls imagining his lips and hands and body on hers. There's no way I'm sticking around for this form of torture.

A nauseous wave of realization rolls over me. I'm going to witness him sleeping with another woman and all I can wish is that it was me instead.

I walk quickly to Tony's vehicle and retrieve a towel and tube of body wash. Once I find my toiletry bag, my hands shake so much I barely hang on it.

"I'm going to take a shower."

"I'll walk you," Tony says, seeing my towel and taking the cell phone away from his ear.

"I'm fine to walk alone." I close the door and leave the campsite like I'm running from Bigfoot. There are lanterns out and a full moon, so it's not too dark. Voices travel throughout the area with people talking low. The sound of a guitar would be pleasant if not for the romantic ambiance it lends, like backdrop music for Gunner and Addison.

Inside the ladies showers, I undress and step into the curtained shower stall. The water is hot. I couldn't ask for better, considering I had expected much worse. I stand perfectly still as water slides down my back and into my face.

My stomach churns and I regret the hot dogs with too much ketchup and mustard. Maybe Addison was smart not to indulge.

I place my hands against the shower wall, not caring about germs. Dropping my hands, I examine the mold growing in the tile grout. OK. I care a little about what lurks in this place.

A choked sound escapes me, and I cry for only a minute. If only I hadn't glimpsed what it could be like with him. If only he hadn't dropped by at the exact moment Dad and Tony wanted to find something new and exciting for the show. If only he'd pretended in the beginning to believe in love, I'd have believed him or convinced him or...

I'd probably have ended up heartbroken. That's what.

My father's question last year echoes in my brain. "Why do you want to do Forever? Honestly, the show's on its way down. I want my daughter to star on something on its way up," he'd said.

"Because everyone deserves a forever."

I step out of the shower and towel dry my hair and body.

I'm better than this. Gunner deserves a forever.

WHEN I RETURN TO CAMP, I twirl around twice, searching for Tony's vehicle. Gone. Where did he go at this hour? And why did he leave me?

I'm in dire need of the wine flask.

Gunner's tent moves as someone bumps against the side. I pivot, ready to bolt because there's no way I'm sticking around to listen and watch like some Peeping Tom.

The sound of a zipper causes me to turn around and then back up in horror.

"Hey, where do you think you're going?" Gunner pokes his head through the tent flap.

"I...um...I..."

He unzips it farther. "Want to come in here?"

"Oh. No. I..." I step back and my heel hits something solid. I freeze.

"What's the matter with you?"

"Go back in there with her," I whisper loudly, my eyes wide. "Quit talking to me!"

"Back with who?"

"Addison!" I whisper-yell slightly louder than I'd intended. I don't want her to stick her head out. I imagine she'll look all satisfied.

Maybe she won't be wearing all her clothes.

I'll want to kick her ass or his. Probably both.

"She's gone," he whisper-yells back. "Your director took her back. Come here and I'll tell you what happened when you left for a campground tour. I'd rather tell you in private."

I do as he says and he holds the flap aside so I can step inside his tent.

He isn't wearing a shirt. Holy Jesus. Abs, triceps, and biceps do a break dance in unison. He's flipping gorgeous, even in the dark.

He switches on a small flashlight. I sit at one corner of the igloo-shaped interior. "What did you do to her?"

"The woman attacked me."

I hold back a grin and an urge to do a victory dance. "And you couldn't defend yourself?"

"She intended to have sex and wasn't taking no for an answer. When I told her that I wasn't in to her, she demanded to go back home. Immediately."

He lays back on his sleeping bag. I see that I'm sitting on a second bag. He'd obviously planned on having a second person in the tent.

Then I remember it was supposed to be me. Warmth floods my belly, and I let my grin break through. I sit on the sleeping bag, then turn to face him.

"You don't have sex on the second date?"

"You suck at math. Second date?"

I put my face into the pillow and then peer up at him. "Well yeah. The speed date was the first one."

"Doesn't count."

"OK. You don't do sex on the first date," I say, trying to get my breathing back under control. Doesn't he remember we had sex with no dates involved? Men!

He shrugs and gets inside his own sleeping bag. "If I do, at least I've bought her dinner first."

"Hot dogs."

"She didn't eat. I watched her."

I snort. "I think she wanted to look good for you. Guys have no idea how hard it is to be a woman. A hot dog can make the difference between feeling like the Pillsbury doughboy and feeling skinny."

"I told you how what I think about skinny. A woman needs to be herself. No man wants a fake."

"Some do. Some want the fantasy. You know...Lara Croft." I smile at him so I won't sound so serious.

He flips the flashlight off and my eyes adjust to the dark. Stars twinkle through the mesh rectangle at the top of the tent.

Gunner puts a hand out and touches my hair. "Why is your hair damp? You're going to freeze," he says.

"Took a shower." Thunder sounds in the distance and I'm glad I made it back before any rain.

"Hm." He scoots closer. "You smell nice. Get inside the sleeping bag or you'll freeze. Keep your head tucked under the blanket."

He reaches over and lifts the edge of the sleeping bag. Wind whistles around the tent.

"Go on. I don't bite," he says.

I get inside the bag and snuggle in. "Thanks."

"You like that guy?"

"Who?"

"Director Tony."

I roll my eyes. "I told you. It's not like that."

"But you were going to sleep in his tent?"

"My relationship with Tony is purely platonic. You were going to have me sleep in your tent and we're only friends."

"Hm." He puts one arm behind his head. "About the other night when you came by. I shouldn't have let you leave like you did."

"No. I needed to leave." The faint tremor in my voice gives away my vulnerability.

"I have a hard time with the opposite sex."

"Please. You should stop right there."

"OK. If you say so."

He puts a hand on my my head and slides fingers into my hair, then pulls it back. "Still wet. You shouldn't have washed it. It'll take forever to dry."

When he reached across to my head, I stopped breathing. Now I realize he was only being practical. I stare at his profile, a strong jaw and wide mouth set in a hard line. "Do you really have trouble with women, or was that a line? Because I'm having a hard time imaging you having trouble with anything."

We're both silent for a while as the wind blows and leaves tumble. I've almost given up that he'll answer when he clears his throat.

"It's the truth," he says.

A powerful gust of wind shakes the sides of the tent. I peer through the darkness, now deeper since clouds cover the previously starry sky. "Can I ask you something?"

"Why do I suspect I won't like it?"

"You don't have to answer."

"I'll tell you anything." There's a raw, honest timbre in his voice.

"Tell me what happened when you moved that year."

"Not much to tell."

"What happened to your mom? How did she die?"

"Cancer. She got breast cancer." His low words hold a sadness that vibrates through the air.

"You loved her a lot." It's so easy to hear in

213

his voice. I reach across and capture his hand in mine, squeezing his big palm gently. He's breaking my heart simply thinking of how hard he had it.

"Yeah. I did. Sometimes you remind me of her."

I draw in air quickly, not expecting that at all. "How's that?"

"She was sassy and bold. She knew what she wanted. She was a strong woman...until the end."

"She'd be proud of the man you are."

"Hm..." he says. "She would sometimes. Right now she'd whip my ass."

"Why is that?"

"She'd want me to be more honorable than I am."

I can hear the smile at the edges of his statement. "Honorable how?"

"I'm trying to think of a way to tell you I pissed Addison off on purpose so she'd leave."

I pull my hand out of his and smack him on the arm while I laugh. "You're kidding. Right? Tell me you didn't do that. I can't believe you admitted it."

"On the other hand, maybe Mom's looking down on me and is proud of my ingenuity."

He grabs my hand again and pulls me to him in slow motion. I'm half in and half out of my bag, unable to resist the tug he has on me physically and emotionally.

His breath tickles the edge of mouth. "Maybe she'd want me to do whatever makes me happy."

Taste

Current Day

Gunner

"DON'T, GUNNER," Kiley breathes with our mouths almost touching. She allows her head to fall back and closes her eyes. "We cannot do this."

"Sure we can." I trail two fingers down the front of her beautiful neck and stop at her collarbone.

Her eyelids fly open and flash murder at me. "You are dating women."

"Not by choice."

She ignores my protest. "I am not one of these women."

"Again, not my choice."

She snorts and wrestles her way back into her sleeping bag. "You signed a contract. You made the decision to do the show." She points her finger at me. "You could've called me after I broke it off with Mason."

Something surprising blooms in my chest. Hope? A drop of cold water slides down my neck. I ignore it.

Then another drop. Rain pelts down on the back of my head. "Don't move," I say. I'd watched the weather yesterday and didn't see this coming. I'm a dumbass who didn't check it again early this morning.

I stand so I can make sure the sky flap is completely closed. Kiley burrows into her sleeping bag to avoid the now steady stream of water dripping on her side. The tent shakes from the onslaught outside. Thunder claps in a sudden sharp sound that makes me jump.

In minutes, I'm back inside my sleeping bag and scooting closer to Kiley.

"Don't come this way. I think there's a leak," she whispers.

"Are you wet?" No response. I unzip my sleeping bag. "Get into mine. I'm dry." I'm talking to myself because she doesn't even make a sound in response. I've never in my life known Kiley to be bashful or speechless.

She crawls out of her bag and stands.

"I don't think so. I...um...I" She crouches, glancing from her abandoned sleeping bag to me and back.

"Is there a problem?" I ask when she stands and stares down at me with her hands on her hips.

"I don't want you to expect anything," she says softly as she peels off her socks and throws them to the side. Kiley stares at her bare feet.

Hesitating so much it makes me grin in the dark.

"Maybe you're the one expecting sex." I roll to my side and hold up the edge of my bag so she can get in.

"Maybe. But I'm not having sex with you, Gunner Parrish. If that's on your mind, you can think again. So stop thinking about it...if you are."

She sits next to me and slides her bare feet into my bag, sticking them on my leg. I jump at the cold feel of them. Her teeth click together in a barely audible chatter.

"Hurry before we both freeze," I say. The temperature outside is dropping.

She grabs her side of the bag and pulls the zipper up until we're zipped in tight.

"Roll to your side or I won't be able to breathe." I can't keep the amusement out of my voice.

"Sorry I ate those last two hot dogs." Her

sweet giggle tells me she isn't sorry in the least. She's having a good time—in the cold and the rain. With me.

"You made me a happy man when I saw that. Even happier when I noticed the mustard on the corner of your mouth."

She sighs, turns and snuggles her ass against me, and I suck in a breath. What the hell does she think I'll be thinking about with her body tucked up in this position?

I scoot back an inch so I'm not poking her in the back with my dick.

"This is nice," she whispers.

"Mm." I bury my nose into her hair and breathe her in.

"I should get into the other tent when it stops raining." Her voice turns serious. "This looks bad. You know—me and you alone in here."

"Who's going to know?" I make an effort to keep the lewdness and the subtle hinting out of my tone, but it's tough.

She turns her head slightly, putting it even closer to my mouth. "Roy will," she says. "And Tony will when he gets back to load up his tent and stuff."

"Roy hopped in and left with Tony and Addison. Didn't you notice he's missing?"

"Why would he do that?" She pauses. "Oh. I guess there's nothing to film. Wow. They were really concerned about me!"

I grin into her hair. Actually, Tony had argued that he was going to stick around and let Roy drive Addison back to the city. But then Roy said he has some night vision thing.

But there's no way I'm telling her all this. Because I can feel her heart beating and her body relaxing. It doesn't matter that the rain is falling harder or that the temperature has dropped.

An odd contentment I haven't felt in years settles over me. I tuck her body into the curve of mine, spooning within the small space.

"When I was a kid, I'd camp in my backyard," I say into her hair. "My mom and dad had this firepit in the back. They'd let me and my friends pretend we were in the wilderness when we were really only a hundred yards from the back door."

"That sounds fun."

"Yeah. Sort of like this—camping in a campground. This isn't real camping. There's no electricity or bathrooms where I'd planned to take us."

"Oh." She yawns. "Whatever you say. This feels pretty primitive to me. There were no hairdryers in the bathroom."

I chuckle and kiss the top of her head. "Sweet dreams."

"You, too. Good night, Gun." She exhales in

a slow, satisfied whoosh.

Gun. It's a nickname used only by the people closest to me. "If you need to go to the bathroom, wake me up. Don't go alone."

"Sure," she mutters, her limbs relaxing even more. My hand rests on her arm due to the close quarters and she pulls it around her as if I'm her human blanket. I don't have the heart to complain that she's torturing me.

I fall asleep to the sound of rain and another sound—her light snoring. It's a damned relief that she's not perfect.

Or maybe she is.

I DRIFT DEEPER AND DEEPER into unconsciousness. I'm inside the local hamburger joint back in Arkansas. No, that's not right. This place is too nice to be Bambi's Burgers, because a waitress walks up to us with pen and pad in hand. She wears a funky dress and has a giant nametag pinned above her right breast with the name Vanessa. I look closer to see it's Vanessa Hudgens from that movie High School Musical—the one my stepsister Veronica watched a million times the year our parents got married. She knows the words to every song.

Waitress Vanessa Hudgens gives us a huge

smile."What'll it be?" she asks and then blows a humongous pink bubble with her gum.

The popping sound startles me in surround sound and I jump. Veronica laughs from the seat across the table.

Veronica kicks me lightly underneath the table. "Are you going to order or are we going to starve?"

"OK. We'll have a couple of cheeseburgers, an order of fries, and another of onion rings. I'll have a Coke. Nicky-girl? You having a chocolate shake?"

"Strawberry," she answers.

"You're going to turn into one big strawberry," I tease.

She throws a sugar packet at me. "It's your fault. You got me hooked on strawberry slushies at the store," she says.

"You're killing my profit with your slushie addiction."

Her face grows concerned. "For real?" she asks in a low voice. "Sorry Gun. You can take it out of my pay."

I push the toe of my boot against her sneaker. "Stop. I was joking. What's mine is yours."

"You're too good to me." She looks away from me and up at the waitress placing our drinks on the table.

I level a scolding eye at her. "We have to

watch out for each other. You're the only one in this world I care about. Don't ever leave me, OK?"

Vanessa of High School Musical brings the burgers on a red tray. She sings, "Don't ever leave. Don't ever leave. Don't ever leave."

We both ignore her as if it's normal to have a singing waitress.

I unwrap my burger from the foil paper and take a bite without looking across from me.

I shouldn't have said it out loud. In this diner, I'm nineteen and she's sixteen. I know this because it's the year she first worked for me at Gimme Gas. We've survived, holding onto each other for stability and normalcy for three years now.

Grandpa saved us. But a heart attack stole him from us.

I don't want to imagine life without Veronica. I don't want her to leave me like Mom did. Like Grandpa did.

Suddenly, I look around and we're not in the diner. We're in the kitchen at home. I'm hot so I shrug out of my jacket. I'm still wearing that stupid letter football jacket, and I'm too old for that.

It's Veronica's seventeenth birthday because I brought her a cake from the grocery store.

"I want to spend time with my friends

tonight," she says. "It's a birthday party for me."

Why does she want to leave me? I think of ways to make her stay, but it's no use. She doesn't see how she comforts me, makes me want to be the best man I can be.

"If that's what you want, Nicky-girl. I thought you might want to spend your birthday with me." I've said too much. I don't need her to stick around out of guilt. I don't want her to feel sorry for me.

From the time we were thrown together as teenagers in a household on the verge of exploding, I've been the strong one, lending her my courage when she had none. Now that she's ready to fly away, I can't bear the thought of being alone.

She gets up from the sofa and comes to stand before me with a small smile. The I'm-trying-to-be-patient one. "Let's do something tomorrow, Gun. OK? I promise."

"Sure. It's fine," I lie.

She turns her back and the kitchen disappears.

I'm sixteen and at the hospital. Mom's hooked to an IV bag. Her colorless face rivals the white of the hospital sheet. I look away from her face and look anywhere but her eyes. I touch the tips of her fingers with one hand. A large purple bruise surrounds the tape over the needle stuck in the vein.

Fuck, fuck, fuck!

"I feel good today," Mom says.

I nod instead of calling her a liar. You can't call out a woman on her deathbed. A woman acting fucking cheerful because she doesn't want to make other people feel sad.

There's a lump in my throat so big I fight to swallow. Finally, I'm able to control my voice. I finger my cell phone in my pocket. "Want me to make Dad come? I'll call him. He can get his ass down here."

"No, baby." She hasn't called me that since I was little. It's enough to make me bawl like I really am one.

"Aren't you gonna tell me to quit cussing?" I grip the sides of the hospital bed rail and my knuckles turn white.

"No," she says. "You're practically a man. Old enough to take care of yourself and old enough to decide the person you want to be."

"Not really," I mumble. "I'm not."

"You are. You'll be a fine man. You're going to be OK."

I let go of the bed rail and back away. Turn two circles, afraid to look at her. Afraid to see that she's been disappearing for a while and soon it will be forever.

"I FUCKING won't! I need you." My eyes fill with tears. I turn and leave the room.

Weakness

Current Day

Kiley

DAWN LIGHT FILTERS THROUGH THE TENT walls, creating a leafy pattern of shadows from nearby trees. A frigid wind buffets the nylon fabric, and I shiver. I roll into the warmth of Gunner's body.

Even though he's worked his upper body out of the sleeping bag, his skin radiates heat. Morning stubble in a color a shade darker than his hair stands out along his jawline. A tiny scar sits perched at the top of one eyebrow. I examine the way his eyelashes curl at the ends. I've never noticed it before. But now I have the luxury of seeing every detail of his face up close and unhurried. He's all man, but those lashes should belong to me.

His breathing quickens and his eyes move beneath his eyelids.

"Need you," he chants several times, as if he's trying to convince the person in his dream. His pained tone sends daggers straight to my heart.

I squeeze Gunner's bicep and gently shake him. "Hey."

He shrugs it off. "What? What is it?"

His gaze darts from the ceiling of the tent to the far corners, but never looking straight at me. His breathing comes in little shallow gulps.

"It's me. Kiley." I need to make the shadows leave his eyes.

He meets my gaze as I lean close to his chest. After several seconds, he licks his lips and gives me a tremulous smile. "Sorry. Did I wake you up?"

"Yeah. You were talking in your sleep."

"Bad dream." He stares up at the top of the tent.

I resist the urge to hug him. He's not a child in need of soothing. "Want to talk about it?"

"No," he says too quickly.

I place my hand on his chest in a comforting way. "It must've been a doozie."

"Yeah. Well," he rakes his free hand over his hair. "I'm not used to sleeping with someone. That must be it. Sleeping with you."

"Are you saying I give you nightmares?" I tease him.

He doesn't laugh as I expect him to. "It's not a big deal." He exhales and looks away. "Drop it."

His words grate, gruff and final.

I want to make him feel better. What makes a guy like Gunner afraid? I don't want to act as though he's hurt my feelings, but he has.

"Sure," I say, my voice tight and my smile tighter.

"Wait." He closes his eyes. "I'm sorry I snapped at you."

I shrug. "It's all right."

"No, it's not." His lids flutter open and his gaze softens. "You don't deserve a shitty attitude."

"I forgive you."

He slings his free arm across and surprises me with a quick hug. His arms feel warm and his body hard. His hand trails over my back and drops casually lower. "Good," he says.

"I was in your face, I understand. But honestly, there's not much choice in this sleeping bag. You're very close." I lick my bottom lip. "And...um...your hand is on my ass, Gunner."

He keeps a straight face. "Yeah. I know."

"Is there a reason why you're not moving it?"

"Yep."

I wiggle away, which is only a couple of inches. He sighs. "I needed comfort and your ass was providing it."

"Gunner!" I widen my eyes, but I'm grinning at his change in mood, his playfulness, and if I'm being honest—the feel of his body and roving hand.

Bad, bad Matchmaker. He is so off-limits he should have yellow caution tape strapped across him.

"Can a man not flirt with a pretty girl when she spent the night with him? I did that cuddling thing and we didn't even have sex."

"Cuddling is not necessarily paired with sex. It's not wine and cheese. And I didn't realize I would be this cold. That's my excuse." I lose the inch of space between us on that note and allow my arms to curl up flush with the side of his chest.

"OK. I was cold, too. Still am." We're practically nose-to-nose.

I cover my mouth and smile beneath my hand. "I'm going to go brush my teeth."

"Don't even think about moving. I like you exactly where you are." His eyes crinkle at the corners. His chest expands as he draws in air. He looks away and then back. "You know this show is stupid."

"It isn't."

"Is. If we weren't on this show, I'd make you

229

want to stay with me all day in this tent. Brushing your teeth would be the last thing on your mind. And then we'd cuddle."

"Dream on. And keep in mind that I am your Matchmaker and we are on this show. Sex would be highly inappropriate." One corner of my mouth quirks.

"Do you remember that majorette skirt you wore on game days our sophomore year?" he whispers as if he's said something really dirty.

"Yeah. I froze my butt off during the winter. Why?" I'm grinning now. I'm so wrong for encouraging him.

"Do you still have it? Please tell me you do."

I can't help but laugh. "I was about a hundred pounds then. So, no. I don't. I couldn't fit one leg into it. Remember, I'm the one who had three hot dogs for dinner."

His lips purse. "Maybe we could find you one in a bigger size."

I poke him in the gut, underneath the covers. His firm abs don't budge. But it's not the hard planes of his body that get to me. It's the liquid heat in his eyes while he stares at my face as if I'm something he worships.

Desire shoots in tiny sparks through my body.

He blinks and gets an odd look on his face. There's no question he's made a mental shift. The playful Gunner is gone. I study him, trying to figure what's changed.

"You know I could get rid of all of my dates, like I did with Addison," he says in a low, husky tone.

I frown at him for more than one reason. I hate that he's said something so appealing. Where are my morals? My integrity? "Gunner. You signed a contract with a clause that you go on the dates without interruption to filming. They'll probably keep this weekend's film. I don't know. But you're going to be in jeopardy of breach of contract."

He winks. "I bet they keep the footage. The audience will love this sort of thing. It's damned funny. But I'm not trying to make you look bad."

I scoot back a couple of inches.

"I have a great idea," he says, his voice all melted caramel and dripping with temptation.

"I don't like the way this conversation is going."

"I can pretend to go on the dates so you'll look good, and no one would know if we…"

He doesn't have to fill in the blanks. My mouth drops. "Are you propositioning me and asking me to lie to the American audience?"

"I'm tempting you."

"You're being a jerk."

"I'm a jerk because I'm telling you what I want? You're a liar if you deny you feel this thing between us. You've felt it since we were in

231

school."

I toss the sleeping bag from me and scramble to my feet. "So, you think we should have a fling. Just like that."

"I wouldn't call it a fling."

With my hands on my hips, I glare down at him. "I don't sleep around. Do you think I'm a whore?"

His mouth drops open. I can't tell what he's thinking, but he should be saying, 'No.'

My eyes widen and my heart accelerates. A giant burning coal of pissed-off sits in my chest. "And as for what happened in the kitchen. You and I weren't on this show yet. I was hurt and you were nice and I..."

"You're accusing me of saying things I didn't. You caught me off guard. I'd never think of you that way. You're getting defensive. And it's not like I met you yesterday. We have history..." He sits up in the sleeping bag with a bewildered look on his face.

"Listen up. I don't know if you think I was going to be some easy lay for you, but think again." My throat tightens and tears gather in my eyes, so I look away and blink.

He rubs a hand over the top of his head. "Sorry. I thought you felt the same way about me. About this," he says and motions between us.

I have been tempted every moment I spend

alone with him. I almost hate him for the way he makes me feel—helpless to fight the pull.

He reaches out to put a hand on my bare foot, as if he's trying to bridge the emotional distance with this one touch. "You know I'm not planning on falling down on one knee at the end of the show for some girl I barely know. I'm going to win the prize. And I'm more into you than I'll be into any of the ones you fix me up with. I tried to tell you. I'm not the dating, engaging, or marrying kind."

His words douse me in cold reality. Show or no show, we are incompatible. "Wow. I thought you were one of the good guys. Do you honestly think I'd want to sleep with you after that speech? You've confirmed you only want to sleep with me. Nothing more."

He stares at me without answering. Finally, he exhales loudly. "I could lie to you, make a lot of promises I can't keep, but I won't."

I search around for my shoes, bending over to flip up a soggy sleeping bag on the opposite side of the tent. "Don't say another word to me. You're making it worse. I hope I find someone to melt that icy heart of yours."

"Kiley. I'm being honest with you because I respect you."

I hold up my hand in the universal sign for stop. My hiking boots are soggy and tight as I slip my feet into them. Sunshine streams into

233

the tent as I unzip and open the flap with shaky fingers.

He scrambles to his feet and takes a step forward. "You need to admit we've always had this chemistry. I've always liked you a lot. Admit you want me as much as I want you."

Like? I can hardly believe I ever harbored feelings for this guy. "I'm calling Tony to see where he is and I'm out of here. I'll be arranging your next date for tomorrow night, so be ready. And Gunner? You are a dick."

I toss my hair out of my face and stomp through the opening of the tent, leaving a trail of watery footsteps behind me.

Feelings

Current Day

Gunner

"YOU'RE A DICK." Dane slides a cardboard coaster toward me. Dastardly Bastards isn't officially open yet, but Dane puts in an order with his cook. Being friends with the owner has its perks. The smell of cooking onions should make my mouth water, but I feel sick.

I'm worse than some teenager with his first bad crush and unable to sleep because I can't quit thinking about a girl.

"Yeah. So I'm a dick." I put my elbows on the bar and lean forward. "I messed up. She makes me crazy."

He nods as if he knows exactly what I mean.

Of my friends, Dane is the one with a string of girlfriends. He knows something about the ladies, or I'd never confess my fuck-up to him.

"Maybe you should back off from her right now," he says. "Get through filming the show and then go after her. What's the hurry? Want me to ask Josie what she thinks you should do?"

I glare at him. "Why the hell would I ask Josie?"

He places a glass of soda in front of me. "Women know these things. We don't think like they do. Plus she's Kiley's cousin."

"Huh. I didn't know that."

Maybe he's right, but I'm not letting him broadcast my dick moves to the world. "This conversation is between you and me and the walls." I pause when the cook brings a king-sized plate of breakfast to me. "Thanks, man," I say to the cook.

The guy nods, passes me a bottle of hot sauce, and disappears to the back again.

I take a large bite of egg. I'm not even hungry, but I didn't eat yesterday after Tony returned to pick Kiley up. She'd spent the morning sitting inside his tent and avoiding me. I swallow, then make a production of cutting my food into tiny bites.

Dane stops polishing a handle on a beer tap. "Listen. You have to do the TV show. You can't

236

get out of it. You're supposed to really try to get to know these women. Why not make that work for you? Make her jealous. From my experience, the minute you're with another woman, you're a chick magnet. If she feels like you do like one of them, it will drive her nuts. She'll reconsider turning you down. Trust me."

"Hm," I grunt, not liking this idea at all. When we were kids, Dane led me into more disasters than I can count, purely on his confidence. "That's a terrible idea."

"You asked what I'd do. That's all I got."

"This kind of thing works for you?"

He grins and shakes his head as if I'm naive. "Every time."

"You're a bigger dick than I am."

He gives me a cocky grin. "I've never said I wasn't. I need to get myself a T-shirt that says, 'Big Dick.' Maybe I'll buy two and give you the other one."

I roll my eyes and stuff another bite of sausage and egg into my mouth. I should've known better than to talk to him about my problems.

"When do you film your next date on the show?" Dane's phone vibrates, bumping along the top of the wood bar, and he checks the screen. "Josie's here."

"She hang out with you a lot?" I glance around at the empty bar. I guess I'd thought I would be the only one barging in on Dane this early.

"She's bringing me something."

"A Big Dick shirt?"

He points at me. "Funny and a very good guess, but no. She's bringing me a book."

"Why?" It's good to have something else to concentrate on besides my own misery.

"She wants me to read it. I'm going with her to a book signing in Bowling Green next Friday night."

I take my time with the next question since Dane seems to be squirming behind the counter. "Why? That kind of thing sounds more like Leo than you. Also, does he know you're banging his sister?"

"I'm doing no such thing."

"Really?" I eye him to see if my bullshit meter goes off.

"We're friends. She doesn't think of me like that."

But it's written on his face that he's not happy about the status with Josie. This is baffling to me since he's never hesitated to go after a girl he wants.

"And you're the one giving me advice," I say. "Man. We're a sorry pair."

The kitchen door opens and Josie— obviously so comfortable she enters through a rear entrance—strolls toward us.

"Oh, hi, Gunner. How's it going?" she says.

I give her a chin nod. "Good. You?"

"Couldn't be better," she answers.

She's a happy little thing. I study her, looking to find a resemblance to Kiley now that I know they're cousins. Both have dark hair, beautiful eyes, and olive skin. Other than those things, they don't really look alike.

Josie's the girl next door, the brainy but sweet girl who doesn't call you out for being a dumbass. Kiley? Kiley's the type guys turn to watch as she walks down a street. She's more along the lines of supermodel next door.

Throwing a new paperback book on the bar, she drops into the stool beside me. "How's the dating show?"

"It's good."

I look down at my plate and cram a large bite into my mouth. I really don't want to talk about the show that has become the worst thing to happen to me since I've moved back to Nashville. Being around Kiley is going to be torture now that she's made it clear she won't have anything to do with me.

Dane places a water glass in front of Josie and picks up the book. "Gunner has it bad for Kiley."

My head pops up and I glare at him. The loud sound of my own heart beating is about the only thing I can hear in the bar. I didn't

239

think it was necessary to tell him to keep his mouth shut about what had happened, but I was obviously wrong.

Josie clears her throat. "Then you and I need to talk, but you have to promise not to tell her anything I say to you."

I shake my head. I don't want to know her secrets and I sure as hell don't like it that she knows mine. "I'm not the one with a big mouth."

Dane gives me an out-of-character serious look. "You weren't around when Kiley had a hard time."

"What do you mean by that?" I frown at him and glance over at Josie for an explanation.

He shrugs. "You'd moved by then and stuff happened in high school. Stupid stuff."

Josie takes a sip of water while she stares at him. "Kiley's been one of my best friends for a long time, but I don't get to see her much anymore. What Dane knows and what I know are two wildly different things. He knows the rumors. I know the facts. And I don't know much, only what I can piece together."

"Is someone going to tell me this big secret or are you both going to hint around all day?" I squirm on the barstool.

"Has Kiley mentioned her mother to you?" Josie's mouth dips at the corners.

"No."

"Uncle Ed and Kiley's mom got divorced

when Kiley was pretty young. They had joint custody and pretty much hated each other. Kiley did this back and forth thing where she'd split her time between houses. Something happened to Kiley when we were juniors. I'm not going to tell you the rumors. They're too ugly. But Kiley's mom threw Kiley out and never spoke to her again."

"Hm. So they had a disagreement." My chest tightens at the thought of Kiley upset. It's tough to have family turn their back on you. I should know.

"No, it was more. Kiley's mom was on husband number four. She kicked him out after Kiley's fight with her. So you can imagine what the rumors were. Kiley changed after that. She'd been bold and confident before. But high school can be a rough place for the gossip mongers. They had a field day because she'd been everyone's princess. You know?"

I stare down at my plate of cold food, definitely not hungry after hearing Josie's story that I almost wish I didn't know.

Josie touches my arm so I'll look up at her. "Kiley has Ed—a man who's never made it a secret that his career takes priority over his daughter. She has me and Leo and really no friends to speak of. And now she has an ex-fiancé. I wanted you to know that she's more fragile than she seems."

An impatient customer jiggles the locked outer door and Dane jogs to open it. Light streams inside and a group of girls stomp into the entry, laughing and ready to start their party. The one in the middle wears a white hat with the word 'Bride' in large glittery letters across the front.

Josie sips her water and shoots eye daggers at the group of young females flirting with Dane as he seats them around a large table.

He might not be banging her, but something is definitely going on.

"Thanks, Josie," I say.

"I did it for her, not you. I don't know what you're going to do about the show, but I don't want you to hurt her."

Even though Dane tries to comp my meals any time I'm here, I throw a twenty on the counter. "I'll do my best not to."

KILEY CALLS ME at sun up saying that we'll be doing a morning date instead of an evening one. She's matching me with a new woman today. No second chance for Addison.

After a night of tossing in my bed, I'll be lucky if I notice I'm on a date. I'm like the living dead today. I rub a hand over my scruffy face and decide to leave it like it is. It fits my mood.

I arrive at the indoor shooting range. Of all the places I'd imagined to do these dates, this certainly didn't make the list. Kiley is missing, but I assume she's running late or simply out of sight.

The empty stalls give off a funhouse vibe. When I approach, I'm a little surprised. My date wears loose-fitting jeans, cowboy boots, and a pale yellow button-down. She's attractive, but not in a showy way. She stands in the middle stall with earmuffs hanging loosely on the back of her neck.

"Hi, I'm Melanie. It's nice to meet you again," she says.

"Gunner." I take her extended hand and shake it. I barely remember her.

"Yeah. I know. I look forward to a good time out here. I hope to stick around longer than the last ones. I would've had a blast on the camping trip. I wouldn't have thrown myself at you."

I raise an eyebrow. Do the ladies share their date information? I'm confused.

She motions to the platform where we'll stand. "I guess you don't read social media."

In this moment, I stumble, mentally and physically. I shift to look at Tony who gives me a meaningful look. The we'll-talk-later look.

"You don't know what I'm talking about," she mumbles in a low voice.

"Hell no."

Melanie furrows her brow and shifts her attention to the range. She puts on her goggles and motions to mine that lay on a side table. "You shoot a 9mm before?"

"No. I have experience with rifles, but that's it."

"Perfect." She radiates confidence. "This will be fun."

My date with Melanie begins with a bang. The camera crew lurks two feet behind us. I've practically stepped on one of the camera guys as he walks on my heels. He certainly isn't worried about a stray bullet.

This isn't Melanie's first rodeo with a gun. She's practically a sharp shooter and teases me with comments about my aim and stance. Although some guys might be threatened by her efforts to give shooting tips, I'm not.

She hasn't asked me about my family or favorite food or the last movie I watched. Melanie is the perfect date for a guy who likes competition and women who don't talk unless there's something important to be said.

Kiley finally shows up after an eternity of me sneaking looks over my shoulder. Even though I can't make out her words, the music of her voice plucks tighter than a fiddle string.

High. Tense. Abrupt.

At least it's directed at Tony and not me.

More worrisome is that she's not looking my way. If I didn't know better, I'd think she's avoiding me. A person might think she doesn't care one whit that I'm on a date with another woman.

Maybe I should reconsider Dane's advice about making her jealous.

When the hour of shooting ends, we take off our gear. Melanie gives me a friendly smile. "I'd love to take you to dinner tonight."

I focus on her. It's really not her fault that I'm so distracted. "OK."

"I know a little pizza place. Can I come pick you up?"

"I can come get you."

"Oh," she looks wide-eyed in Tony's direction, then returns her gaze to me. "I'm supposed to pick you up. Those are the rules. I'll be at your place at seven."

So much for being a gentleman and for spontaneity. "Sounds like a plan."

Melanie leans forward to give me a loose hug. "Here's my phone number," she whispers and tucks something into my hand. Then she pretends she hasn't said a thing as she waves at me and leaves the building.

I have no idea why her request makes me nervous.

Tony strides across the room and claps me on the back. "That went well."

The camera crew back off and Kiley hangs close to the makeup artist who powdered my nose earlier. She's wearing a loose black dress that covers her from neck to ankle as if she's ready for a funeral.

Tony waits for my reply and I fold my arms across my chest. "I thought the show was being recorded for later. What did Melanie mean by social media?"

"Due to the stunt you pulled this weekend, we're in jeopardy of fans losing interest. Someone leaked some clips from the camping weekend."

"What do you mean someone did? Who?"

"Exactly what I said. I don't know who or how. Roy swears that the cameras haven't been out of his sight. There were other people at the campground. People with cell phones now are as bad as the paparazzi."

"Can I see the social media you're talking about?"

Tony's eyebrows knit. "Go look it up on Facebook or Twitter. Tumblr. It's everywhere."

"Will do," I say, even though I really don't. I do understand what he means, only I don't use any of those tools. I'm connected with the people I want to stay in touch with in real life, not some pretend world online.

Kiley pulls her thin silver bracelets up her arm and lets them fall. She does this a couple of times as she talks to the makeup girl. We make eye contact and the air vibrates with energy. Wild, electrical, burn-your-house-down energy.

I frown at her.

She turns on her heel and disappears outside. I stroll quickly after her until I reach the parking lot, only to see her pulling out in her SUV.

My phone buzzes in my pocket. I answer, half-relieved that it's Dane. Otherwise, I'd be tempted to jump in my Jeep and haul ass after her. It's best to let her go for now if she's needing some space.

"Hello." I peer around to see if I'm alone or if some camera guy is two feet behind me as the case has been all morning.

"Man, you sure know how to make the news."

"What?" I don't ask it because I feel the bad thing coming. This is tied to the conversation with Tony and the reason I never trusted that guy in the first place.

"You look at the news today?"

"No." My stomach churns. What could it be? That the show has realized they don't want me to be their guy? Yeah. Of course that's all it is.

"Infrared footage," he says. "Kiley going into your tent on that camping date and a timestamp. Kiley leaving the tent and another timestamp. And there's an audio clip playing on one site."

I'm silent. I cannot wrap my brain around it. Who took pictures? And more, who is the son of a bitch posting them?

Tony. That SOB has to be guilty.

I've let the phone fall away from my ear without realizing it until I hear Dane whistle into the phone.

I pull the phone back to my ear. Then I remember the second part of what he said. "I'm here. What's on the audio?"

"Holy shit man. I really don't want to repeat it. I think you need to hear it for yourself. I'll send you a video link in a text message."

"Thanks," I say, my voice strangled as I think about Kiley's behavior this morning.

"Settle down. Do I need to come help you beat somebody?"

"No. But do me a favor. Can you ask Josie to call Kiley and check on her?"

"Yeah. Of course."

"And one more thing. I need you to show me this social media stuff. I need to get up to speed before tonight. Also, I might need a lawyer."

The Internet is on fire today with sneak peeks of filming for Forever. Sources say that Gunner Parrish, this season's bachelor, has been fighting off inappropriate advances by the show's Matchmaker, Kiley Vanderbilt. While many skeptics had their doubts about Ms. Vanderbilt's ability to match Gunner Parrish to the perfect mate, they didn't predict she'd stoop to bribery in the form of hanky panky. Shame on you, Ms. Vanderbilt. Even the producer's daughter must play by the rules.

We captured some tweets of the outraged public:

"@RealityGirl823:   Beauty   queen @KileyLoveWins keeps relying on her looks to win. #Skank #ForeverLoses #loveormoney"

"@PiousPixie0: Poor guy. Can we get a Matchmaker   with   morals?   #Forever #sexisnteverything #Gunnershouldcallme"

"@StudHasGame: Will you marry me, Gunner? All of the honesty, none of the games. #Forever #kileyisahoe"

Entertainment Deets, America's Real Source:

Interview Excerpt with Mason DuMonde.

Entertainment Deets: You were recently engaged to Kiley Vanderbilt and that's no longer the case. Did Gunner Parrish have anything to do with your break-up?

Mason DuMonde: Absolutely not. Kiley was the love of my life and we'd honestly been talking about calling off the wedding long before we parted as friends. Kiley's goals are more career-oriented. Mine are family. It was simply a clash of what we want in life. She wasn't ready to settle down and I am.

Entertainment Deets: As an entertainment attorney, should the studio investigate whether or not there are grounds for sexual harassment by Gunner Parrish?

Mason DuMonde: This would be a contractual issue, if any issue merits an address. I'm not assuming there is. Mr. Parrish or Kiley are not subordinates of each other and both are under contract on the show; therefore, it can hardly be sexual harassment.

Entertainment Deets: So, do you believe she's sowing her wild oats now that she's no longer engaged?

(Mason DuMonde refused further comment and our interview ended.)

Heartache

Current Day

Kiley

A GIRL CAN ONLY TAKE SO MUCH DRAMA before she needs therapy.

I sit alone in the movie theater with a large bucket of buttered popcorn, extra salt. I've purposely chosen an empty theater in case I should succumb to blubbering into my movie snack.

At least the bucket can catch my tears.

Once, when I competed in Miss Junior America, I overheard some girls whispering about me backstage. They said I slept with all of the judges to get where I am. The judges consisted of two former pageant queens and one male who was a day short of ninety.

My cell buzzes for the forty-billionth time. I dig into my bag. It's Josie again.

If I don't answer, she'll continue to distract me from the marvel of Chris Hemsworth on the big screen and then the crying will ensue.

"Hey," I say in my cheeriest voice. "Sorry I couldn't answer, but I'm swamped today. What's up?"

"Where are you?"

"Well, I..."

"I would appreciate a straight answer. When you wouldn't pick up, I called the studio and the hospital. Now, where are you?"

I sniffle. "You saw the news."

"Of course I did. Anyone who isn't dead has seen it. Or they will."

"Gee, thanks. It's not what it looks like."

"Honey, I know. If you don't tell me where you are, I'm going to think you're standing on the Cumberland River Bridge about to jump."

I heave a surrendering sigh. "I'm at Grand South Cineplex watching a movie with Chris Hemsworth."

"With Thor? You're at a movie with Thor? And you didn't ask me?" she screeches.

I roll my eyes. "No. He's acting. I'm worshiping him on the screen."

She doesn't say anything for several

seconds and I imagine Josie speeding over in her little convertible.

"You're not coming, are you?" I sit straighter and nearly upturn the popcorn bucket in my lap.

"Do you want me to come?"

"No. I don't. But thanks. I'm fine."

She promises to call me later and I toss my phone back into my purse. Josie—friend, accomplice, nuisance. Sometimes a girl needs time to drown her sorrows in butter.

I lose myself in Chris's earnest gaze, grabbing handfuls of popcorn like there's no tomorrow.

Thump. I jump at the sound. Someone has taken the seat directly behind me. I purposely chose an empty theater and some creep has the nerve to sit where she or he can breathe on my neck for the rest of the movie. I look right and left.

This is awkward. Moving will be obvious. Staying in my seat will be torture.

"I haven't seen this one," he says.

I twist around at the sound of Gunner's voice. "You have got to be kidding me. Josie is a dead woman."

"I forced her to tell me."

"How did you do that?" I mumble the question and turn back around so I don't have to look at him. I shove popcorn into my mouth.

He doesn't answer. Instead, he leans in with his forearms draping my seat back and the one next to me. "I don't care what anyone thinks about the photos."

"I do," I say through a mouthful of popcorn.

"I figured."

"You realize all the bad press is about me. Not you. It's a double standard world."

"Hm." He stands behind me and I tense. In another thirty seconds, he's moved to the seat beside me. I don't look at him and stare straight ahead. My stomach is beginning to churn from the onslaught of butter and salt.

"I'm fine," I say as my eyes fill with tears. "I just needed a movie."

"I need one, too." He reaches into the bottom of my popcorn bucket to help himself.

We sit together while the images flicker across the screen. He doesn't fling his arm around me or anything to suggest we're more than two friends seeing a movie together. I never glance at him, knowing I won't be able to hold it together if he smiles or gives me a pitying look.

When the movie ends, we continue to sit until the dim lights illuminate the theater. It's still only the two of us. I get to my feet, wordless and empty. Well, not totally empty, since I'm stuffed with a pound of popcorn.

"We can't leave together. I don't know if

paparazzi are following either of us."

"We're leaving together."

"Gunner. Are you listening to me? They are calling me Vixen Vanderbilt. One tabloid said I'm teaching you how to please your dates."

"What does Ed say about all this? Is he going to fire Tony? It has to have been him that leaked this stuff."

My face burns with the rush of embarrassment. "Tony was doing his job. He can't treat me differently. It's what he would've done in the case of any Matchmaker on the show. My dad says not to worry about it. All press is good press."

Gunner tilts his head and gives me a flinty look. "He's your father. He can stop it."

I laugh, the sound bitter and crackly as dry leaves. "No one can stop it. He said, 'Toughen up, Buttercup.' And Dad's right when he says gossip comes with the job. We are public figures now and it's going to happen. No one wants to report the sweet, innocent stuff. So they find the dirt or they make up something."

"Then we should do whatever we want if they're going to make it up." He reaches a finger out and tucks my hair behind my ear.

"Easy for you to say."

"I talked to a lawyer about my contract. About quitting the show."

"What? You can't do that."

255

He shrugs and turns, walking down the aisle and leaving me with no choice but to follow if I want to talk to him. "I can," he says. "But I'll forfeit all compensation Rolling Hills Productions owes me so far. Still...money isn't everything."

He strides down the rest of the aisle, his long legs leaving me behind.

"No. That's crazy." I grab the back of his shirt.

Gunner whirls and takes both my hands in his. His gentle grip comforts me, his thumbs stroking the tops of my hands. "Everything about our conversation at the campground went wrong."

My belly does a little flip and I lean forward, so tempted to lay my cheek against his chest and give into the pull of his body. I'm weak. After berating myself all morning that I've brought this on myself, only one touch and I want to fall into his arms.

I say the only thing I can think of to push him away. "We can only have a professional relationship. We can be friends later. But for now, I need you to respect me enough to back away."

He releases my hands. "You need to take some time to recoup from today."

"You've got that right. It's only a matter of time before they start saying I broke off my engagement because of you—"

"That's not true."

"I know that and you know that, but the press will love spinning it. Gunner," I pause and inhale. "I can't handle the bad publicity right now."

He shakes his head and rubs a hand along the back of his neck. "I know you're taking the heat. I can take some of it. I can make a statement on social media."

"That will make it worse."

"I can confess that I have it bad for you and you tried to tell me to back off."

"And you'll come off looking great and I'll still be the whore. Let it die. I have to get ready for the filming tonight. I'm supposed to interview Melanie on her thoughts about you before the date. Then you and I do the same thing afterward."

"But I want to talk about us."

"There is no us. You are my bachelor. I'm the Matchmaker. You have a date later."

He doesn't move and I feel as though the walls are closing in on me. "Please," I say through gritted teeth.

"I came here to say it's not your fault and that we are OK. To offer to quit the show. To tell you that I was an ass for acting like it was all about sex the other day when you know that isn't true."

"Oh really? How am I supposed to know that? I need some space right now. I'm sorry."

I follow him out of the screening room and into the theater lobby. A girl working behind the concession stand points at me. "I knew it was her."

She holds her cell phone, obviously taking video. I panic, my feet stuck in place on the red theater carpet as if in concrete.

Gunner backs up, takes my hand, and guides me to walk on the opposite side from the girl, effectively shielding me from her phone. It's the nicest, yet worst thing he could possibly do.

In the parking lot, I stalk to my vehicle and hit the unlock button on my key fob. "Why-why-why?" I pace five steps past my SUV and then back. "Couldn't you just go on? Her video will be on YouTube before we make it out of this lot."

"I'll go back in and take her phone. She won't be putting it online if her phone is busted."

I shake my head, horrified. "Listen to yourself. I'll be bailing you out of jail next. No. Go home. Please, for my reputation, go home."

AT HOME, I PULL A COUPLE OF PIECES of popcorn from my hair. Oh so attractive. I'm lucky I don't have a ring of butter circling my lips. It shouldn't surprise me after my fiasco of a drive home from the Grand South Cineplex Theater where I wiped my tear-filled eyes with salty fingers.

Mistake.

I have exactly forty-five minutes to prepare myself for the evening's filming. The camera crew will set up in Dad's study and record. Normally, we'd film interviews like this one at the studio downtown, but not tonight.

"Kiley, have you got a minute?" Dad's voice surprises me.

"Sure." I open my bedroom door and step back to let him in.

"I thought we'd chat before the filming." He examines my face. "What the hell happened to you?"

"Nothing." The popcorn would've been a clear sign of something amiss, but I'm hoping I simply look tired.

He points to my eyes and then to my hair. "You look...not like you normally do."

"Well, yes. I've been a little distracted today."

"It's like a train wreck."

"What is?"

"This media coverage. I keep telling myself not to watch, but then I can't look away."

"That's what you wanted." I walk to my

vanity and sit in the chair. Picking up a hairbrush, I drag it through the mess.

He sits on the edge of my bed. It's the first time he's come into my room in ages. "You want to call a decorator in to redo this room?"

I chuckle under my breath and pull my hair back in a headband. "I'm not living with you forever. I thought I'd be moving into Mason's after the wedding. I'll find an apartment. Do I need to move soon?"

He rises and strolls across to a wall filled with photos. He's removed his suit jacket and loosened his tie. Still, he hasn't taken the tie completely off. That would be far too relaxed. "You could stay," he says. "I don't mind. It's a big house."

"I appreciate the thought." I grab a tube of makeup remover and a cotton pad. In the mirror, I notice he's studying all my photos. "Is that what you wanted to talk about?"

He's silent until he takes a photo off the wall and turns around while gazing down at it. "Did I go to this?" He holds up my Teen USA photo.

I scrunch my forehead. "I don't remember. But I'd guess not."

"I'm sorry I missed it."

I shrug and never take my eyes from him. "It wasn't important."

He meets my gaze. "It was. Do you mind if I take this and make a copy? I'd hate to think I don't have one."

"You can have it. I have a box full of photos."

Dad studies it for another moment. Then he lifts his gaze to meet mine in the mirror. "Elena called me today."

I raise one eyebrow. He never mentions Mom. But I don't either, so we're even on that score. "Why?"

"To tell me how embarrassed she was over the show and the news."

I stay silent. I forget how much I despise her until times like this.

He fidgets, shoving one hand in the pocket of his jacket. "It's water under the bridge, what happened between you and your mother when you were younger, but I'm ashamed that I wasn't more vocal in defending you."

"It's in the past," I say, swallowing hard. "Really, it was a long time ago—"

"I told her today that she'd better not state her asinine opinion about you to me, the press, her friends, or her husband. I promised I'd make up some scandalous story about her. She'd never be able to show her face in public again."

"Daddy." The corner of my mouth twitches. "You wouldn't."

"Tit for tat. She did it about you." He pauses. "I wanted to apologize for not being more sensitive about the photos."

"You treated me like you would anyone."

"You're not anyone. You're my daughter and I wanted to do something the minute Tony told me he did it."

"Dad—"

"Hear me out. I don't apologize often."

Never have truer words been said.

"When we run the camping trip episode, I predict ratings will be like never before."

So much for apologies.

"And I'd give up those ratings to have stopped the social media. But it's too late and I've always been taught to make lemonade out of lemons."

"Hm," I say, channeling the response that Gunner seems to give me every time we talk.

"Tony honestly thought the cameras would capture what happened between Gunner and Addison. He never dreamed it would be the two of you in that tent. We're still trying to figure out how the footage was leaked."

I look down at my vanity table, unable to meet Dad's eyes. The man who never tucked me into bed a day in my life shouldn't pass judgment on whether or not I was alone in a tent all night with a guy.

"Kiley?" he prompts.

"Yeah, Dad?" I search through my makeup caddy for foundation and eye concealer. A truckload of it.

Maybe I should skip the concealer and look for a ski mask. It's going to take more than a swab of goo to hide this much unhappy.

He lays a hand on my shoulder and squeezes. "I want you to know I'm proud of you. You always hold your head up high and never let anything beat you. You're the best daughter a man could have."

My throat tightens and my bottom lip wobbles.

He nods and stares at the framed photo in his hand. "OK then. I'm going downstairs."

Filming begins in a half hour. "Thanks," I say in a husky voice.

He slaps me on the back once. "Melanie's downstairs and they need you ready for makeup. Let's show them how Vanderbilts do television."

"I've got this," I say in my boldest tone.

After he leaves the room, I close my eyes and count to ten. When I open my eyes, I'm better.

Melanie Vance is perfect for Gunner. She's attractive and bright and real. I vetted her like she's running for Congress.

I'd never pass my own vetting if I were in the running for Gunner. My colorful past always comes back to haunt me and I pray the tabloids don't dig it up. I shouldn't be in the spotlight.

Melanie's background is spotless.

Gunner and the American audience can fall

in love with Melanie. If I were gay, I'd want to date, love, and marry her.

With my arm on the vanity table, I drop my forehead down to rest on it. I imagine Gunner kissing and holding Melanie.

Being the person he can count on.

He'll be happier with someone like Melanie—stable and sensible.

I hope I can lie well enough on-screen to hide my feelings. I'm falling hard for Gunner and no one can know.

Fling

Current Day

Gunner

I GLANCE AROUND MY CABIN that's been transformed. Rolling Hills Studio sent over a staging coordinator a few days ago. I now own fluffy pillows arranged across the back of the sofa and a watercolor of a forest above it. I look like I live in some lodge, ready to take visitors out on a hunting expedition.

Dane sits on the sofa and swipes across his cell phone screen, doing an irritating headshake of sympathy every so often.

"Social media is the devil's playground," he says. "You guys are now making national news.

Dateline will probably do a feature on you all about immorality in the current dating scene."

"How can they print all these lies and get away with it?" I close my laptop on the news story titled, "Matchmaker Makes Her Move."

"They assume photos tell the truth. It's tough to argue when you see it with your own eyes."

"There's nothing to see, man. She slept in my tent. Period."

"What about the audio?"

"Somebody spliced that in all the wrong places. It wasn't like that." Guilt over the way I treated Kiley haunts me so thickly I cannot catch my breath for a moment.

"Listen." Dane holds up his phone and plays it with his volume on high.

I cringe and listen to the track, even though it's my one-hundredth time to hear it.

Kiley: "I like the way this conversation is going."

Gunner: "I'm tempting you."

Kiley: "We should have a fling."

Gunner: "I wouldn't call it a fling." Pause. "We went to school together," Pause. "I thought you felt the same way about me."

Kiley: "You're making it worse."

Gunner: "I'm being honest with you because I respect you."

Dane lowers his phone. "Kiley knew she would be in the spotlight. She should've warned you."

"No. Don't blame her."

"But taping you guys when you didn't know? That's wrong."

My hands tighten, gripping the edges of my closed laptop. "Tony's attorney says the audio was leaked somehow. They didn't tamper with it, but the person who got it did the work. The conversation doesn't even make sense. Kiley never said she wanted to have a fling. I don't know how they twisted it."

"There are experts who do it. Mess with photos, alter audio." Dane checks his phone. "I guess I'd better head out since your new lady love is picking you up in a few."

"Lady love," I mutter. "At least she's not trying to rip my clothes off like that last one."

"Kiley?"

"No, you ass. Addison."

"Oh yeah, her. I'm kidding with you. Lighten up. This will pass and you can get on with your life."

"I thought it would be easy. Kiley..." I can't finish my thought.

Dane stands and tucks his hands in his pockets. "The reporters are like wolves. Wave something juicier in front of them and they'll forget all about the camping trip. Give them better news to report."

"Like walking out naked for my date tonight?"

"Yeah. That'll work." Dane walks to the door, giving me a glance over his shoulder. "Throw the press a bone. Give 'em new things to report. Flirt with your dates and get the focus off Kiley."

"You're a wealth of bad advice. Like I want to give them anything else to talk about."

I frown as he closes the door. Give the social media hive something more? Shit. He's a genius.

THE FOREVER PRODUCTION CREW arrives and I ignore them as they take over my house. A woman forces me to sit at my table so she can do my makeup. Two people set up lighting in the living room so they can get a good shot of me showing Melanie through my cabin, a task that'll take all of five minutes.

Kiley's dad, Ed, stands in one corner of the room with folded arms. He's pissed with me, no doubt, but his face doesn't reveal it. Usually, he's friendly with me, but today he's yet to say hello or go to hell.

It's as if I've become invisible to him as a person.

Kiley enters and every muscle in my body bunches into knots. She's wearing a long, fitted skirt that molds to her body and a silk shirt buttoned to her neck. I think she's trying to look professional and untouchable, but it has the exact opposite effect on me.

My gaze runs down the length of her body from her hair slicked back into a high ponytail all the way to her spiked heels.

But she's not even looking at me tonight. She stands with Tony and talks low so I can't hear their conversation. She's really not looking at him either and I'm sure he's on her shit list.

The sound of a vehicle pulling into the driveway distracts me from watching Kiley's every move.

Tony stops talking to Kiley and looks at me. "We need you to answer the door," he says. "We'll show close-ups of your face and Melanie's. You'll ask her in for a drink and then we'll cut film. We'll not film the car ride, but cut to the restaurant."

I nod. I hate this guy more than he can imagine. He's a con artist and I shouldn't be surprised at the way he's betrayed Kiley's trust.

He continues, "Kiley interviewed Melanie before the date and she'll interview you afterward."

"Got it." I walk to the door and put my hand on the handle. "Answer it now?"

"Yes, but we may have to do a couple of takes for us to get something natural."

I roll my eyes. When I open the door, Melanie smiles brightly, a genuine excitement on her face. "Hi, come on in."

"Hi." She walks inside and glances around. "You have a nice place here."

"Thanks. Have a seat. Would you like a drink before we leave?"

She sits on the sofa and leans back comfortably. "Sure. Anything is fine. How was your day?"

An honest answer won't work in this situation, and I don't plan on doing multiple takes until Tony gets the response he wants. "Things were hectic, but I'm ready to relax with you. Iced tea OK?"

"Perfect." Melanie wears jeans and a sweater. She's casual and non-intimidating. She fingers the edge of her sweater and I wonder if she's nervous.

Handing her the iced tea, I sit beside her—not on the opposite side of the sofa since I'm sure this will send the rumor mill into overdrive.

"Tell me about landscaping," she says and sips from her glass.

"It's hard work. I don't like to be behind a desk all the time, so I'm always out with my crew on a job site."

"I could guess that. You seem to be more comfortable outdoors."

"Yeah. I like everything about creating spaces people can enjoy. People nowadays spend so much time on their phones and in front of a television. I want to change that, one outdoor job at a time."

She grins. "Changing the world. That's a big goal."

"Come on. I'll show you." I glance up at Tony and Kiley. I'm not supposed to look at them. Ever.

But it's ridiculous for me to act as though we don't have a roomful of people watching this scene play out.

Going off script earns me some annoyed looks from the cameraman. He prepared lighting inside the cabin for an entire hour, and Tony's not happy. But Tony doesn't stop it. I think he's curious about what I'm doing and he can always cut it from the footage.

Melanie follows me out the back doors onto the deck. Fall colors fill the backyard with orange and red maple trees everywhere you look. A squirrel flees from the closest tree and Melanie grins at me. I smile back because the fresh air feeds my sense of well-being.

Kiley stands to the side of the deck behind the second cameraman who follows us. She turns away after we make eye contact.

Her avoidance makes it difficult to think. Melanie points out a deer grazing in the valley. She tells me about bow and gun hunting with her dad. I pretend to be interested.

Of all the women Kiley could've chosen, Melanie makes sense. We like the same things, have similar values, speak in easy conversations.

Everything should make her the perfect match for me.

When I look at Melanie, I see a pretty woman I could do things with on weekends. I appreciate her smile and her humor.

She's sensible, from the clothes she wears to her lack of jewelry or makeup.

And now I catch a glimpse of Kiley in her ridiculous tight skirt and high heels that are probably going to get stuck in my lawn and I'm jealous of the way she leans to hear what a camera guy says to her. It's not how she looks. It's because I want to know what she says and how she thinks.

I want to be part of her world.

She grins and one dimple appears, then her lips smash together like she's afraid to show the smile.

Her gaze flicks up to meet mine and I'm there inside her world.

Our chemistry promises the perfect storm,

even when we're a hundred yards apart.

Everything about Kiley is so wrong but so right.

Melanie touches my arm. "Ready to go?"

I agree it's time and she loops her arm around my elbow. "I'll drive," she says.

I'm glad the cameras won't be following us inside Melanie's vehicle. I feel suffocated by all the filming and the show. She drives us toward downtown Nashville.

"I thought you might call me," she says and looks away from the road at me.

I'm not only hurting Kiley, now I'm stringing along this very nice woman who thinks she stands a chance.

"Melanie, I think I need to be straight with you. I—"

"Don't see me as a future wife," she finishes. "I know."

"You tell it like it is."

"I do. I'm crazy for what I'm about to do."

"What is that?"

"I don't want you either."

"Why are you on this dating show then?"

The corner of her mouth quirks in a rueful grin. "I do want to meet a guy like you. I'm ready to get married, have kids, and settle down. But my future husband will look at me the same way you look at Kiley."

I close my eyes. "I'm friends with Kiley."

"If you'll forgive me for saying so, that's utter bullshit."

"If you feel this way, why are we on this date?"

"Because I'm the nicest girl you'll meet and I'm not going to play you. The director paid me a visit and I think someone less nice than I am will take him up on his offer."

"What did he say?"

"He hinted that if I slept with you, that if I seduced you, I'd probably have a guy like you offering me a ring. He offered it as friendly advice if I want to make it farther in the show."

I clench and unclench my fists. Tony's crossing the line in too many ways. I don't know if show business has any ethics at all, but I'm positive it wouldn't be good for social media sites to catch on to that bit of behind-the-scenes.

"You said no, of course." I shift in my seat. I'm too big for this small car and now the interior feels like a cage.

"I said I'd think about it."

I raise my brows. "I don't understand."

"I gave you my number for several reasons. You're a nice guy. And I've been so disillusioned by all the bad ones over the years, it was like a godsend when I got this chance to know you better. Now that I'm here, I realize I like you. A lot. So, I'm doing the right thing."

"And what's that?"

"I'm helping you. You don't want anyone but Kiley."

I shrug. "I'm attracted to Kiley and we're good friends."

"Wake up. If you could see the look on your face when she enters a room, you'd know. I've been dating like it's a competitive sport and I've never, ever found anyone who looks at me like that."

We pull into a public parking lot with the production team ready to meet us at Poppy's Pizza. Melanie places her hand on the door handle and pauses.

I can't get out of the car. If people can be frozen out of fear, I'm shrouded in ice. Her knowing look indicates she's aware of the way I'm uncomfortable with the internal war in my head.

"Gunner?"

"Yeah."

"We have to get out and follow through with the date. It'll be pretend. We'll make pizza consumption look so exciting, the social media will go wild with things to speculate about."

"So we go inside and eat pizza. It doesn't fix a thing."

"It keeps you from having to date a lot of other women. At least you know I'm on the same page as you."

Desperate

Current Day

Kile

I WAKE TO THE SOUND of my dog's gentle snores. I roll over in my bed and snuggle the furry head beside me in bed. Westley growls and moves away from me.

Grump.

I glance at my cell phone for the time and notice a series of missed text messages.

Gunner: We need to talk.

Gunner: What do I have to do to get a minute of your time?

Gunner: Are you awake?

Gunner: I guess not. I'm talking to myself. I

hate text messages.

Gunner: I hate the Internet. I hate not seeing you. I hate the fact that I'd like to beat Tony's ass and you'd be so mad at me.

Gunner: And my lawyer said not to

Gunner: But I'll do it anyway if you want me to

Gunner: I'm stopping now. Shooting the breeze with myself has made me sleepy.

The texts stopped over an hour ago. Still, my fingers hover over the keys. I'm tired and jealous and furious. Melanie flirted with him last night and he flirted back. It's the whole point of Forever and that's what makes me pull the pillow over my head. I sling it to the side when my cell beeps with an incoming text.

Gunner: Please answer me.
Kiley: Hi. Sorry I was asleep.

The dots light up immediately indicating he's typing back. My belly flips anxiously. It's a silly schoolgirl reaction.

I have a problem on my hands and should not be texting with the root of my problem.

Gunner: Come over. I can't come over there. The press or your dad will catch me.
Kiley: A braver man would do it.

277

The problem with texting is once you hit send, you can't get the message back. I throw my arm over my eyes. Why would I act this way when it's courting trouble?

Gunner: Is that a challenge?

Kiley: Absolutely not.

Gunner: Putting on pants.

Kiley: No threats

Gunner: I will be in your front drive in 5 minutes

Kiley: You're crazy. Don't do it.

Gunner: Then come to my house.

Kiley: There's probably reporters in the bushes.

Gunner: Good. I'm gonna step out naked and give them something to report.

Kiley: Behave yourself.

Gunner: I want to talk.

Kiley: Being together in the tent got us in a lot of trouble.

Gunner: Fuck in tent.

Gunner: opps. Meant fuckin not fuck IN tent

Kiley: Um...

Gunner: I'm coming.

Pause.

Gunner: Over there.

Gunner: I hate texts.

Gunner: Is there a way to do this so everything doesn't sound dirty?

Gunner: Unless you like that

Gunner: Kidding.

The grin on my face hurts. How can he do that to me when I'm so mad? I hold the phone above my face in the dark, the cell phone's light dim and comforting. His words on the screen connect me to him across the miles.

Kiley: I'll meet you to talk. Not your place.

I don't trust myself to be alone with him here. He'd be the perfect gentleman, I'm certain. But one heated look or word and I'd succumb to what I really want. One word about Melanie and I'll cry.

Gunner: Dastardly's. I'll ask Dane if we can go in early. I'll text you the time after I ask him. There's a party room in back.

Gunner: I'll buy you breakfast.

As if he has to feed me. I'm pathetic.

I jump from the bed, Westley grousing that I've disturbed him. In minutes, I'm dressed and ready to head out the door. Gunner's text lets me know I have half an hour to meet him. When I walk downstairs, a light shines from the kitchen.

"Kiley?"

"Yeah Dad. It's me."

"Where are you off to this early?"

This is the problem with being an adult in my parent's home. Finding an apartment needs to move higher on my list. "I'm having breakfast with a friend."

He studies me over the rim of his coffee cup. "You have a minute?"

"Sure." I walk over and grab a mug. It's rare that he visits with me, always in a hurry to get to the next appointment and take care of the business he's worked so hard to build. Every day—even Sundays—he goes to the studio, directing filming and edits. Forever isn't the only show he produces.

After making my coffee, I sit at the island bar across from him.

"I've been doing a lot of thinking." He stares into his mug.

"What about?"

"Ratings. Viability of new show pilots in the works."

I gulp a mouthful of too hot coffee at the topic. "Ratings on Forever. The camera likes you. I should've known it would capture your grace and the sparkle you've had since you were a girl."

My face heats at his praise. "Thanks, Dad. But right now the tabloids—"

"Our ratings are higher now than they've been since season one when we had that psychic who predicted the bachelor would marry a professional soccer player before we'd even begun the season."

"Oh." I check my cell phone for the time.

"Our audience loves you. It's the damnedest thing. It's why I'm upset."

"I don't follow."

"If the ratings were low, I could pull you from the show due to all this controversy. Redeem us so to speak. You could step forward and resign. You'd recover from this with a reputation that's been salvaged. We could find another project for you. We'd choose another Matchmaker. Audience would tune in to see who replaced our bad girl."

I cringe at him calling me this. "Dad. Me and Gunner...I didn't—"

He holds up his hand. "Poor choice of words. Sorry. I don't like to see my daughter's name in the headlines like they are now. Contrary to what you might think, it's not all about the show. It's you I'm worried about."

"I'm fine." I walk to the sink and pour my coffee down the drain. With my back to him, I stare at nothing out the window. "The fact that you've been worried about me—about how I'm dealing with this—means more to me than you'll ever know."

"You're my daughter. How did you think I'd feel about it?"

I turn and face him. "I don't know. I really don't. You don't talk to me much. And when you do, it's about the studio and shows and production schedules."

He gets to his feet and brings his coffee cup to the sink. "I know. I have to say something that I should've said years ago." He pauses. The sounds of the kitchen amplify in the quiet. The refrigerator dumps ice into the bin. The clock on the far wall ticks.

"I should've talked to you after your mother lost her mind and accused you—"

I grip his forearm. "Dad, I don't want to talk about this."

"You may not need to talk about it, but I do."

My skin flashes hot. I can't do this. I can't relive that year of drama. "Dad, please, let's not."

He stands, probably seeing the panic I can't contain. "Kiley, I'm sorry. I thought the counseling helped. I—"

I give him a tight smile. "I have to be somewhere to meet a friend. I need to go. Can you please let Westley out and feed him?"

In that moment, he's not the man I know.

His shoulders slump forward and with his hands on his hips, he looks at the floor and shakes his head. He's inside there somewhere and as miserable as I am.

"Yeah. I'll take care of it."

I've never wondered how everything affected him or even if it did. I'd always assumed it was more of an embarrassment than something he was emotional about.

I run through the house, the tears pricking behind my eyelids, my heart threatening to explode from emotions I've not felt for five years.

In thirty minutes, I'm at Dastardly's. I'm late and worried that Gunner has given up on me. When I enter through the front door of the restaurant, the lights are dimmed and tables empty. It's obvious they aren't open for business yet. Lights above the bar shine on glass surfaces. In the mirror, I see movement and turn to find it.

"Hey," Gunner says. His eyebrows dip. "What's wrong?"

"Nothing," I say. "Nothing at all." But I'm a liar. My throat cinches together and I can't swallow or talk.

He strides forward, meeting me in the center of the room within seconds. Without saying another word, he grabs my shoulders and pulls me into the warmth of his arms. "I thought you changed your mind."

I shake my head instead of answering. He lets me step back from his arms. I suck in a steadying breath. "So. Are you feeding me this morning or what?"

My voice belongs to someone else. It's sad and unsure. The voice of a girl from high school who couldn't deal with betrayal.

"Follow me." Gunner leads the way and we walk through a winding corridor. "Here." He pushes open a door to a room with a long table to seat at least twenty-five people. There's a stage at the end.

He hits a switch and low lights come on at the opposite end of the room. "Tell me what you want and I'll go let the kitchen know. They're not really open yet."

"Anything."

"Be right back." He winks and pulls out a chair for me.

I sit and wait for him to return. The privacy of the room lets me know I don't have to be paranoid of someone with a cell phone taking photos or video. For the first time since talking to Dad, I relax.

When Gunner returns, he sits opposite me at the end of the long table. "No one will bother us back here. A friend of mine works here and will bring our food when it's ready."

"OK." Sitting across from him intimidates me. I don't know where to look besides him. I don't have anything to do with my hands.

He leans forward with both his elbows on the table putting him even closer to me. "Thank you for coming to meet me."

"Sure." I pick up the rolled silverware and put it back down.

He reaches a hand out and puts it on top of mine, stilling my nervous movements. "I have a hard time being open with people," he says.

I widen my eyes. "Isn't that a guy thing?"

He laughs in a low tone. "I'm pretty sure it's a me thing."

"That's not true. And maybe I shouldn't be sexist. I can be closed off."

"OK. It's not a contest. But I'm positive I'd win."

"Don't be so sure."

"Man, you're competitive." He looks up as the door opens.

"Hi." A girl dressed in jeans and a Dastardly Bastard's T-shirt comes inside with a tray. "Here's coffee and juice."

"Thanks, Harper," Gunner says to her.

The girl doesn't even look at me while she places the drinks on the table. "I'll be right back with the food and then you won't be interrupted again."

She returns with the food exactly as she's said she would. I dive into my pancakes to avoid conversation.

"Do you forgive me for the whole camping thing?" he asks.

"It's not your fault. You didn't know better. I do. Plus, I tricked you with it being a date for the show."

He drizzles syrup over his pancake stack. "I still had a good time."

"You said you wanted to talk. Are we rehashing this whole thing about the camping trip?"

"No. I need a favor."

I eye him and the way he licks his lips between bites of food. "What's that?" I ask around a bite of pancake.

"This Saturday. I have to go somewhere. I don't want to go alone."

"You want your date night to be Saturday instead of the Friday night on the schedule?"

"No. I have a wedding to attend. I don't want anything filmed. I don't want a stranger to go with me. I want you to go."

"Why?"

He shrugs. "It would mean a lot to me."

"You have to give me a little more than that." I shake my head. "Why do you need me? You could ask Melanie."

"Why do you have to be so stubborn? Melanie and I are giving the audience and social media what they want. Nothing more. Aren't you glad to have the heat off you?"

"Whose wedding?"

He spends a few minutes taking slow bites and looking at the wall. When his gaze returns to me, he looks torn about his next words. Finally, he says, "It's my stepsister."

"Oh," I say. "I didn't remember you having a sister."

"Stepsister," he clarifies as if there's a huge difference. "My dad married Veronica's mom when I moved to Arkansas. We were close. Now she lives in St. Louis. Please. Go with me."

"We have a taping tomorrow. You have to choose to keep dating Melanie or ask me for the next contender."

"Yeah. I already know what I'm going to say."

"Let me guess. You're going to ask for someone new because you can't stand Melanie and you're so sure that I can't find the right person."

"I want Melanie," he says.

I dig my fingernails into the tops of my thighs. In one way, I should expect the unexpected with Gunner. But my world tilts at the thought of him being attracted to her.

"That's wonderful." I resurrect the pageant smile.

"And you'll go with me to my stepsister's wedding? As a friend to support me?"

I nod slowly. "I will."

"Don't sound so happy about it."

I stab a piece of sausage. "I'm thrilled. I love going to weddings. That's my job. To hook-up people who end up walking down the aisle."

Tenderness

Current Day

Gunner

"Is there a reason we're meeting in the airport parking garage? We're driving, not flying," I say. I grab Kiley's overnight bag from the bag seat.

"So I can leave my car without the paparazzi noticing. See how empty it is?"

"You don't come here alone do you?"

The corners of her mouth tip down. "All the time when I fly."

"It looks dangerous." I open the rear door on my Jeep and place her bag inside. "You have any mace?"

"Don't worry. I'll protect you," she says.

I rest my hand on the small of her back

while opening the passenger door for her. "I'm serious."

"I go places all the time."

"I don't want anything to happen to you." I close the door behind her and jog around to my side.

We pull out of the secured parking garage and drive toward the interstate. It's early enough on a Saturday morning that there's not much traffic.

I glance at Kiley. "I appreciate this."

Her brow crinkles. "It's no problem. I really do love weddings. Did you get along with your stepsister? What was her name?"

"Veronica and yes," he says.

"What about your stepmom?"

"What about her?"

"Did you like her as much as your stepsister?"

"I don't know. She wasn't much to like or dislike." I loosen my white-knuckled grip on the steering wheel.

"I always wanted a sister."

"Veronica's special. Good and sweet. She never deserved the shit life that her mom gave her."

My protests sound extreme even to my own ears. The silence continues for several miles.

"What about you?" I ask. "Do you see your mom?"

Kiley tenses, her rigid posture indicating I've hit a nerve I should avoid like a buried gas line.

She doesn't answer.

"It's not important," I say, not sure how to salvage the tenuous friendship we have. Kiley coming with me is so much more that I'd expected. I'd been sure she'd say no.

"No. I don't see her."

"Hm." I rest a finger on the stereo button. "Music?"

"No."

I drop my hand. "I'm going to stop for fuel. Want a drink?"

"My mom thinks I slept with her husband," she blurts out. "So, we don't talk. She's not part of my life anymore."

Her confession surprises me and doesn't. I didn't think she'd tell me, even though I'd guessed as much from what Josie hinted.

"I know that hurt you." I reach over and place my hand on the edge of her seat. "I don't know how it went down, but sometimes people do crazy things. Maybe someday your mother will apologize."

Kiley stares out the passenger window at the landscape. "I don't know. I kind of think it made her feel better if she had a reason for her failing marriage."

"It sounds like you're better off without her in your life."

"Mom is now on husband number five. I've never met him and don't plan on it."

"Good. I like that plan."

She laughs at me. "Glad you approve. Thanks."

"So how does a girl who grows up with a serial divorcee end up believing in marriage and a show called Forever?"

"Because I have to. There has to be more than my dad's lonely existence and my mom's desperate one." She pauses and licks her lips. "I'm scared Gunner. Maybe I'll never find it. Maybe I'm screwed up."

"No, you're not. There's nothing wrong with you."

"I want that feeling, the kind you don't doubt. What if I don't know what to look for?" Her voice wobbles at the end.

She's so afraid. I know how it is to want safety and love.

"Hold my hand," I say.

"What?" She looks over at me, alarmed. "Why?"

"I'd like to pretend for today that we're what you imagine is out there." Maybe I should tell her I'm crazy about her. Pretending might lead to reality. If I can do this thing with her for one day, maybe I can take a step toward more.

I glance at her and see a flush rising in her cheeks. "Are you mocking me, Gunner

Parrish?"

"No. I'd like to see what it feels like for a day—that thing you have in your head."

"I'm not playing." She shakes her head at me.

"Please. One day. Hold my hand. Pretend I hold your heart and you hold mine."

"Oh my. The cynic wants to take a walk on the wild side."

"You're contagious. If you don't humor me, I'll refuse to go on any more dates on Forever. I'll also tell the viewing public that you snore. Loudly."

She stretches her fingers out and wiggles them as if she's testing the thought. "Holding hands. That's it."

"All day. Like we're in love and can't keep our hands off each other."

"This isn't a license for you to cop a feel when you get the chance."

I nod in agreement. "That applies to you, too. No grabbing my ass."

Her mouth quirks. "If you can keep it PG, I can."

"OK. Good, clean handholding like we're going to a church social."

"I've never been to one, so I guess." Kiley skims her hand along the console. "When does this fantasy end?"

I shrug. "Does it matter?"

"Yes. Let's say the coach turns into a pumpkin at midnight," she says and then slips her hand into my outstretched one.

Her hand feels right in mine. It's the same sort of right as seeing a perfectly shaped tree, a sunset of oranges and reds, or the blue sky of a cloudless day.

We ride in silence and I reluctantly release her hand while I get fuel. She runs inside to the restroom, returning with a bag of snacks. I make sure to grab it again when I get back into the Jeep. She grins at me and rolls her eyes.

"I'm starting to feel a little claustrophobic," she says.

I frown. "That was fast. You're tired of me already?"

"I'm not used to this."

"You and Moneyclip didn't hold hands all the time?" Now why in the hell did I bring up the douchebag?

"No. We didn't."

"Tell me your favorite thing we'd do if we were actually dating."

"Maybe movies."

"Ah yes. Movies with popcorn. Lots and lots of popcorn. Would we make out at this movie? I never did that with a girl, but it sounds like the best part of going to the theater."

"No. We'd watch the movie and eat lots of popcorn—you got that part right. And you'd put your arm over the back of my seat and hug me close during the scary parts so I could hide my eyes."

"Horror flicks? All right. I could do that. Then what? What comes after the movie?"

"Then we'd take a midnight cruise on the river."

"I'm not sure I can afford you. You're an expensive date. Movie tickets and riverboat cruises," I tease.

"I can go Dutch," she says.

"No. That doesn't work in my book. I'll be paying for all the tickets."

"Then don't complain."

"Do you let me kiss you at the door?"

"You aren't coming inside?"

"Are you going to hit on me?"

"No."

"Then why do I come inside?"

"To see my place."

"I've seen Ed's place."

"We're pretending I have my own place." She pokes me in the ribs. "I am going to find a place soon."

"Is this pretend talk or real talk?" I ask.

"Real. I can't live with Dad forever."

I don't like the thought of her moving into a place by herself. Man, I'm too overprotective and I know it. Plus, what if she moves farther away?

What if she moves somewhere besides Nashville?

"Ed can't be all that bad. I imagine he's gone a lot."

"Yes, but I never planned to move back in with him. I only wanted a temporary place until I got married..."

"But you'll be local, right?"

She shrugs. "I have no idea what my future holds now. When I thought I'd marry Mason, I pictured a career for a couple of years. Maybe a kid or two sometime in the next ten years."

I don't like talking about her with Mason, even though the wedding didn't happen. "What's after the show? You ever think about working in your dad's studio?"

She tilts her head and leans back in her seat. "Maybe. I've always wanted to work in television."

"But you want to get married."

"Let's not talk about this anymore, OK? Tell me about you."

"Nothing to tell."

"Come on, Gunner. Give me something. I've told you my life story and you're blowing me off."

"I was a happy kid. You know about my mom. My dad pretty much checked out on me and started doing drugs. Actually, he was doing them before she passed. Then he met a woman online and we moved to Arkansas."

I'm silent then because it's not something I talk about with people. Is this what she wants to know?

She squeezes my hand. "Your dad met Veronica's mom online?"

"No. He met Jodie after we'd moved."

"Jodie is Veronica's mother?"

"Right."

"How old is Veronica?"

"Nineteen."

"And did you get along with Veronica?"

"Yeah."

"That's all you have to say about her? It's not convincing me."

"She..." I pause, not knowing how I want to finish. "She's a good girl. The best. I've missed her."

Kiley stares at me. "I can tell."

I don't take my eyes off the road. "She's the only family I have left that I care about."

"We are such a pair."

"Aren't we?" I chuckle. "Damn. Can we talk about anything positive?"

"Yes. Tell me what you're going to do with the money if you win Forever."

"Ah, now you're talking. I want to open a storefront."

"What? Seriously?" She gapes as if I've said I want to open a brothel.

"Yes, I want to have a store with outdoor furniture, pottery, and fountains. You know. Customers could come in and pick out merchandise to go with their landscape plans. I'd like to draw up plans for people on the fly and price the projects so they can get excited and see they don't have to be rich to do it."

She grins and tightens her fingers laced through mine. "You want to make people happy."

"I guess."

"You do, you big softy." She looks out the window. "That's what I want on Forever. To see people happy."

We're silent for a while. I turn on the satellite radio and we listen to some country music. The song we danced to plays and I glance across to see her smiling.

Sentiment

Current Day

Kiley

I DON'T TELL GUNNER how much I dread attending a wedding today. Usually, I'm the one who wants to attend, even if I barely know the bride and groom. There's nothing more beautiful than a bride walking down to meet the person she's to spend the rest of her life with.

Gunner's fingers tighten around mine, his grip making my rings bite into my flesh.

"I'm not going anywhere," I say. "Loosen up."

He relaxes his fingers. "Yeah. Sorry."

I nod. "Let's have fun. Don't break my

fingers. You've got me. I'm sure you could catch me if I made a run for it. And remember that I agreed to pretend for today. I'm all yours."

He gives me an uncomfortable smile bordering on a grimace. "Sure. OK."

The door opens before we ring the doorbell. The dark-haired girl who answers it tilts her head. "You must be Gunner."

"Yes. Is Veronica here?" He looks over her shoulder into the house.

"Come in. I'm Malerie," she says, stepping back so we can enter.

"Thanks." He walks inside and releases my hand. Before I can miss it, he places his hand on the small of my back. "And this is my girlfriend Kiley."

I love the sound of the introduction—fake or not—and restrain my goofy grin.

"Hi," Malerie says and walks backward. "I know Veronica will be so happy you're here. She's been antsy that you wouldn't show."

"Of course I'd come. Where is she?" he asks. His gruff tone surprises me.

Malerie doesn't seem to notice. "She's upstairs. You guys make yourselves at home." Malerie waves in the general area of a room to the left. "I'll get her."

We walk into the next room and take a seat on the sofa. "What a great house," I say.

"Hm," he answers. He sits arrow straight

and uncomfortable.

We've returned to the monosyllabic Gunner, and I try not to let it bother me.

I rest my hand on his knee and squeeze. "Relax."

He leans back to recline with me on the sofa. "I'm fine."

"Liar," I say, my mouth curving into a smile at his denial. Men. So weird.

"Gun?" A blonde stands in the threshold, looking like an angel in a long, white dressing gown with a mass of curls waving gently down her back.

He doesn't answer, but stands.

She runs forward and flings her arms around his chest. "You came."

"I said I would." He smiles down into her face. "Nicky-girl, everything OK?"

"Better than OK," she answers. She places her head against his chest. "I've missed you."

The moment stretches out for hours, a definite figment of my imagination as I wish it were me in Gunner's arms.

He pulls his head back and looks at her. "I want you to meet Kiley."

She lets her arms fall and takes a step back. "You brought a girl. I'm so glad."

Then she does the most unexpected thing. She grabs both my hands in hers and kisses me on the cheek. "Hi," she says. "I'm Veronica."

Her friend Malerie steps forward. "I hate to break up this reunion, but Gunner needs to go out back with the guys so he can get instructions on giving away Veronica. Ace and Collin are in the pool house."

"OK." Gunner can't take his gaze from his sister. "You look beautiful."

"Gun! I'm in my robe. Go on so you'll know what to do and I can get into my gown." Veronica gives him a friendly shove.

"Kiley?" he asks.

Veronica grabs my hand. "Kiley comes with us. I need help with my hair and getting into the dress."

I gulp past the giant lump in my throat. This scene isn't anything like I'd expected. I'd thought we would be ushered into a place to wait for guests to arrive. It's also a surprise that he's giving away the bride. Had I missed that detail when he invited me?

Somehow, I don't think so.

Veronica rushes away and talks the entire time. Malerie walks behind her and throws glances over her shoulder to make sure I'm still following. She gives me looks that say she's amused at her friend's non-stop chatter.

"How long have you known Gunner? Did you know he's on a television show? I really can't believe he would agree to do such a crazy thing. Do you watch it?" Veronica doesn't even pause to listen to my answers.

We walk through double doors at the end of a long hallway. The suite is huge with clothes strewn everywhere.

Malerie closes the door. "You're Kiley Vanderbilt," she says.

She knows who I am. So much for pretending to be dating Gunner. A set of French doors lead to the back lawn, framing a wonderland that I can see from across the room. The decorations seem elaborate for a small backyard wedding.

I hadn't thought through how I'd be received or if anyone would recognize me.

Veronica twirls around. "I know that name. You're Kiley from the show? The Matchmaker?" She frowns.

"The one and only." I stand awkwardly to the side of the door. "Gunner asked me to come along as a friend. I went to school with him," I add awkwardly.

Malerie examines me with a knowing look, but doesn't say a word. I'm so paranoid that I imagine everyone has seen the social media. Maybe not.

Veronica sits on a long chaise at the end of the bed. "You went to school in Shelby City?"

She seems unfazed by the fact that I've been named the harlot tempting her brother.

"No. I'm from Nashville." I walk to the

window and look out at the lawn. There's an area at the far end with gas lamps lined up on each side of a purple velvet runner. At the end, massive standing floral decorations in apricot and white mark both sides of a trellis wrapped in white lights.

Beyond, white tents shelter tables with covered serving platters. Lanterns hang from all the trees. Even in the daylight, it's enchanting.

A stage flanks the right side of the tents.

"How many guests are there?" I begin to panic.

"Only a few. Veronica wanted it to be small." Malerie studies me. "Beautiful, huh?"

Veronica sighs happily. "I'm surprised Gunner brought you. You must be very special to him." She hands Malerie her hairbrush and several clips while tilting her head back to look at her friend. "Do your magic."

"He thinks you're pretty special." We make eye contact in the mirror.

Veronica gives me a tight smile. "I worry about how he is. Since I left home, he doesn't talk to me much."

I raise an eyebrow. "Did you guys fight over something?"

She lowers her gaze and searches through the makeup on the countertop. "No. Gunner had a fight with my ex-boyfriend. You could say I ran away from home after it happened.

Gunner didn't deserve that, me shutting him out. We'd been close."

"I can tell he's happy to be here." I stare at this beautiful girl and experience an overwhelming desire to be in her place. Ready to join lives with a man she loves.

She looks up and smiles. "There's not a better wedding present in the world he could've given me. I think he's forgiven me for letting him down. I'm so glad he's here. And so happy he has you."

Heat rises into my cheeks. "We're only friends."

"You're more than that. Gunner wouldn't bring someone who's only a friend."

I want more. This girl is the key to everything I want to know about Gunner. "I think you've got the wrong idea. I've matched him with Melanie on the show. She's so into him. And I think he's into her. They've had more than one date."

Veronica wrinkles her nose. "Oh, sorry." Her brow wrinkles. "Melanie from the show is OK, I guess."

Now, my curiosity's peaked. "You don't think she's the one."

Veronica hands Malerie a hairclip. "I know she's not. Watch the last show of their date. He smiles at her like he would his teacher. You know, respectfully."

"Oh," I say.

"Has he touched her back like he did yours?"

"I don't know. They went on a date. Surely he touched her."

"He likes you a lot."

I give her a tight smile. "No, I told you. We're—"

"Just friends," she finishes. "OK. Maybe I'm making all that other stuff a bigger deal than it is. But the truth is he'd have found a way to bring her to my wedding if he really saw a future with her. Instead, he brought you."

"You're sweet."

"So you really like him a lot, too. Gunner needs someone who can be true to him and never waver. He needs someone special. He deserves someone devoted to him. I hope that person is you."

My heart slams against my chest. "A girl would be lucky to have his love. It's my job to find her."

"Maybe you're looking too far." Veronica pulls a strand of blonde hair down to curl along her neck and Malerie shakes her head at the unsolicited help.

"I have a job to do." I look out the window so I won't have to meet her gaze.

Veronica inspects her hair in a hand mirror. "Some things in life are more important than a job. Now, I need help getting into my wedding gown without messing up my hair or makeup."

Malerie exits the room and returns with an apricot colored creation, a breathtaking swath of fabric. "Let's get this girl married today. Kiley? Can you help?"

Veronica stands and removes her dressing gown. "I'm ready."

LESS THAN TWENTY PEOPLE SIT in the chairs to witness the wedding. I sit on the front row beside Malerie. I've never been to a wedding without bridesmaids or groomsmen.

Only the groom stands underneath the trellis with the woman minister.

A wedding song begins and we turn. Gunner escorts Veronica down the outdoor carpet runner leading to them. My breath catches in my throat. Veronica's a vision with her arm linked through his elbow. He occasionally glances down at her with overwhelming affection on his face.

Such love in the way his eyes crinkle in the corners.

I've attended hundreds of weddings, yet this single moment surpasses the sweetness of all the others. Veronica's focus is on two men today—Gunner at her side and the dark-haired man standing beneath the trellis.

I should be enjoying all the tiny details of the wedding—the flowers, the fairy lights hanging from trees, the rock ballad playing as they walk.

But instead, I'm mesmerized by Gunner.

Malerie sniffles beside me. It would be totally ridiculous to cry at the wedding of someone I've only met today.

My eyes water and I quickly blink back threatening tears. I thank the cosmetic gods for waterproof mascara.

Gunner turns his head. The moment his gaze meets mine, I lose my ability to hold back. I feel the weight of the world on my chest, smashing into my ribs and crushing my ideas about my future beneath an overwhelming realization.

I cannot take my eyes off Gunner. His crooked, jubilant smile feels like helium in my heart.

He could be the one, my forever.

We've both chosen to play a silly game of matchmaking for money or fame or whatever reason, and I don't want to play anymore.

Because my heart can't understand why he feels so right when others felt so wrong.

My previous vision of my future was clear.

My future husband woos me and knows I'm the only woman in the world for him. We talk until dawn because we have so much in common. He introduces me to his friends as the woman he knew he'd marry from the moment we met.

None of this fits Gunner.

Gunner scoffs at the institution of marriage and the idea of love.

I try to get out of the crazy thoughts in my head. The tears flow down my cheeks. I'm going to be a mess.

Someone hands me a tissue.

Gunner puts Veronica's hand in her future husband's. He nods at the man I know is Collin.

An empty chair waits for Gunner beside me. When he sits, he places a hand on his knee. He flips his hand up indicating he wants to hold mine. I thread my fingers through his, but return my attention to the couple reciting their vows.

"You may now kiss the bride," the minister says.

As Collin kisses Veronica, a loud rock song from Jelly Bean Queen blasts from hidden speakers and Malerie hops up from her seat. She begins clapping and gives a few wolf whistles.

"Time for champagne!" she yells. She and her husband Ace wave us to follow them. I begin to stand, but Gunner pulls me to stay.

He leans forward and puts his lips to my ears. "I'd like to go."

His hot breath tickles the shell of my ear. "Already?" I ask.

"Yes. I want to be alone with you. They won't expect us to stay." He strokes his thumb along my hand he still holds.

A thrill of anticipation dances in my belly. "OK."

He's still holding my hand as I use my free one to wave at Malerie. She seems to accept that we're sneaking away. This is far from my normal concept of a wedding with mandatory congratulations and tradition.

What about the cake? And the first dance?

None of that matters. I catch a last glimpse of Veronica embracing her husband, kissing him as if there are no guests.

Gunner releases my hand, but flings his arm around me and hugs me to his side. "Trust me?"

"Scary things come after a phrase like that."

"Everything worth something is scary. So, I'll ask again. Trust me?"

"OK. I guess."

He laughs. "You don't trust me one bit, but I can deal with it."

As we drive away, he reaches across to grab my hand again. He brings my knuckles to his lips and places a soft kiss on them.

"Are we still pretending?" I look out my window instead of at him. It'll be dusk soon and time to head back to Nashville. It will be a long drive if he plays with my heart the entire way back.

"I think I'm getting better at it," he says and leaves a kiss on the back of my hand. "Am I doing this in-love thing right? Guys aren't born knowing the rules of romance."

"Practice makes perfect," I say under my breath as we pass a small-time carnival.

"I'm very competitive."

"Stop," I yell and point at a Ferris wheel, its festive lights glowing in the dimming evening.

"Lord, woman. What is it?"

"That!" I wrest my hand from his and point like a kid. "Please Gunner. I haven't been on one in years. That's romance."

He squints at me and shakes his head. "OK. But it's going to be tough to find someone who'll ride it with you."

I poke him hard in the ribs. "You owe me for this wedding."

Closeness

Current Day

Gunner

"Get me off this thing." I close my eyes and hope I won't vomit on the people below me. For some mechanical reason, we've been stuck at the top of the Ferris wheel o' death for the past hour. It's dark and Kiley insists on swinging her feet in a pendulum motion.

"Isn't this great?" She sighs happily. "Look down there!"

I crack open one eye and regret it. She points below us at a tool belt-wearing guy who climbs several spokes of the wheel.

"Hey," she says to me.
"What."

"Put your arm around me. I'm cold," she says around a smile.

"I can't move."

She snorts. "You should've told me you're really scared of heights."

"I told you I didn't want to ride."

"Not the same thing. I thought you didn't feel like it. I thought you'd have fun once we were going."

"Which part of this is fun? I completely missed whenever that happened." I lift one finger at a time from the metal bar and attempt to lift my arm without causing us to move. I plan to put my arm slowly around her and everything will be good.

She immediately swings her feet and we rock back and forth.

"Kiley," I warn.

"What? Scaredy," she responds.

"Paybacks are—"

"Hell. I know, I know. You've said it plenty of times." She laughs low and diabolically. The motion vibrates our seat.

"No laughing." I inhale and open my eyes, looking straight ahead.

"Oh my God!" a voice below us squeals. "Did you see that guy almost fall?"

I fling my arm around Kiley and hold on for dear life. "I'm going to die. Right here on a metal paperclip four billion feet in the air."

Kiley's laughter distracts me. She wipes tears from her eyes. "It wouldn't be so..." snort. "...funny," another snort. "If you weren't this big, fearless type."

"Everyone's afraid of something."

She pulls in a huge gulp of air. "Yeah. But usually, it's something actually scary."

"Scary like what? What can I get revenge with?"

She swings her feet. I swear under my breath until she stops.

"Well," she says. "Like stage fright."

"I need to push you onto a stage? That's all you've got?"

"No. I'm not really scared of the stage. I was when I first started the pageant circuit, but it passed. Let me see," she says, tapping her lips.

"Snakes?" I offer.

"No. I don't know. I guess I'm scared of people. People you love have the power to hurt you. They take away their love or they use it against you."

Her confession makes my fear of heights seem ridiculous. Is she talking about her mom?

I hug her closer and gaze out at the multi-colored lights of the fairway. It's actually beautiful up here. "I was scared of seeing Veronica today."

Silence can be deafening, and this moment of honesty stops every carnival sound at once.

We both freeze, her swaying feet stilled, my lungs no longer expanding and contracting.

"Why?" Her voice is serious, like mine.

"We were close and she left home. Disappeared for a while. I'd had a fight with her ex-boyfriend where I tried to take his head off. I thought she might not want to see me."

Kiley doesn't respond.

The guy below us yells for the carnival operator to hurry and get us down. The smell of funnel cakes drifts up from the fairway.

"I'm telling you because I don't think I could've come alone. But I'm glad I did. It made her really happy."

"Why were you so afraid?" Kiley whispers.

"You told me earlier that you're afraid of people and the way their love can be gone. I guess I thought I'd lost her. She left home and moved on in her life."

"She loves you," Kiley says.

I sigh and look up at the stars, then back to her. "I know. Deep down I know that. I was used to taking care of her and then..."

"Then what?"

I sit taller and shift in the metal paperclip of a seat. "It's like she didn't need me anymore."

The admission sounds immature. I wish I could take it back.

Kiley runs fingers over the knuckles of my hands gripping the safety bar. "Veronica asked you to give her away because you're really important to her."

"She's the only family I have. After Mom died, she kept me from folding in on myself. I wanted to shut everybody out and she refused to let me." Time for a change of topic. I glance behind me and up to the other riders who don't seem distressed over our predicament midair. "Do you think they could send some corn dogs up here to us? Maybe string up a—"

She leans forward so I'm forced to look at her. "Don't change the subject. I know guys can't talk about their feelings, but you asked me to come for a reason."

"I asked you because I trust you." I want to say that she makes me feel stronger. Surer. Sane.

Certain.

I can be certain of few things in my life. The sun will rise in the morning. My new horse, a Missouri Fox Trotter named Tilly, will only nuzzle my hand if I bring her a carrot. My best friend Aiden will razz me for missing workouts this week at the gym.

And Kiley Vanderbilt. She's a woman I can trust.

I put my hand on her cheek and lean forward to kiss her. Before I can touch her lips with mine, a motor churns to life. The Ferris wheel lurches into movement.

The riders leave their seats, with me shakier than most. I've never told anyone what I've confessed to Kiley. She lets me take her hand as we walk down the midway.

We walk quickly to the field where I parked the Jeep. I start the engine and heater. A frost covers the windshield and we wait in silence for it to clear.

"It's after eight." She checks her cell phone.

"What would you think about getting a couple of hotel rooms? It's late to drive back."

"Oh. I...Yeah. It's not a good idea."

"Why not? Do you need to be back for something?"

"Yeah. I need to return to my sanity. I'm sure I left it back home." She directs the vents toward her hands and rubs them together.

A corner of my mouth quirks. "I make you a little crazy?"

"A lot. But really, I don't think we need to be seen together. It'll only take one person with a phone camera to start up all the rumors again."

I need more time with her. "I'll go to a motel that has outside entry. I'll pay for two rooms. You can stay in the Jeep until I get the keys."

"I don't know, Gunner. It's risky."

"I'll be careful. We'll drive out of the city and stop at one of those places along the road."

"OK. Find us a place. But I'm telling you now. No monkey business." She gives me a sidelong look accompanied by a grin.

"Yes, ma'am."

THE REMOTE MOTEL BOASTING 'VACANCY' and 'Special Rate' on their sign reminds me of a horror flick for some reason. I don't mention this to Kiley since she already seems nervous, twisting her rings and staring out the passenger window.

I return with the keys—not keycards like you see in nicer places, but real keys they've probably used since before I was born. We don't have bags, since we'd never discussed staying the night.

Kiley steps out of the Jeep and follows me.

"We're all set." I glance at her and hold up the keys. "Last two rooms."

We walk toward the long building of ten rooms in a row. Only half of them have an outside light on. I spot numbers 9 and 10 at the end.

"I'll look inside yours." I insert the key and jiggle the sticky lock. "They need to invest in new locks."

"They need a new motel," she says under her breath.

"You want to go somewhere else?"

"No. It's fine. Sorry. I'm not complaining."

I forget sometimes that Kiley's the sort who stays in the Ritz-Carlton. Not a girl who'd normally set foot in a place like this. I open the door and go in first, since I'm a little creeped out by the dark room.

Flicking the light switch, I squint at the glare of five naked light bulbs secured to the bottom of an old ceiling fan. "Home sweet home."

She walks in behind me. "Wow."

I follow her gaze. There's actually a mounted deer head over the headboard of the bed. "That's amazing. It's a ten-point." At her frown, I grin. "Joking. It's not the usual decoration for a motel."

Kiley takes a step back. "I'm not sure I can sleep underneath a dead animal."

"Let's find another place. We'll find a nice hotel."

"No, you're tired. I'm tired. Maybe your room is better."

"Let's go see. I'll take this one." I guide her, my fingers barely brushing her back. I've tried to quit thinking about how nice it would be to draw her into my arms. How nice it'd be to forget everything but her naked body.

Walking around the corner, we stand in front of room number 10, the last one in the row of rooms. I insert the key, but don't even turn it when the door swings open. I test the knob. It pivots around in a circle. "You're not staying in this one. The knob is broken."

I flick the light on. It's a match for number 9, except for a black silk painting of Elvis Presley over the bed.

"You're not sleeping here either. Are you kidding? Someone could come in and murder you in the middle of the night."

"Elvis will protect me." I smirk.

"No and hell no," she mutters unhappily. "We'll both stay in the taxidermy lounge."

"It's hardly a taxider..." I trail off at her murderous expression. "Yeah."

"We can share the bed without you know..."

"Having sex." I complete her sentence matter-of-factly. "Sure."

I pull the door closed on number 10. The knob rotates loosely, and I know we're both staring at it and reconsidering this stay.

"I hope you didn't pay much for these rooms." She steps hesitatingly to the previous door.

"Bargain basement prices."

She snorts. "They should pay us to stay here."

We walk inside the room and a Pine Sol scent hits me as I close the door behind me. "It smells clean. There's that much."

Kiley eyes the mounted head and walks to

the bathroom to flick on the light. "Looks clean."

"It'll be OK for one night." I stand behind her in the bathroom doorway.

"Do you think it's safe?"

Safe? Do I really have to sleep next to her without touching her? "I'll let you have the bathroom first."

Kiley deposits her purse on the dresser top and glances around the room. "OK. Thanks. I'll hurry. I think I'll take a quick shower here at the Bates Motel."

I chuckle at her horror movie reference. "Sure. Take your time. I'm not going anywhere." I grab the remote control and find a station. "If I step out, I'll be getting ice and drinks."

Her eyes widen as if I've said I'm going to bury a dead body. "No. Wait. I'll go with you."

"Now who's the scaredy cat?"

She purses her mouth. "Now is not the time for revenge. Got that, Parrish?"

I grin at her use of my last name and attempt to lighten the mood. "Paybacks are hell, remember? I thought it would be much tougher than this."

"Not funny." Her eyebrows rise. "Gunner. Really. Do. Not. Leave."

I laugh. "I'm not leaving. I'm only teasing you."

She steps forward and stares above my shoulder. I turn my head and see the deer head.

I turn around and wink at her.

"Oh my God. You are so enjoying this." She walks to close the distance between us. "You are a bad man."

"And you're too easy to tease." I brush strands of dark hair from her eyes.

Her lashes flutter for a second. She stands inches away from me. Her lips part into a smile. "You know this is a terrible position for us to be in."

"We're not in any position," I say, my voice low and regretful.

"You're on a reality show. I'm not supposed to engage in personal relationships with you while I'm trying to find someone for you to marry."

"It's not going to happen. I've told you. I don't plan on marrying anyone."

Her frown deepens, creating tiny little creases along her forehead. "I wish you believed that sometimes people find the person they should be with."

"I want to believe. I do. Don't get me wrong. Take Veronica for instance. I'm happy for her. She loves that guy, Collin, and it's clear that he's crazy about her."

I sense her shallow breathing, her tensing muscles, and her sadness. She's giving up on me.

I turn my back on her and walk to the heavy

curtains covering the window, lifting the corner to peek out into the darkness rather than face her. "I'm not ready to make promises to you. I'm trying hard to be honest. You deserve that. I want you to know I haven't felt this close to anyone in a long time. The things I've told you? No one else knows those things."

I release the curtain and drop my head, rubbing my hand over the back of my neck. It's not enough. Why can't I let go of my fear that she'll leave me like so many other people in my life? Am I a pansy-assed wimp? Emotionally stunted?

"I'll be out in a minute," she says to my back.

I rub my hand over the top of my head. I don't want her to give up on me.

The shower starts and I pick up the phone book on the room's nightstand. Maybe if I read the yellow pages, I won't think about her in there, water coursing down her naked curves.

Soap bubbles sliding along her skin.

Her head thrown back, long, wet hair sticking to her back.

I groan and flip the yellow pages to the landscaping section. Work. Think about bushes and backhoes. Flowerbeds and fruit trees.

Soil. PHP levels. Irrigation—

"Gunner?" she calls.

Fuck.

"Yes?" I yell back in the nicest voice possible.

"I need something."

I shake my head. Places like this don't stock up on body wash and scented soaps. She's probably in there already soaking wet and tempting as sin.

I stride to the door and lean my head against it for a second. Deep breath. "What do you need?"

"You can open the door."

She is a devil.

"Please," she adds.

I open the door a crack. Steam rolls out.

"What is it?" My temper threatens. I've never thought of her as a tease, but this is plain torture.

I hear the sound of a curtain sliding along the metal bar. "Join me?"

Heart

Current Day

Kiley

THE WATER SPRAYS from the showerhead in erratic spurts, an old plumbing fixture from some other decade.

Gunner steps closer to the shower, his gaze flicking hungrily down my body and back up to my eyes. He doesn't look away from my face again. "Are you sure?"

I nod. "Come here," I plead, my voice husky.

He closes the distance between us, placing his hands on both sides of my wet hair, slanting his mouth against mine in a deep kiss.

His tongue strokes the softness of my mouth and he hums, low and deep in his throat.

I push him back. "Your clothes."

The fabric of his dress shirt clings to his chest in wet spots. He straightens and unbuttons his shirt without ever breaking eye contact.

Shivers run along my spine in a dance of pleasure. My breasts feel heavy, my nipples pebbled like flowers reaching for the sun.

His gaze drops to my body and he smiles with a devilish lift of one side of his lips, a flash of white teeth.

Gunner kicks off his shoes, pushes his slacks down and steps out of them. His boxers follow. He takes only a moment to place his clothing and wallet on the counter.

My mouth goes dry and anticipation pools at my core.

His wide chest tapers perfectly to a slim waist. A hard V of muscle leading to his manhood.

Forget Michelangelo's David. Gunner is a living piece of art. I could stare at him all day. But it's more than his perfect proportions. Or the way his muscles in his powerful thighs flex when he takes a step.

He exudes confidence and power. He's not embarrassed for me to see him.

Gunner steps naked into the bathtub with me on the opposite side from the showerhead. He's already fully aroused, and I shyly look away from his thick cock.

He gently drags me against the full length of his body, allowing me to revel in the hardness of every inch. The throb between my legs aches as I run my hands over the muscles of his broad back.

His mouth cascades kisses down my neck and across my shoulders. Stubble scrapes the sensitive area along the swell of my breast. He lingers for a second over my nipple, then draws it into his mouth and sucks.

Every nerve ending in my body fires at once, tingling in a burst of need for more. My fingers dig into his shoulders, his muscles bunching underneath my hold.

"Gunner," I moan.

"I'm here." He twirls me around to face the spray of the hot water and wraps one arm around me, teasing and tweaking my sensitive nipple as he places openmouthed kisses on the back of my neck.

Desire pools at my core, throbbing and needy.

All I can feel is hot, slick skin.

His cock juts against me, prodding me to let him in.

"Put your hands on the wall, sweetheart." He slides his other hand low, between my thighs. His long fingers trace along my folds until he inserts a finger.

My legs tremble, but he holds me with his arm around my waist. I'm weightless and completely under his command. Willing to do whatever it takes to ease the urgency filling my body.

"Good?" he asks.

He expects me to talk? I nod, hoping it's enough. That he won't stop what he's doing. He slides his finger in and out of my center, then back inside.

He curls his finger and a building pressure pushes me to beg. "Yes, yes, yes."

"Fuck, yes," he agrees. The low growl of his voice sends thrills into my belly.

He stops and pulls away. There's the sound of the sliding shower curtain. I panic, looking back and ready to pull him back to me. Curse him. Plead with him.

Instead, he turns back to me and rips a condom wrapper open with his teeth. Sheathing himself, he returns to stroking me from behind.

I wiggle my ass against him, moaning and wanton. Desperate.

He moves his hand forward, stroking my clit as he enters me. Each slide of his body into mine increases the foreign sounds emerging from my throat. Silence is beyond my control. A blinding desire rushes through me to take all he will give. "More," I demand. "Oh, Gun—"

The moment he slides inside me, I'm lost.

Only aware of his skin and the way his hands grip my shoulders. He enters me with the measured skill of a man intent on drawing out each moment.

Painfully slow.

"Tell me what you want," he murmurs, his lips touching the spot between my shoulder blades. "You are my heaven. Mine."

"Faster. Gun. Please, please, please." I should be embarrassed to beg, but I'm not.

His big hands move to my hips and his thrusts come faster, eliciting needy sounds from me.

I'm losing myself. My body only knows the pleasure of him.

Joy.

Need.

The luxury of his touch. The surety of something being right.

My core pulses around his cock and I'm barely conscious of his own throaty moan as he releases. He folds me into his embrace, nuzzling into the back of my neck.

GUNNER MASSAGES THE SHAMPOO from my hair and tenderly kisses me under the spray of the water. We make love a second time and I wonder if the water will run out in this place.

Our lovemaking is intense and confusing. At least it's confusing to me.

He doesn't act like it's just sex.

Sex, I might be able understand from a man who says he can't give me more.

He whispers sweetheart and beautiful and darling into my skin.

He caresses me, vows to tell me all his secrets.

When he places his hand gently across my throat and holds me still only so he can tenderly place kisses along my cheeks and across my eyelids, I think I'll die from pleasure.

The water begins to run cold and we step out, laughing at the sudden change in temperature, and drying each other with the stiff, cheap towels of the motel. He finds a blanket in the closet and wraps me in it. Then he dries my hair with the motel's hair dryer.

We sit on the edge of the bed. The paper-thin comforter scratches me where it touches skin. I sit between his thighs, running my hands along the muscles of his long legs. He uses his fingers to comb through the strands of my long hair, seeming to revel in the feel.

Gunner points the dryer into my hair, then kisses my neck, then dries some more strands. He seems fascinated with smoothing out my hair, and the thought makes me smile.

We crawl into the covers naked and I love the way he wraps his arms and legs around me. "No snoring," he says into the top of my hair.

"No hogging the covers," I reply.

"I am your covers."

"Then make sure you don't go anywhere." I snuggle into his arms. Fine hairs tickle my nose when I kiss his forearm.

"I'm not leaving this bed," he yawns. "Not even to get a bag of chips, and I'm starving."

"You'd better not go anywhere."

He lifts onto one elbow and leans over me. "Hey."

"Hm?" I lift one eyebrow.

"Do you think you could match me up with this hot brunette? She's about five-six. Fine junk in the trunk. Tits that taste like ambrosia..."

I smack him on the shoulder with my palm. "Shut up."

He returns to holding me. "We do need to talk about the show later."

"Later," I agree and block it from my mind.

I WAKE TO A DARK ROOM with light bleeding in around the edges of the heavy window curtain.

My phone beeps and I slip from Gunner's arms to check the text.

Tony: You'd better not be in there with him. I'm outside a motel in bumfuck Missouri.

I swing my feet off the side of the bed and carefully stand. What's Tony doing here and how did he know where to find us? Maybe I can ignore it.

Tony: Are you trying to kill your father's show and all the hard work he's put in for years? What's the matter with you?

Kiley: One minute. I'm coming out.

My clothes are neatly piled on the chair in the corner of the room. I tiptoe over and get dressed. Gunner never stirs. I grab my purse, since I can probably find a vending machine while I'm out there.

Once outside, I see Tony's SUV parked next to Gunner's Jeep.

What the hell? He signals for me to get inside his running car.

I hop in and he backs out. "Where are we going?" I ask in a panic.

"You know what? I'm tired of taking the blame for your impulsive stunts. You're a big girl and you should know how bad this looks."

"Hold up. You are way out of line. Turn around and take me back."

"Put your seat belt on," he orders. "And listen to me."

"You can't just show up and kidnap me." I glare at him. "How the hell did you know I was in there?"

"GPS app on Gunner's phone. It's part of what we do to keep up with the stars of the show. And you should know that every yahoo between here and Canada has a smartphone and could be taking pictures of you two."

"No one took a photo and no one knows. Take me back before Gunner wonders what happened to me."

"You are not going back with him. Someone took your picture already. Posted it on Twitter. Did you stop at a convenience store yesterday, by chance?"

I sit silent.

"How is the Forever show supposed to work when my bachelor and Matchmaker can't keep their hands off each other?" Tony pulls over on the side of the road. "What do you suggest I do for damage control?"

I shrug like a sulky teenager.

"It's hard to sell a match for Gunner when you're sleeping with him."

"I messed up," I answer and look miserably

333

out the window. "I don't know how to fix it."

I check my cell phone to see if Gunner's noticed I'm gone. He'll panic if I'm gone without a word.

"Listen, we've known each for a long time. I know you don't want to ruin your father's show. And hell, it's probably much worse for your reputation than the show. But your dad can only take so much of his daughter being called a whore on social media. OK?"

My face heats in indignation. I'm pissed off and regretful at the same time. "You know how all this social media stuff works. It's part of the business."

"I'm being blackmailed." He looks at the roof of his SUV and then back to me.

"What are you talking about?"

"I never meant for any of this to come back on you. I even thought you and I would end up together someday, after you broke off your engagement."

"Can we get to the blackmailing part? Who and what does it have to do with me?"

"I slept with Addison." He rubs a hand over his face. "That night I took her back home from the camping trip. We ended up having a little fling. Then my laptop went missing for a day or two. She stole files from my computer. The show has a complete background check on Gunner. We have to do that to know what might come up. She's threatening to sell the info to the highest bidder."

"Turn her into the police." I look at him horror. "It's pretty simple."

"It'll be hard to prove she's blackmailing me. She's threatened to expose everything about Gunner's family—his father being in prison. The stepsister. The tabloids will make it more sordid than you can imagine. Addison says they can print stories about Gunner and Veronica. They can twist it more ways than you can imagine. Headlines about him sleeping with his underage stepsister when they lived together."

"That's all a lie." I twist my hands together in my lap. Bad press about Gunner. He would hate me. I would hate myself. I've lived through rumors and venomous lies. But Gunner doesn't deserve to be flayed in the public eye.

Neither does Veronica.

"What does Addison want?"

"More money than she can get from the tabloids. I have to be the highest bidder." Tony grabs my hand. "I'm giving her everything she's asked for."

"Why?"

"Your dad's been good to me. Between the bad press pointed at you and some shitstorm media that could surround Gunner, it would be too much for the show. It could affect the reputation of Rolling Hills Productions." He releases my hand as I numbly pull it from his. He glances out the window and then back at me. "Ed has a heart condition. He found out this year and didn't tell you. He didn't want you to know."

I stare at him. "Why? Why wouldn't he tell me?"

Tony gives me a sad smile. "Of course he didn't want you to know. Ed's a legend for being a hardass. He can't have his daughter feeling sorry for him."

"He should have told me."

"I told Ed about Addison. I offered to resign and take the heat for what she's done, but he said no. He said we'll deal with it."

I nod and squeeze my eyes closed. "OK. What do I need to do?"

"You need to stay away from Gunner. Addison's crazy. She talks non-stop about how we're staging a reality show because you and Gunner have something going on. I didn't know a jealous woman could be so dangerous. It's not about the money. I think it's all revenge."

I swallow and fight the tears. "Let's go home. I'll text Gunner that you picked me up."

"Stay away from him except for the on-screen shots. I'll come up with something to pacify the social media frenzy that hasn't died since you two got caught at the campsite. And for what it's worth, I'm really sorry."

"Don't be sorry. Help me fix this." I cover my face with my hands.

Gunner will never understand why I left. If I tell him the truth, he'll say the press doesn't matter.

But other people are involved. My dad. Rolling Hills Productions and their employees.

Most of all, Gunner would regret ever being part of the show and meeting me.

My reputation doesn't matter, but Gunner doesn't deserve to have his relationship with his sister, his landscaping business, and his entire life ruined.

Longing

Current Day

Gunner

SHE'S GONE.

The rumpled sheets and her scent—I swear I smell her hair on my pillow—tell me it wasn't a dream.

"Kiley?" I hop from the bed and walk naked to the bathroom. Push open the door.

Empty.

The plain white shower curtain is pushed to the side. A towel lays discarded on the floor. The towel I'd used to dry her body and then her hair.

Perspiration bursts onto my forehead and I gulp in a breath.

I search the room for her clothes. A familiar

feeling, panic and dread mixed together, hits me like a Molotov cocktail. My sanity thins as I imagine the possibilities of her disappearance from our room.

I convince myself that she's stepped outside. Maybe she went to my Jeep, not realizing that it will be locked.

Heading to the door, I'm stopped midway by the buzz of my cell phone. I lunge for the nightstand, pressing the button without even confirming it's her.

But in the way of déjà vu, I know. It's her. People have left me before.

"Gunner?" she says. Her soft voice strokes along my skin.

"Where are you?" I ask, my tone abrupt.

"I...um..."

Silence.

She coughs. "I had to go. Tony gave me a ride. Listen. I think it's best if we keep our distance right now. For the show. We don't need all this bad press and I made a mistake by—"

"You made a mistake?" I stalk to the window and pull open the curtain. Blinding sunlight pours into the room, unable to defeat the darkness and anger spilling into my soul.

She called Tony? Did our time together mean so little to her?

"I'm sorry," she says. "I'm so sorry. I can't be with you right now."

Dejection and anger consume me, prodding the need to protect myself. My gut roils and a burning sensation rises in my throat. I cover my eyes with one hand to shield the sunlight from the window. Inhale deeply to steady myself.

"Don't be sorry," I say. "It's what I wanted. A good time. Thanks, sweetheart. I'm sorry we didn't have time together this morning. Tell me. How does Tony feel about picking you up from another man's bed?"

She doesn't answer. A whimper comes over the line and for a second, I'm positive she's crying.

I look at the rumpled sheets on the bed. The indention in her pillow. I squeeze my eyes closed.

Fuck, fuck, fuck. Why did she run to him?

"I'll have my assistant contact you." There's a long pause and an intake of breath. "He'll tell you what to do about the last shows," she says, her voice catching. "Bye, Gunner."

The call ends.

I should've known better.

She came into my life telling me what she expected—the real deal, a relationship.

But I lied to myself and said I didn't want that.

Turns out, she granted my wish. A good time. Now, it's too late to tell her I was wrong. I really wanted more.

THE GYM IS ABOUT THE ONLY PLACE I can get some relief from my tension after Kiley's disappearing act. I've wavered between wanting to beg her to talk to me and never speaking to her again.

"I saw you spent every day for a week with Melanie. That hot tub show must've been tough to film." Aiden stands at the end of the weight bench, towering over me in my reclining position. He's my personal trainer at the gym.

I roll my eyes at his sarcasm. "Yeah. It's a real turn-on to sit next to a half-naked woman with a camera crew audience hanging over my head."

"She seems like a lot of fun." He adds more weight to my bar.

"She's nice." I wish he'd talk about anything else.

"Tomorrow you film the finale, right? Isn't this show supposed to end in a proposal?"

"Nope. Not for me, it doesn't. I'm leaving with cash."

"Heard from Kiley?" Aiden spots me as I pull the bar from its racked position.

"Nope," I say through a grunt and perform the repetition of the bar with more weight than normal.

"Easy, there. Last one." Aiden steps up, ready to grab the weight if I've overdone it. He watches me a little too closely.

"Quit waiting for me to talk. I don't need a counseling session." I blow out air and lift the weight back to the rack.

"I didn't say a word."

"You don't have to." I curl up and swing my leg over the bench.

"But if you want to, I'm here for you."

"We're not a couple of chicks."

"For all the women in the world, I take offense to that statement." He marks my reps on his clipboard.

"I thought I'd get away from the third degree by coming here. Dane's already drilled me. Leo's sister Josie tried to kick my ass. Then Leo's girlfriend gives me a piece of her mind and I don't really even know her. Actually, every woman I pass gives me a dirty look."

"Isn't that normal for you?" He chuckles and looks up from the clipboard. "I'll open up for you after hours if any of the ladies here are giving little Gunny a hard time."

"Fuck off."

He grins and signals for me to follow. "Pull ups. Let's make it twenty-five."

"You trying to kill me?"

"No. Trying to make you shut up and stop

feeling sorry for yourself."

I grab the bar and pull up to my chin. "So what would you do?"

"Man. You're still talking. I thought you didn't want to talk about it."

I roll my eyes and let my body down. Then I pull up to the bar. "You don't know what you'd do, do you?"

"Do you want to date other women?"

I didn't want him to turn the questions back to me. "Not really."

Hell no.

"Do you want to see her date someone else?" He raises an eyebrow.

"No, what kind of question is that? You know the answer." I puff and pull up. Then reverse to the ground.

"Do you want to see her fall in love and have some babies with somebody like me?" He makes eye contact with a curvy redhead who passes us.

I grind my teeth at his comment but don't respond to his jab. It's obvious that he's trying to piss me off.

He rubs his jaw and grins at me. "She's a beautiful woman. It's only a matter of time. Maybe I should throw my hat in the ring."

The muscles in my neck tighten and I mash my lips together. One thing we don't do—date each other's exes. Dane, Leo, Aiden, and I know it's an unspoken rule.

Hands off.

"There's a reason I should hang out with Leo more. You and Dane both think you're God's gift to women." I pull up and hang there for a minute, enjoying the burn in my biceps.

"All I'm saying is be sure about what you're throwing away. You've been in love with that girl since we were kids."

"Whoa. Nobody said anything about me being in love." I drop to my feet. "She's unpredictable. She broke off with her fiancé weeks before their wedding. She ditched me after Veronica's wedding so she could be with the show's producer."

"And does she realize how you feel about her? I figure this show thing has to be messing with her head. I feel really bad for her."

"Well, don't. She and I had some fun. The show ends soon. Life will go back to normal."

He nods. "I get it. You're being careful. Maybe she's not the right one."

"You sound like her with all this 'right one' business." I grab the gym towel and wipe my neck. "I need to cut it short tonight. I'll see you later."

Aiden shakes his head. "Whatever. Take care."

I grab my gym towel and stalk out of the gym. Halfway to my Jeep, I spot a note tucked underneath the windshield wiper blade. I break into a run.

Unfolding it carefully, I curse at my expectations. Kiley has made it more than clear she doesn't want to see me. I slam my fist against the Jeep's door, leaving a shallow dent.

The note from Melanie says she looks forward to the show finale tonight. We'll be on location in the studio. She's been a good friend to me, but she knows where I stand.

Melanie and I have an easy friendship. I could sleep with her. Hell, I could probably marry the woman and be content.

Content.

Life should be full of surprises, not planned out with a script.

I ball up the note and toss it into the backseat of the Jeep.

AT THE STUDIO, I SIT BACKSTAGE. A studio audience waits for the taping to begin and I'm supposed to go out after all the women from the dates talk about me.

Half an hour passes. I watch a small screen showing all the women in interviews—even the ones from the speed dating rounds. The audience laughs along with the women who talk about me.

A man I don't recognize questions each of the ladies. "Where's Kiley?" I whisper to the woman who applies powder to my nose.

"They replaced her for the finale. Didn't you know that Bob Targis will be hosting?" She dabs the sponge on my forehead.

"They can't replace her. She's the Matchmaker." I hold up a hand and block the makeup sponge. "Where's Tony Tolino? I need to talk to him."

"You go on in a few minutes. You'll have to wait."

"You're on in five," a guy wearing a headset says and holds up his fingers.

I glance at the screen in front of me. The camera pans the audience and Ed Vanderbilt sits in the front row. I get up from my seat and look around for Tony. He'd been by to say hello a few minutes earlier.

He stands in the wings with the nearby studio lights glowing on his face. His pensive expression does nothing to alleviate my worries about Kiley. I stalk to him, my temper rising because someone should be telling me what the hell is going on.

The guy with the headset holds up four fingers.

"Why isn't Kiley here?"

"Shh," he answers.

"Where is she?"

He draws me down a hallway by the arm. "She couldn't be here today."

"Why not?"

"She thought it best if you didn't share a stage."

I shake my head. "Does she hate me that much?"

Tony frowns at me. "No. She's protecting you."

"From what?" I'm livid, my hands balling into fists because he's not giving me the information I need.

"You have to get out there," he says and points to the stage. "Go."

"Not without Kiley."

"You'll forfeit the prize money. If you don't fulfill the contract, you lose the million. Think about it."

I grab him by the collar. "Tell me where she is."

Tony exhales and pulls my hand off his shirt, smoothing down the wrinkles I've created. "I don't know. Honest to God."

The guy with the headset rushes to me and holds up two fingers, then points to the entrance of the stage.

I shake my head at him. "Who does know?"

"Ask Ed after the show. He agreed to pull Kiley off."

I back away from Tony and run to the stage. The bright lights blind me momentarily as I walk out with a forced smile. I wave at the women, all seated around a U-shaped sofa with my chair at the open end.

The audience chuckles.

Bob, the replacement host, walks forward and sits in the chair beside me. "It's good to see you, Gunner," he says as if we're old friends.

"Nice to meet you," I say and hold out my hand to shake. "I'd expected Kiley Vanderbilt."

He looks awkward for a split second. We haven't rehearsed the windup since they wanted genuine reactions.

They should've warned me if they didn't expect me to balk.

The replacement host folds his hands in his lap. "There was a last minute obligation she had to fulfill, or she wouldn't miss it. So, here we are. I guess you've been watching backstage and have heard some of the stories from these lovely ladies."

I nod.

He continues. "You've spent the most time with Melanie."

For the first time, I notice she sits on my left at the end of the nearest sofa. "Hi Melanie," I say.

"Hi Gunner." She gives me a warm smile and rises to give me a hug.

I glance around at the rest of the women: all the speed dates—including the mime-girl who sits silent with a residual pissed-off expression. There are several women I saw for only one night. Addison from the camping trip and Melanie sit nearest me.

"What is it about Melanie that drew you to see her again and again?" Bob the Host asks.

"We have a lot in common. Fishing, hunting, the outdoors."

Bob nods.

"Kiley matched me with someone who makes a lot of sense for a guy like me. Melanie has it all—beauty, brains, a four-wheel-drive."

The audience laughs and so does Bob. Melanie smiles at me.

"Kiley certainly knows me well. Hell... Sorry, I'm probably not supposed to curse on television. Melanie is exactly the type of girl I'd choose to date."

More laughter from the audience.

At the side of the stage, Tony grins as if he wrote a script for me himself.

Bob stands. "Before you continue, let's bring out another guest. We'll come back to Melanie."

When I see the girl in the wings, I decide I hate live television. With a passion. I'm never watching anything but football, ever again.

Why is Veronica here? She's not part of this

349

process.

She walks onto the stage with a grin and a wink before sitting on a sofa opposite Melanie and Addison.

"Welcome," Bob says. "I know Gunner's surprised to see you."

"Probably. I'm glad to be here and give my two cents about what Gun needs in his life." Veronica straightens her long skirt. "He took time off from the show to help me get married and I wanted to be here for him."

She beams at me, no longer the scarred girl from so long ago. A happily married woman.

She didn't let her past dictate her beliefs. Her goals for a healthy relationship.

Bob leans in, folds his hands over one knee, and adopts an intimate tone. "Congratulations on your recent marriage, Veronica. We can't wait to see if Gunner chooses love or money today. Before we find out, all of America wants to know the real Gunner. The man he doesn't show to the camera."

"He's a private kind of guy, so I'm risking a lot by telling you this." Veronica's directs a sad smile toward the studio audience. She doesn't look at me immediately, and when her gaze flicks to mine, blood freezes in my veins. I know I won't like whatever she says.

"Tell us," Bob says. He prods her with a nod.

"Gunner, Gunner." She says my name and

shakes her head. "You put up this wall against people. But I know you love hard and true. I never doubted for one minute that you'd protect me from all the bad things in the world. And even though you never said how you felt, I knew. I felt this incredible love. I felt it every time you worked overtime at the store to put food on our table. I knew it when you helped me with algebra when I vowed to quit school over math."

I look away from her to the audience, mostly women, who all grin. Heat flushes up my neck and into my face.

"I couldn't ask for a better brother," Veronica says. "But you're also dense as concrete when it comes to picking out a match for yourself."

The audience laughs.

She continues. "You and Melanie have zero chemistry. So what if you like to fish and shoot guns with her? Are you looking for a pal or the love of your life? Do you want to touch her right now? Do you want to tell her when something good happens to you? Do you want to make sure she's happy, because it makes you happy?"

Bob holds up a hand. "Let's give Gunner a chance to answer."

He looks to me and I exhale, attempting to relax so I can answer the damned question. I

351

should get paid triple wages for this inquisition.

"So many questions. I'm not sure where to begin." I say. "Melanie's easy to be with. I care about her." I know I'm not choosing Melanie at the end of today's show, but I don't want to embarrass her, either. She's been a trooper—hanging out with me so I can get through the rest of the season.

Veronica's brow crinkles in disbelief. She's planning to scold me on national television.

Bob motions off stage to someone. "Let's bring on one more guest."

I turn slowly, daring to hope. It has to be Kiley. She's the only one from this show who hasn't been on stage. I need to see her, touch her.

Ed strolls out and takes the seat beside Veronica.

Disappointment cuts through me.

Bob sits in the chair and says something to Ed. It's all background noise in my head as I glance back to the stage entrance again. I'd been so sure she would walk out.

My gut clenches. Something is wrong. Maybe all my worst fears will culminate in this moment and I won't see her ever again. "Can someone please tell me where Kiley is?"

Ed turns to face the camera instead of me or Bob. "I'm the producer of Forever. It's been a good long run of this fantastic show in its eighth season. But this is the end. It's not because I don't believe in it, but because I think it's time. And because I don't want it to end on a sour note, I'd like to clear the air."

The women on the sofa all look to one another. Veronica keeps her gaze on me. Bob doesn't look surprised at all.

"I allowed my daughter to serve as Matchmaker this season because she's good at it, not because she's my daughter, although she's wonderful in that role as well. She asked that I pull her from the show because she didn't want to compromise the production's integrity. It seems she's become involved emotionally."

Bob signals to the wall behind my back. "Our Matchmaker, Kiley Vanderbilt, and Gunner have known each other since they were young."

I turn in my seat to face a giant projection screen filling the entire wall. A class photo of little kids appears on-screen. It's a photo I don't recognize. A drawn heart appears around a little boy. It's me. Me, back when I didn't worry about anything but playing outside with my friends.

When I had a whole family and a carefree life.

Next to me, another heart pops up framing the face of a dark-haired beauty.

Wow. Even at second or third grade, Kiley was beautiful. Her huge smile and shining eyes glow so brightly, it draws the eye.

Another photo of Kiley on stage in a school play. She's the Statue of Liberty. The girl didn't need a torch to look regal.

I can't stop smiling. She's always been so vibrant. No wonder the kids at school gravitated to her. She's like the sun. Always has been.

"Let's take a look at some footage that made headlines."

A montage of images from the camping trip flicker in boxes. Kiley smiling at me. Me watching her.

Kiley's face as she focuses on my every move while we hike. When did that camera guy film this? My shoulder muscles bunch.

Ed motions to the screen and doesn't seem phased by what he's about to reveal. "We had to mount a special action camera to get some of this. Then a night camera. No one but Roy even knew about the extra cameras. Cameras tend to make people uncomfortable and we wanted genuine moments. The real deal. At first, we hadn't planned to use any footage."

Ed folds his arms over his chest and sits back like he's going to watch some home movies.

Hell, this guy is going to show real moments all right. Moments between me and Kiley. Things she'll hate being televised. How could he do this to his daughter?

Then her face fills the screen. Her wet hair sticking to her high cheekbones. Man, she's beautiful. My lungs stop functioning.

We're inside the tent talking about my mom. I'm not embarrassed about the emotional timbre to my voice. I'm never ashamed of loving Mom. I focus on what we're saying.

Kiley: "She'd be proud of the man you are."

Me: "She would sometimes. Right now she'd whip my ass."

Kiley: "Why is that?"

Me: "She'd want me to be more honorable than I am."

Kiley: "Honorable how?"

Me: "I'm trying to think of a way to tell you I pissed Addison off on purpose so she'd leave."

There's the sound of Kiley smacking my arm.

Kiley: "You're kidding. Right? Tell me you didn't do that. I can't believe you admitted it."

Me: "On the other hand, maybe Mom's looking down on me and is proud of my ingenuity."

The film grows dark and our heads pulls together. It's tough to tell what's going on from the angle, but I know.

Me: "Maybe she'd want me to do whatever makes me happy."

My pulse ratchets and blood rushes into my ears. I'm always happy with Kiley. Deliriously happy.

Fear sinks deep into my soul, so leaden I can't move for a moment. Can't breathe.

I shake it off.

"Ed, I—" I get to my feet.

He continues like I haven't said a word, like he hasn't been watching me make out with his daughter. "And I'm so very proud of her moral compass, her spirit, and her belief in love. It's a hard world out there and hard to find the right one," he says. "She knows love isn't measured in time. People sometimes simply know when it's right."

One person in the audience begins applauding and the studio fills with the sound. It dies, but I still stand, wanting to get off the stage and find her.

"Where is she, Ed?" I take a step away from my chair.

Veronica nods as if encouraging me. "Finally."

"Patience, Gunner. I also want to point out an unscrupulous contender who unwisely blackmailed my staff." He stands and points at Addison. "Criminal charges will be filed for theft of property. You took computer files of this footage from the home of our director. Those files belong to Rolling Hills Productions. Lady, I want it on national television that you're scum."

Addison's face turns bright red and she

attempts to stand. Melanie grabs her arm. "You should stay," she says. Melanie nods toward two officers waiting off stage.

Bob nods as if this is all part of the show.

"Gunner," Melanie says to me. "It's been a good run, Buddy. I think you and I don't have to pretend. We've both known all along what you really want. I'm disappointed that Bob didn't bring Gunner's real match on the show today."

The studio audience cheers deafen me.

I step closer to Ed. "I need to go talk to her."

Ed smiles and looks to me. "Kiley went back to the house for some boxes. If you hurry, you might be able to stop her from moving to Dallas."

He winks at me and I run off stage to prevent the thing that scares me the most in my life.

Losing a chance with Kiley Vanderbilt again.

Amour

Current Day

Kiley

I SIT WITH AN EMPTY BAG of miniature candy bars in one hand and a glass of wine in the other. Westley romps around the obstacle course of boxes in my bedroom.

A torrential rain outside matches my mood. Lightning flashes, illuminating the dark room.

Dark except for the glow of the television.

Melanie looks so pretty. She dressed up today in a blue short skirt with spiked heels. It's a good look for her. She should do it more often. I've never seen her dress like this during the entire season.

Bitch.

I sigh, knowing it's not true. She's one of the nicest people I've met this year.

Does she really think Gunner's going to propose or say they have a future together? Probably.

I barely hear Veronica's questions as I stare hard at Gunner. He's wearing black slacks with a gray dress shirt. Fresh haircut. Purposeful stubble along his jaw makes him look even more masculine.

The camera zooms in on his face, caressing the sharp angles of his cheekbones and his square jaw. "So many questions," he says. "I'm not sure where to begin. Melanie's easy to be with. I care about her."

I suck in a breath. He might propose. He might do it after I'd assumed he wouldn't this entire time.

Black panic bleeds over my vision. I'm dizzy with fear.

Lightning streaks across the sky and a loud boom immediately follows. I jump at Westley's barking. He hates any loud noises, but especially thunder.

Pop. The television blinks and goes black.

I frown at the blank television screen. "No, no, no." I scramble around for the remote at my feet. I press the ON button.

Nothing.

Looking up, I realize all the lights are out.

Power outage. How much bad luck can one person possess?

I sit on the floor, thinking about Gunner's last words. He cares about her.

A storm of grief threatens like dark clouds.

He must be in love with her. He said he wouldn't, couldn't, didn't believe.

Self-pity sneaks up on me. I roll the cool wineglass along my flushed forehead. Another glass of wine will help me feel less. Hurt less.

I'm another half glass in when I realize the wine won't numb the pain of knowing he didn't want me.

Putting my unfinished drink on a dresser, I curl up on the carpet. Westley licks my face.

"Yes, I know. I know you love me." I stroke his body until he relaxes.

My eyes drift closed and my breathing steadies. Hot tears slide down my face, and I wipe them away. Rain lashes against my window and thunder vibrates through the house.

Bam. Bambambambam.

Someone pounds on the door downstairs. Disoriented in the dark, I get to my knees and then stand. It's probably Josie, feeling sorry for me and coming in like the cavalry to save me from my pity party.

Taking a quick step, I stub my toe on a twenty-pound free weight, a reminder of my good intentions about doing squats.

Someday. Someday, I'll do those squats and quit eating chocolate bars with my wine, and I'll find a guy who thinks I look beautiful without mascara. The tears come harder.

I'll find someone, but he won't be Gunner.

"Just a minute," I yell and walk down the stairs. "Coming!"

I peer through the front door glass. Lightning streaks across the sky, illuminating the outline of the man outside. Gunner stands in soaking wet clothes with his back to me, but I'd know those broad shoulders and that compact butt anywhere.

"Shit-shit-shit-shit!" What is he doing here?

I back away from the closed door. Maybe he didn't hear me. I can't talk to him now.

Darkness envelopes the house and I stumble along the corridor, using my hand to guide me toward the back. The pounding on the front door continues.

My head feels stuffed with cotton due to the excess wine and crying.

I love Gunner Parrish and I hate him.

Hate him for not falling in love with me.

And I love him for being a man who said he wouldn't fall, but does.

Westley runs around my feet while barking. I stride to the back of the house, as far from Gunner as possible.

"Shush," I scold and hug my arms around my chest.

Westley runs and jumps along the back door. Gunner appears, his clothing drenched by the rain. He tries turning the back handle, but it's locked. He spots me. "Open the door!"

I shake my head at him. "Go away."

"You're not getting rid of me."

We stare at each other. He's come to thank me for putting him with Melanie and there's no way I can keep my chin up when he does.

I unlock the door anyway. Might as well get it over with. He immediately opens it, stepping inside. Water drips from his hair into his eyes. He uses his forearm to draw it from his face. Westley steps back, out of the growing puddle, but doesn't attack.

Gunner takes a step forward. "Why weren't you at the finale? I needed to tell you something."

"Leave me alone. If you even care about me a little bit, you'll leave me alone."

Gunner grabs me and pushes his body against mine. Then he places both hands on the sides of my face. "Are you drunk, woman? I'm sorry for not telling you sooner. I need you. I'm here to lay it all out in plain English. No more hiding from what I really want."

"Not Melanie? I saw you on the finale telling her..."

"I don't know what you thought you saw. Are you sure you're not drunk?" He leans in and sniffs.

I shake my head, tears clouding my vision. "No. A little wine to get me through the show. OK. A lot of wine. But not drunk."

He sweeps a finger along my cheek, catching a tear. "I can't promise you that I'll be easy. I need to take this slow. People in relationships need to spend more than four weeks to get to know each other. But I'm not letting you get away. I know it sounds crazy, but I've spent my whole life waiting for you. I'm begging you to take a chance on me. I'm sorry I don't know how to say all the romantic things, you'll have to teach me. I'm trying to figure it all out. I even watched The Princess Bride to see what this Westley guy is all about."

I blink away more tears. I think this is the most he's ever said without taking a breath. "Gun..." My lips tremble and I smash them together. Hot tears drip down my chin. "You big jerk. You are romantic."

He takes his thumbs and wipes them away. "Nope. I was an idiot. You were my dream girl at sixteen and nothing's changed. I'm just saying whatever's necessary to make sure you never get into the backseat of a car with anyone but me."

I pull his mouth to mine and kiss him hard.

"I'm parked by the garage," I say against his mouth.

Gunner lifts me to him and I wrap my legs around his waist. He carries me all the way there.

Epilogue

Five years later

Gunner

"DARLIN', WE DON'T EAT BROTHER'S CRAYONS." I take Kami's chubby fist and pry her fingers open. She bats long eyelashes at me and two deep dimples appear in her cheeks. "I wub you, Daddy. I wub bwother. I wub cwayons."

Lord, she's like her mother. Obstinate and charming. A little on the devious side. Someday, a man will be in as much trouble as I've been these last five years.

"Yeah. Well, crayons are yucky. No more. Got it?"

She nods with wide eyes and pulls a crayon from the pants of the stuffed koala bear in her arms. Presenting it to me, she flashes a smile of two glowing white teeth. "Cwayon."

"Thanks, darlin'." I eye her diaper. I'll be

doing a crayon check for sure.

"Dad? You said you would help me." My boy Cameron pokes a sharp object into my back. I can't fault him. He's been more than patient in his wait for my attention. "How long does a tea party last?"

I glance over my shoulder to see a building block spaceship in his hand. "I'll be there in a few minutes after I put Kami down for her nap."

"She's supposed to take a nap at two," he says with a stern expression. "Mommy said."

"Yeah. A few more minutes." I turn back around as Kami holds a tea pitcher and dumps pretend tea into my boot I left behind her when I took them off to play. "Time for a nap."

"No nap," Kami says with a pout. "Dwink, Daddy." She throws the tea pitcher on the plastic table and grabs my abandoned boot with both hands. "No nap," she repeats, her delicate blonde eyebrows knitting together in the middle.

Although she looks like me, her attitude is definitely her mother's.

Cameron places his hand on my back. "Do you need my help?"

I look over my shoulder again and nod my head. "Let's read sister a story, OK?"

He scampers away to his bedroom, his bare feet flying across the carpet, deftly avoiding the landmine of toys.

"Don't run!" I yell after him.

When he returns with an oversize book, I carry both kids across the hall to the master bedroom. We pile onto the bed, Kami in the middle. She snuggles in and puts her head underneath the little blanket she carries around the house.

"I weady to weed," she demands from underneath her shroud.

Cameron shakes his head at me and grins. "She's crazy."

"No, Camwin." Kami flings the blanket off. "You cwazy."

"Hush. We're all crazy." I open to the first page of the book. Kami covers her head again, and I read to them in soft tones. After three pages, I uncover Kami's head and tuck the blanket around her. I glance over at Cameron, ready to tell him we can play now.

It's too late. He's asleep too, his small hand placed on his sister's shoulder. I glance up at the sound of footsteps in the hallway.

Kiley leans against the doorway, her hands behind her back. She smiles and mouths, "I love you."

I nod. It's a given. No doubt in my mind that my piece of heaven sits within these walls. "Did you get the test?" I whisper the question.

She brings one hand around and holds the stick in front of her. A blue dot clearly marks the end of the pregnancy test.

Kiley beams, a damned light shining from the joy on her face. She tucks a dark strand of hair behind her ear. "We've got to figure out what's causing this." She smirks.

I exhale, a fear letting loose in my chest. I'm grateful she's not upset. We didn't plan this baby. Heck, we didn't plan the first one. Not that she ever complains about the two little monkeys sleeping soundly beside me, but it's a lot in a few short years.

Years I wouldn't trade for a billion dollars.

Between the growing landscaping business and our store, our lives get busier every day.

I insist Kiley fulfill her dreams. A person needs to work with something that makes them grow and bloom. I get a high from seeing the beauty I shape from outdoor spaces.

Kiley needs something different.

Audiences love her new television show, Magical Beginnings. She films one couple from the time a guy gets down on one knee, through all the drama of wedding preparations, and all the way to the altar.

And she loves every minute of it.

Still, she gives most of her attention to our family. We're not stupid. We know what we have.

Sometimes, I'm so lucky it scares me. I'll begin to fuss over things like life insurance policies and health insurance. I insist we make every moment count. Kiley kisses away my paranoia and promises me that no matter what life throws at us, we have each other.

Now, she pads over to the edge of the bed and sets the pregnancy test on the nightstand. Slipping in beside Cameron, she kisses the top of his head and rests her arm over both kids.

I lay my hand on top of hers and caress it, tracing my finger over the ring on her left hand. She closes her eyes, a grin tipping the corners of her mouth with some secret thought I hope she'll share later.

Maybe she's wondering if she'll need a bigger vehicle, like a minivan. At the rate we're going, we'll need a bus. But she's way past due for a new vehicle. Still, I hate to get rid of her SUV, since I'm pretty sure it's where we conceived Cameron.

In private, I've often called him our backseat baby. In private, I tease that she knew I was husband material in the second grade. In private, I tell her how she saved me from a lonely life.

In public, I tell all my friends that I'm lucky to have found my forever.

THE END

Secrets are exposed, trust is betrayed and two people face the beauty of lies.

Leo Jensen has a secret—he is Mr. Expose, a blogger that reveals the truth about liars and frauds. It's a way to make a living, and he's had a motherlode of experience with liars. Cheaters. Women who live for drama and carry more hidden baggage than a Boeing 747. Even his twin sister can't seem to admit the truth about her relationships, so finding an honest woman is about as likely as finding a unicorn in the middle of Nashville.

Harper Wade wishes life had a do-over button. She'd press that sucker and reset the last four years. Now, she has the chance to start fresh and make things right, but first she has to retrieve the damning evidence of her past from an annoying blogger. She's doing all the things she knows she shouldn't--breaking and entering, lying by omission, falling for the hot guy next door. Too bad he holds the key to her clean slate.

Find The Beauty of Lies and all Brinda's books at major retailers online.

Sign up for her newsletter at
http://www.brindaberry.com/mailing-list.html.

Also by Brinda Berry

Adult Novels

Chasing Luck (A Serendipity Novel, #1)
Tempting Fate (A Serendipity Novel, #2)
Seducing Fortune (A Serendipity Novel, #3)
Serendipity Boxed Set (Books 1-3)
The Beauty of Lies (A Stand By Me Novel #1)
The Fiction of Forever (A Stand By Me Novel #2)
Fit for Love (A Stand By Me Novel #3)

Young Adult Novels

The Waiting Booth (Whispering Woods #1)
Whisper of Memory (Whispering Woods #2)
Watcher of Worlds (Whispering Woods #3)
The Waiting Booth Box Set (Books 1-3)
Wild at Heart II (An Anthology)
Lore: Tales of Myth and Legend Retold (An Anthology)

Twitter: @Brinda_Berry
Facebook: BrindaBerryAuthor
Website: www.brindaberry.com

Made in the USA
Lexington, KY
04 April 2017